WITCHFINDER
Dawn of the Demontide

For Johnny, my nephew,
whose magic surprises me every day.

WITCHFINDER
Dawn of the Demontide

WILLIAM HUSSEY

OXFORD
UNIVERSITY PRESS

OXFORD
UNIVERSITY PRESS

Great Clarendon Street, Oxford OX2 6DP

Oxford University Press is a department of the University of Oxford.
It furthers the University's objective of excellence in research, scholarship,
and education by publishing worldwide in

Oxford   New York

Auckland   Cape Town   Dar es Salaam   Hong Kong   Karachi
Kuala Lumpur   Madrid   Melbourne   Mexico City   Nairobi
New Delhi   Shanghai   Taipei   Toronto

With offices in

Argentina   Austria   Brazil   Chile   Czech Republic   France   Greece
Guatemala   Hungary   Italy   Japan   Poland   Portugal   Singapore
South Korea   Switzerland   Thailand   Turkey   Ukraine   Vietnam

Oxford is a registered trade mark of Oxford University Press
in the UK and in certain other countries

British Library Cataloguing in Publication Data

Data available

ISBN: 978-0-19-273190-6

1 3 5 7 9 10 8 6 4 2

Printed in Great Britain by CPI Cox and Wyman, Reading, Berkshire

Paper used in the production of this book is a natural,
recyclable product made from wood grown in sustainable forests.
The manufacturing process conforms to the environmental
regulations of the country of origin.

Contents

THEN
The Sacrifice

'HELP! Someone—anyone—please, *help me*!'

A roar of thunder drowned out Luke's cries. Step by stumbled step, the strangers dragged him across the bay. The boy's pyjamas dripped with rain and his bare toes squelched in the wet sand. A rope had been tied around his wrists and, with every tug, he looked up at the figures that held his leash. Robed and hooded, the strangers appeared ghostly in the moonlight.

'Who are you? Where are you taking me?'

No answer—just the rumble of the sea, the screech of the wind and the whip-crack of lightning.

There were three of them in all—two men and a woman. Normal human beings, Luke assumed, though he could not be sure. For thirteen years, he had grown up surrounded by tales of wicked creatures that preyed upon the young, the weak, and the helpless. Luke shuddered.

Perhaps these 'people' were the same monsters from his bedtime stories.

Perhaps there really were such things as *demons* . . .

The group struggled across the rocks, keeping as close as possible to the cliffs. It was high tide and the sea had eaten away most of the shore. The crash of the waves rang in Luke's ears and salt water stung his eyes. He tried once more to wrench himself free but the man (the demon?) that held him was strong. Luke could not escape. By the time they reached the cavern, he was shivering and soaked to the bone.

Most of the caves in the bay were just small nooks bored out by the sea, hardly big enough for a cat to creep into. Crowden's Sorrow was the only large cavern. It had an entrance the size of a cathedral doorway and reached back further than the eye could see. Time and again, Luke had been told never to come here. It was a warning he had always taken very seriously. The cavern had a dark, dripping mouth and the stalactites that hung behind its upper lip looked like a set of razor-sharp teeth.

The group came to a halt just inside the mouth of the cave. Water fell from those fang-like rocks and dripped onto Luke's head. He shivered as icy trickles ran down his neck and along his spine.

The cloaked figures gathered around him. Luke's gaze passed between them. Even with the occasional burst of lightning he could not see the faces beneath the hoods.

The tall man spoke up.

'Let it be done here.'

Luke's heart lurched in his chest. Since being dragged

from his bed, this was the first time that he had heard one of his abductors speak. Now he forgot all about his parents, who were out of town for the weekend. He forgot about Mrs Grady, the housekeeper, who was supposed to be looking after him, but who had not answered his calls for help. He even forgot about Mildred, his little sister. All he could focus on was the man's voice.

'Very well,' the woman said, her words heavy with despair, 'but afterwards we must go deeper. Into the chamber, up the stairs, all the way to the Door. I just pray that we're still in time. That his blood will be enough . . .'

'We're sure that there is no other way?' asked the third figure—a man, small and stooped. 'You know that if we do this then we are no better than the Coven and their demons. We should keep our hands clean. We should remember the mistakes of our ancestors.'

Luke felt sick with horror. These people were neither monsters nor strangers—he knew them very well indeed. He called out their names. Only the little man flinched.

Ignoring Luke, the tall man said:

'We have no other choice. We must act or the world will fall into darkness.'

The sea boomed, the sky shrieked.

The woman slipped a hand inside her cloak.

'Just stop a moment and let's discuss this,' the little man pleaded.

Luke saw the man's stubby fingers reach out and touch the woman's arm.

'There is nothing left to discuss,' she said. 'Can't you feel it in the air? The Demontide is upon us. The blood—*all of it this time*—is the only way to stop it.'

'And next time? What will we do then?'

'We have a generation to ponder that question,' the tall man said. 'But only if we do this now. Tonight. Proceed, sister.'

The woman withdrew a long, curved knife from her cloak. The blade shimmered in the moonlight. Luke saw the letters carved into the hilt and began to understand what was about to happen.

'You can't!' He fought against the hands that held him. 'Let me GO!'

'Turn him around,' the woman instructed.

An arm locked across Luke's chest. A hand cupped his forehead and pulled his head back. He saw the knife flash before his eyes.

'Please . . . '

Three voices rose up from behind him in a sing-song chant.

'Hobarron—Elder of Elders—showed us the light, and so we fight against the darkness. Let us spill the Finder's Blood. Finder's Blood to seal the Door. Finder's Blood to vanquish Evil. Finder's Blood to hold back the Demontide . . . '

Luke could not look at the knife. His gaze swept out of the cave and into the bay beyond. Sprays of sea foam frothed around the mouth of the cavern like spittle on a madman's lips. Little fishing boats moored on the beach broke into splinters under the fist of a mighty wave. On the far side of the bay, he could make out movement on the clifftops. Two figures stood side by side, staring down into the dark entrance of Crowden's Sorrow. The children's coats whipped about them as they staggered against the wind. The boy held his sister close, comforting her.

'Adam!' Luke cried. 'Joanna . . . !'

The knife swept across his throat. Pain, as bright as lightning, etched itself behind his eyes. He could feel the coolness of the blade, the sting of its brilliant edge. Blood steamed the night air and Luke fell to his knees. Sliver by sliver, the pain slipped away.

As his life left Luke Seward, the wind streamed into the cave and back out again. The murderers in their cavern, the children on the clifftop, and the people of Hobarron's Hollow—snug in their beds—heard it as a low, mournful howl.

25 Years Later

Chapter 1
Horror Boy Harker

The teacher's voice droned on in the background . . .

Meanwhile, an army of vampires flocked down from the hills.

'*Feast, my brothers!*' the master vampire cried. '*Rip out every throat! Drain every artery! Tonight we shall bathe in blood!*'

Jake licked his thumb and index finger. Resting on his knee under the desk, the comic book crackled at his touch. He turned the page to find a scene of vampire frenzy—all flared nostrils, bloodshot eyes, and bared fangs. He yawned and flipped the page.

The title of the comic shrieked out at him: *TALES FROM THE CRYPT!* Jake's eyes widened. Amazing! Tucked inside this collection of old terror tales bought from a charity shop was the first horror comic he had ever read! The sight of that famous title, and the ghoulish image on the cover, sent Jake's thoughts scurrying back six years. His ninth birthday. The day when his obsession with all things grisly had begun.

He remembered his dad pushing a big cardboard box across the kitchen table. With one eyebrow raised, Jake had flipped back the sides, plunged his hand into the box and brought out the first in a bundle of dusty old comics.

'I collected this lot when I was about your age,' his father had said, beaming. 'They used to scare me stupid! The comic you have there was one of my all-time favourites: *Tales From The Crypt!*'

Jake stared at the cover. It showed a picture of a terrified man locked in the embrace of a zombie.

'I treasured these comics, and now they're yours. Happy birthday, son!'

That night, hunkered down under the duvet, torch in one hand, horror comic in the other, Jake had begun his journey into the world of monsters. There were four fully-illustrated stories per issue. By the end of the first tale, he'd felt pretty scared. Two stories down and he was well and truly spooked. The third slice of gruesomeness, a story about a man changing slowly into a flesh-eating ghoul, had to be abandoned halfway through.

Weeks passed and the comics gathered dust on his bookshelf. Eventually, Jake plucked up the courage to take down Issue 2 of *Tales From The Crypt.* By the end of the month he had finished his dad's collection. By the end of the year, he was a certified horror nut.

With his dad's encouragement, Jake moved on from comics to books. He searched libraries for tales of haunted houses, blood-hungry beasts and creeping corpses. He loved zombies (*Ber-ains! Ber-ains! BER-AINS!*), werewolves (*vulnerable only to silver bullets*), vampires (*like Jake, allergic to garlic*), golems, ghosts, and gremlins. He read everything he could find and, at the age of fifteen, Jake considered himself something of an expert on monsters . . .

'HAR-KER!'

Mr Kilfoy's screech jolted Jake out of his memories.

'Sir?' he said, stuffing the horror comic into his bag.

'*Macbeth*, young man,' the English teacher sneered. 'I'm sorry to have woken you, but in the living world we were talking about one of Shakespeare's greatest plays.'

Kilfoy stalked down the room. He reached Jake's desk and slapped down a dog-eared copy of *Macbeth*.

'Witches.'

'Sorry, sir?'

Kilfoy picked up the play book and, with each word uttered, rapped Jake on the head with it.

'The—Three—Witches—in—*Macbeth*! What is the point in me giving extra classes to prepare you for A Level English if you just sit there like a brain-dead moron? Listen—to—the—text, numbskull!' Kilfoy cleared his throat. ' "*Fair is foul, and foul is . . .*" '

Jake snatched the book from Kilfoy's hand and shot to his feet. He was tall for his age, his legs lanky, his arms long and thin. Towering over the teacher, Jake felt the blood roar in his veins.

Kilfoy noticed the look in the boy's eyes and took a step back.

'"*Fair is foul, and foul is fair: Hover through the fog and filthy air,*"' Jake quoted. 'Spoken by all three witches at the end of Act One, Scene One. The witches in *Macbeth* believe that they have power but, in the end, their magic is just an illusion. Was that the theme we were discussing?'

Kilfoy's mouth fell open.

Jake glanced around the room to see if his victory had been noticed. Anyone else in 5B could have expected a few sniggers and the odd thumbs up but, in his heart of hearts, Jake knew he would receive no such sign of approval. 'Weird' Jake Harker was regarded by his class-mates with almost as much dislike as Killjoy Kilfoy him-self. It was surprising, then, to see a face in the front row smiling back at him. Jake's heart snapped into a gal-lop—it was Rachel Saxby, hands down the prettiest girl in the year.

The end of day bell rang out. Chairs scraped back and mobile phones bleeped into life.

'Bell's for me, not for you,' Kilfoy barked.

Whatever he had seen in Jake's eyes—whatever had unnerved him in those deep brown pools—had vanished. Now Kilfoy's old authority returned to him.

'If you're taking part in the short story competition this term, leave your efforts on your desks. I guess we'll have the same old rubbish from you, Harker? Ghoulies in their grave-yards, vampires in their vaults?'

Jake took a folder from his bag and handed it over.

Kilfoy slipped his spectacles onto his nose and flipped open the folder.

'*A Hungry Heart* by Jacob Josiah Harker. OK, let's have a quick look . . . Hmm. A pretty young schoolgirl falls in love with . . . Ah, of course, should've known it—a werewolf with a taste for human hearts!'

'It's not a werewolf,' Jake protested, 'it's a wendigo. There's a difference.'

'Oh really? And what, pray tell, *is* the difference?'

'Well, a wendigo's an animal spirit from Native American mythology while a werewolf is a creature that looks kinda like your mother. Only less hairy.'

'What did you say, young man?'

'Nothing, sir.' Jake picked up his backpack and headed for the door.

During his chat with Kilfoy, the class had emptied. With an eye out for Rachel Saxby, he squeezed his way through the crowds in the corridor. Calls and shrieks—the excitement of another school day done and dusted—accompanied Jake into the entrance hall, through the large double doors and out to the school gate. He saw no sign of Rachel.

The wind howled through the streets like a mischievous ghost, rattling letterboxes and throwing litter into gutters. Head down, Jake trudged away from Masterson High and towards the Hobarron Institute. It was a half-mile walk but on that day, with the wind cutting through him, it felt like a twenty-mile trek. He marched through the Tesco car park and into the New Town housing estate. Beyond the houses, out to the west, scarlet streamers blazed in the sky.

Jake emerged from a side street and onto a long stretch of tarmac. The road to the Hobarron Institute rolled out through acres of cornfields like a black line scored through yellow parchment. He had walked a few paces when a Vauxhall Corsa roared up beside him. The passenger window slid down to reveal Rachel Saxby.

Jake had known Rachel all his life. Their parents were colleagues at the Institute and they had seen each other at various Hobarron events over the years. He even had a vague memory of dancing with her at a Christmas party when they'd both been about five years old. Since then they had never really talked. Despite this, Jake saw Rachel often in his dreams.

Now her sea-green eyes held him where he stood.

'Hey, Jake, need a lift?'

'Rachel. Hi. Um . . . I'm walking actually. I mean, obviously I'm walking—it's the one leg in front of the other motion that gives it away. Ha-ha.' *Shut up, shut up, shut up!* his brain screamed at him. 'But, yeah, I think I'm OK. OK walking, I mean.'

'Come on, Rach, why've we stopped to talk to this freak?'

It was the driver who spoke, one of Rachel's girlfriends from the year above. Like Jake, Rachel had few friends in their own year, although in her case it was a matter of choice. Trendy, hip, sophisticated Rachel was more at home with the in-crowd of Masterson High's Lower Sixth.

Ignoring her friend, Rachel asked, 'Are you going to the Institute? We could drop you off, no bother.'

'I don't think that'd go down too well with your mates,' Jake muttered.

'Oh, don't worry about them, they're cool. Us Institute kids should stick together, yeah?'

'I guess.'

'Jump in then.'

Jake glanced through the rear window. A girl sitting on the back seat narrowed her eyes and shook her head.

'I'm good thanks,' he sighed. 'Think I'll walk.'

'Come on, Jake, it's not like you need the exercise, there's nothing of you.'

Always conscious of his stick-thin body, Jake bristled.

'Look, to be honest, Rachel, I don't really understand this.'

'Understand what?'

'You being nice to me.' Blood rushed into his face and he heard his voice crack into an embarrassingly high pitch. 'This is, like, the first time you've *ever* spoken to me and . . . '

'Hey, I was only offering you a lift,' Rachel snapped. 'I wasn't asking you out on a freaking date! Listen, I just read one of your stories, right? One of those you posted online. The one about the guy haunted by his mother's ghost.'

'*Mother's Day*,' Jake said, surprised. 'I posted that anonymously.'

'I recognized your style.' A smile fluttered across her lips. (*Beautiful, cupid's bow lips, shining with pink gloss. Don't stare, you moron!*) 'Anyway, I think you're really good. I write a bit myself, poetry mainly. Maybe we could've talked. Wish I hadn't mentioned it now. See you around.'

The Corsa's back wheels kicked up a cloud of dust into Jake's eyes.

You bloody idiot! You had the perfect chance to talk to her—maybe even get her number—and you blew it! Jake scuffed his trainers against the tarmac. Perhaps it wasn't a total disaster. She liked his stories—that might be a way in. His parents must have the Saxbys' number in their phonebook. He'd get home, have a shower, relax a little, and then summon up the courage to call her. Play it cool . . .

'Heads up, gimp boy!'

Something sharp struck Jake on the back of the neck. His fingers went to the spot and found it soft and tacky with blood.

'Ow, baby's been hurt,' a familiar voice sniggered from behind.

Jake swore under his breath. Silas Jones, a boy made up mostly of muscles, tattoos, and broken teeth, loped along the road towards him. Jake hadn't seen Silas for a while—he had been expelled from school last year for beating up Mr Cable, the geography teacher. A single punch had broken Cable's jaw.

The street was otherwise empty and the windows of the houses facing it had their curtains drawn. Jake was all alone with the biggest mentalist this side of the Closedown Canal.

'What d'you want, Silas?'

'That's a funny tone to take with me, Jake,' Silas smirked, showing a mouthful of black fillings. 'Seeing as how I could beat the crap out of you right here and now. Unless you think you could take me on?'

Silas thrust his face to within inches of Jake's. It was a great, flat, ugly thing, peppered with yellow-headed pimples. Jake could smell a tuna paste lunch on Silas's breath and tried not to gag.

'Anyway, what're you doing talking to Rachel Saxby? Don't tell me you think you stand a chance with *her*? You're outta your skull if you do. She'd never look at a scrawny scrap of nothing like you.'

Jake started to walk away. Silas trotted alongside, like some kind of psychotic pet dog.

'Where you off to?'

'Meeting my mum.'

'Oh, baby needs his mummy to walk him home. Still, I guess that's about right. It's not like you've got any friends to keep you company. What's it they call you at Masterson? Gimp-face? Ah no, I remember: Horror Boy Harker, the Creep Freak.'

Jake had a dozen witty comebacks. He swallowed each of them down. He bit back his anger too. There was no point starting a fight with this human demolition machine—not unless he wanted an ambulance crew to scrape him off the road.

'So where does Mummy work?'

'The Hobarron Institute.'

'*La-di-da*. You know, my dad says that only bad things have happened to this town since *they* came here. Everyone knows they're messing around with dangerous stuff— nuclear junk, gamma rays, chemical weapons. My dad says they'll probably blow us all up one day. 'S that what your mummy's gonna do, Harker? Blow this piece of crap town to Kingdom Come with all her stupid experiments?'

Rage burned in his stomach but Jake managed to stay silent.

'Yeah, bet that's what your silly cow of a mother is up to. They've probably got a bunker or something under that tower. They'll cause some massive explosion, kill everyone, and you guys'll be nice and safe in your bunker.'

Walk quicker. Don't listen.

'You'll be laughing at us then, won't you? You and your sick mother.'

Stay calm. He'll get bored soon. Go away.

'Answer me, Horror Boy. I said, is your silly cow mother gonna blow us all up?'

Jake stopped. His hands clenched into fists.

'Are you stupid or something?'

Silas's left eye twitched. 'What d'you say?'

'I said, are you *stupid*?' Now the anger spread out through Jake's entire body. It felt as if he was on fire. 'The Hobarron Institute is a charity. It's a scientific think tank. Do you understand these words, Silas? Are they too big for your dumbass brain to comprehend? Am I talking too quickly?'

'I—it's—my dad,' Silas floundered, 'he says you'll blow us all up and . . . '

'Well, if *your* dad said it then it must be true, Silas. After all, he obviously has first dibs on the family brain cell.'

Silas responded the only way he knew how. His tattooed fist slammed into Jake's stomach. Jake fell to his knees, eyes streaming, choking as he tried to breathe. Another blow, this time to the head, knocked him sideways. *Ceerr-ack.* His left cheekbone hit the kerb and pain splintered across his skull.

Through tears, he saw Silas's heavy Doc Marten as it flew towards him. The boot buried itself in his ribs. Pain again, this time reaching into every part of his body. Silas's rants sounded distant in Jake's ears.

'Take the piss out of me and my dad, you little git? When I've finished with you, you won't be laughing. I'm gonna pound you into the pavement. I'm gonna crack your stupid skull open.'

The sole of the Doc Marten pressed down against Jake's face.

'OK, after three I'm gonna slam my boot into your nose. It's breaky-breaky time.'

Pleas for the psycho to stop rose and stuck in Jake's throat. Whatever happened, he wasn't going to beg.

'Any last requests?'

'A change of footwear?' Jake said, grinning through the fear. 'Gotta tell you, Silas, no one wears Doc Martens these days.'

'Think you're funny, don't you, Harker? Well let's see if you're still cracking jokes in a minute. Ready? One, two, thr—'

A smooth, silky voice cut Silas short.

'I wouldn't do that if I were you.'

Silas balled his fist—he wasn't afraid of adults.

He spun round to face the stranger. 'What the hell's it got to do with y—?' and his words dried up.

With one hand cradling his gut, Jake managed to stagger to his feet. He looked over to where Silas gawped at the new-comer.

The sun fell behind the houses. Streetlights blinked on, bathing the road in an orange glare. In this sickly half-light, the face of the Pale Man gleamed.

He was dressed in an old-fashioned style: shiny leather shoes with pointed tips, pinstriped trousers and waistcoat. A scarlet tie had been fastened to his shirt with a flashy diamond pin. His clothes were immaculate and tailored perfectly to fit his emaciated body. Jake had immediately thought of him as the 'Pale Man' because of the deathly shade of his skin. In fact, now that he looked closer, it seemed that the skin was almost translucent—that the brilliant white of the man's skull could be seen shining through.

'Who are you?' Silas said, his voice quivering.

Blue eyes shifted between the boys.

'I am a friend of young Master Harker.'

'I don't know you,' Jake said.

'Not yet,' the Pale Man agreed. 'And now, Master Silas, as there are grown-up things to discuss, I bid you goodnight.'

Silas's face flushed red. He looked as if he was about to attack the stranger.

The Pale Man shook his head and wagged his finger. 'Now, now, I wouldn't try anything if I were you. My friend Mr Pinch is waiting in the car. He is my—how shall I put it?—my guardian angel.'

He nodded towards a long black limousine parked a little way down the road. Its tinted windows reflected Silas, Jake, and the Pale Man, but kept the mysterious Mr Pinch hidden from view.

'Best you run off home, Silas, or my "angel" will come out to play.'

A silhouette moved against the glass of the windscreen. It was a small form, no larger than a cat. Its movements struck Jake as odd—smooth, stealthy, and then suddenly ragged and sharp, like a string puppet being jerked this way and that. What was it? he wondered.

Jake glanced to his right and saw that Silas was watching the shadow, too. All the ferocity had drained from him and he looked like a frightened little boy. Without a word, Silas turned and shuffled away down the street.

When he reached the end of the road, the Pale Man smirked and called after him. 'Now be a good boy, Silas, or one day I might come looking for you.'

Silas put his head down and walked on.

'That's better, isn't it?' the man said, and held out his hand to Jake. 'Very pleased to make your acquaintance, young Harker.'

Jake tightened his grip on the straps of his backpack. Sweat sprang out at the nape of his neck. There was something very wrong with this man, he could feel it.

'Come now, I am sure your parents have told you that it is impolite not to shake hands when a stranger introduces himself.'

'My parents told me not to talk to strangers.'

'Very sensible. Indeed, I should have expected nothing less from Adam and Claire Harker. But tell me, how are your parents?'

'Fine.'

'I am relieved to hear it. And they are both still happy in the employ of the Hobarron Institute? I wonder what fascinating projects they are working on these days . . . ' Eyes dazzling, he closed in on Jake. 'If you tell me, I could make it worth your while. Whatever your heart desires could be yours. Money, clothes, the latest gadgets. If there's some girl you like, I could arrange things so that she looks favourably upon you. Or that boy just now—would you like something *unpleasant* to happen to him?'

Jake took a step back. 'I have to go.'

'What a pity.' The Pale Man looked genuinely saddened. 'But perhaps you will do me *one* favour before we part—if you are now on your way to the Institute, I wonder if you would place this at the memorial?' He took a scarlet flower from his buttonhole and handed it to Jake. 'In memory of the tragedy. And now, as we have nothing left to say to one another, you had best go on your way, Master Harker.'

'How do you know my name?'

'Your father and I are old, old friends.'

The Pale Man smiled and fear wriggled in Jake's gut like a ball of worms.

'What . . . ' Jake's breath shortened. 'What's your name?'

Spots of rain started to run down the stranger's face and into the hollows of his eyes.

'Quilp,' he said. 'Mr Quilp, at your service. And I am sure we shall see each other again, young man. Very soon, in fact.'

Chapter 2
Clown Killer

Rising to a height of over a hundred and fifty metres, Hobarron Tower, headquarters of the Hobarron Institute, dominated the landscape. A thin structure of steel and glass, it resembled a great shining needle that had been driven into the fabric of the countryside. One road, running out from the town, provided the only point of access.

A lonely figure on the road, Jake hobbled towards the tower. The whole left side of his body ached from Silas's attack and it felt as if his face was ballooning. The cool rain on his skin eased the pain a little.

'Welcome to my lair, Mr Bond.'

He always made this joke when approaching the Institute, because it *did* look something like the hideaway of a James Bond villain. Jake's eye ran around the chain-link fence that circled Hobarron Tower. Coils of barbed wire twisted along the top of the fence while a dozen or more security cameras craned their necks around the perimeter.

Jake approached the cabin at the gate and waited for Brett, the guard, to look up from his newspaper.

'Afternoon, fella!' Brett beamed. 'How was school?'

'A big pile of crap-ola.'

'Hey, you kiss your mother with that mouth?'

'No, just your wife.'

It was the same old banter. As usual, Brett guffawed as if it was the funniest thing he had ever heard. The guard folded his paper and stepped out of the hut. He caught sight of Jake's face and did a double take.

'Whoa, what the hell ran into you?'

'Sports accident. Footy practice.'

'You're sure that's what it was?'

Jake nodded. Although obviously not convinced by the lie Brett didn't press the point.

'OK then, big fella,' he said, his tone more serious. 'You know the drill. Assume the position.'

Jake walked towards the cabin, spread his feet apart and rested his hands on the wall. The guard took a moment to look through his schoolbag. Then he patted Jake down, checking, presumably, for weapons. It was odd. Jake had been coming to the Institute once a week after school for the last four years. The security staff, the science boffins, even the tea lady, knew him. Dr Holmwood, the chief egg-head here, never failed to say hello and ask about his home-work. All the same, he was never allowed through the gate without having to go through this rigmarole. The strangest part of it all was the final check.

Brett pulled on a pair of latex gloves and turned Jake's neck from side to side. Sometimes Jake would sneak a sideways glance and was always amazed by Brett's intense concentration. Maybe the Institute was scared that a rival company could implant surveillance bugs under the skin. Seemed far-fetched, but what else could the check be in aid of?

Brett snapped the gloves from his hands.

'Clean as a whistle,' he said. 'Go on through.'

He ducked into the cabin and pressed a button. A second later the gate rattled into the air.

An open-plan plaza in the shape of a horseshoe surrounded Hobarron Tower. It was filled with sculptures, flowerbeds, benches, and fountains. Nowadays the plaza was only ever used at lunchtimes as a place to eat, to smoke, and to exchange office gossip. Up until eight years ago it had also provided the setting for the Institute's annual summer gala. The Hobarron Fete had been legendary in the local area. There had been fairground attractions, circus performers, animal rides, and food of every kind.

All that was before the murder.

Jake walked to the monument that stood at the centre of the plaza. It took the form of a stone table upon which flowers could be laid. He took out the scarlet flower given to him by Mr Quilp. It felt wrong to leave it here, but he could think of no logical reason not to do as the stranger had asked. As he placed it among the other floral tributes his eye ran over the inscription on the plaque.

IN MEMORY OF OLIVIA BROWN
WHO DIED HERE ON 11 JULY 2001

Jake still had the nightmares.

From early morning, the weather had seemed to be toying with the crowds. As soon as umbrellas were unfurled the rain would stop. The moment they were packed away again, the sky would rumble and a thunderous downpour would break over the Hobarron Fete.

Jake was too young to be bothered by a little rain. He ran through the crowds, calling over his shoulder as he went. Annoyed at his dad's slow pace, he dashed back, grabbed hold of his hand and dragged him between the stalls and sideshows. Jake's excitement mounted with every fresh sight. There were contortionists bending themselves into impossible shapes and acrobats cartwheeling through the crowds. In one corner of the fete, he found a dog that could bark the national anthem and a woman sporting a white Father Christmas beard.

After trying his luck on the hook-a-duck stall, and winning a goldfish in a bag, he caught sight of the face-painting booth. Jake and his dad waited in the queue, debating between them which face it should be: Tony the Tiger or Scooby Doo.

'If you want my opinion, Jakey, I think Tony the Tiger would be grrreat!'

Jake rolled his eyes. 'Dad, that's *so* lame. I reckon Scooby D—'

An unwelcome voice cut in—

'Hello, you two.'

Jake looked up to find Dr Gordon Holmwood, the head of the Hobarron Institute, smiling down at him. Unfortunately, the old man's smile always looked more like a sneer.

'Is this fine fellow I see before me really Jacob Harker?' Holmwood said in mock surprise. 'Growing into a proper little gentleman by the minute! And where's your good lady wife, Adam?'

'Claire's working.'

'Working on the day of the Fete?' Dr Holmwood cried. 'But I won't have that! I must go and find her—drag her out of that damned laboratory.'

'Good luck,' Adam murmured.

Holmwood frowned and glanced at Jake. 'Everything all right at home, is it? Between you and Claire, I mean?'

'Sure, why shouldn't it be?'

'No reason . . . Well, she's a silly girl, cooping herself up indoors when you two are out enjoying yourselves. By God, what a day! Have you seen the elephant yet, Jacob?' The doctor snapped his fingers. 'Sharon!'

One of his eager young personal assistants appeared out of nowhere.

'Yes, Dr Holmwood?'

'Ah, Sharon, my dear. Could you take Jacob here to see the elephant? Get him a ride, let him feed the brute. I just need a quiet word with Dr Harker about his work in the psychology department.'

The assistant's face fell.

'Come to the Hobarron Institute, the job ad said,' Sharon grumbled, leading Jake across the plaza. 'Enjoy the challenge of working for a world-leader in scientific research, the ad said. Some challenge, babysitting a snot-nosed brat . . . No offence, kid.'

Jake didn't reply. He glanced back to find both Dr Holmwood and his father watching him. Holmwood looked thoughtful while his dad appeared lost and a little sad.

Jupiter the elephant occupied a patch of ground just outside the plaza. It was late in the day and most of the kids had already had their ride. An exhausted-looking Jupiter sank her trunk into a bucket of water and took a well-deserved drink. A thick chain had been tied around her neck and secured to an iron peg driven deep into the ground. Jake looked into the beast's tiny eyes.

'She's unhappy,' he observed in a solemn voice.

'Ain't we all,' Sharon sighed.

'I need a pee,' Jake said.

Sharon nodded towards a block of toilets that stood next to the big circus tent just outside the plaza.

'Knock yourself out.'

Jake traipsed towards the toilet block, his heart heavy in his chest. Jupiter had given pleasure to dozens of kids that day. Now, her purpose served, she was left all alone. It wasn't fair. If he were a character in a book, he guessed that he would probably creep back here during the night and free the elephant from her captivity. Then they would travel the byroads of England together, making friends and having wonderful adventures. He shook his head sadly—he knew deep down that such ideas were just childish nonsense.

Jake's hand was on the toilet door when he heard the voices.

'And tell me, Olivia, does your father work at this magnificent institute?'

'Yes!' Olivia Brown cried. 'Now, please will you let me go?'

'All in good time.'

The voices came from inside the big top. The large red-and-white striped tent had been put up earlier in the day to host the circus entertainment. An hour or so ago, Jake and his father had sat on the tiered wooden benches and watched the various acts: clowns and tumblers, tightrope walkers and trapeze artists, lion tamers and jugglers, all performing under the careful eye of the ringmaster. Now, pulling aside a section of the canvas drape and peering into the vast empty space of the tent, Jake saw that it was the ringmaster himself speaking to Olivia. They stood alone in the centre of the sandy performance area.

It was dark in the tent. The only illumination came through a hole in the cone-shaped ceiling. The shaft of light gleamed against the ringmaster's top hat and black leather boots. His burgundy tailcoat looked like a smear of blood in the gloom. The man held Olivia firmly by the hand while she strained with every muscle to break free. As she turned her head away from her captor, Jake saw that Olivia had visited the face painting booth. She had chosen to be a clown.

Her white face and bright red lips were set in an expression that made Jake's blood run cold.

He should do something—call out or run for help—but, as the ringmaster pulled Olivia close, Jake felt a paralysing terror root him to the spot. His throat tightened and the cry that passed his lips was little more than a whimper.

'The other children call you names, don't they?' The ringmaster's voice sounded almost sad—very unlike the booming, cheerful tones he had used when announcing the circus acts.

'Please . . . ' Olivia pulled away again.

'Sticks and stones will break my bones but names will never hurt me. That's probably what your daddy says when you run home from school, bleating like a little baby. *They call me horrid names, Daddy. They make me cry!* Sticks and stones, Daddy says. But we know, don't we, Olivia? We know how much it hurts. But don't be sad, my child, pain does not last for ever.'

'Let me go!'

Olivia kicked out. Her foot connected with the ringmaster's shin and he released her. A yelp of victory escaped Olivia's lips and she started to run. Jake looked past her and saw the smile on the ringmaster's face. He was not hurt. He had let her go on purpose. This was a game.

Jake tried to call out, to step forward and wave the girl towards him. He could do neither. The shame of his cowardice burned beneath his skin.

'Sticks and stones, sticks and stones!' The shriek echoed through the tent.

Olivia screamed. Grinning, the ringmaster stalked after her. Although Olivia ran at full speed towards the entrance, he started closing the gap between them. Jake watched, amazed. The man in the red tailcoat seemed to stretch out like a piece of chewing gum. Step by step, his legs grew ever longer, the bones crackling as they lengthened. It must *really* hurt, Jake thought, but the ringmaster showed no sign of pain. His strange shadow leapt across the big top in grasshopper strides. By the time he had reached his prey, the monster appeared to be at least three metres tall.

Olivia tore the tent flaps apart. Daylight flooded into the big top. Before she could escape, the ringmaster's hand blocked her mouth and Olivia Brown was pulled back into the tent.

'Your suffering will end soon,' he promised. As he dragged Olivia into the performance area, his limbs crackled back into their normal dimensions. 'Then we will show them all, won't we? Show those spiteful name-callers. Show your ignorant father. Show the great Hobarron Institute itself. Show them that everyone is vulnerable and can feel pain.'

The ringmaster grabbed the little girl around the throat. Without the slightest effort, he lifted her into the air.

'And to achieve all that, Olivia, all you have to do is *die*.'

That was when Jake found his voice. The moment he screamed, the ringmaster's face snapped in his direction and lips curled over a set of strong white teeth. He turned back to Olivia Brown. The girl was blue, her arms and legs twitching as she tried desperately to breathe. The ringmaster spat out his frustration in two words.

'No time.'

With a twist of his wrist, Olivia's neck snapped like a dry twig. Dust billowed into the air as her body hit the ground.

The ringmaster looked down at the corpse with something like regret in his eyes. It was then that Jake noticed *the rat*. A large, hairless thing, it sat on the man's shoulder, its pink eyes shining with an unnatural light.

'Such a waste, is it not, Mr Smythe?' the ringmaster said, his words addressed to the rodent. His gaze moved back to Jake. 'But perhaps we shall not be wholly disappointed. Today the Elders will realize that they are *not* untouchable. Today the Coven will be victorious.'

Still unable to move, Jake watched the ringmaster step over Olivia's lifeless corpse and stride towards him. Once again, the monster's arms and legs stretched out. His spindly shadow danced across the canvas walls of the tent. He came closer . . . closer . . .

Jake's little-boy heart hammered. Tears spiked into his eyes. Through the clouds of dust kicked up by the ringmaster's boots, he saw Olivia's dead face staring back at him. Those unmoving eyes screamed *RUN*, but there was no chance of escape. Not now.

An impossibly long arm reached out for Jake.

Fingers closed around his throat.

Flexed.

Tightened . . .

And then he heard the sound of running feet. The roar of frightened voices. Hands tore back the tent flap and dozens of men poured into the big top. Barely able to contain their fury, they fell upon the murderer and restrained him. Jake watched as the monster struggled beneath them.

'See now, you fools, how weak you are? You think your-selves safe in your mighty tower? But *we* are everywhere. We laugh at your science and your protections. We will rule this world long after your Institute is dust upon the wind of history. *It* is coming, gentlemen, and this time there is nothing you can do to stop it. The Demonti—'

A hand blocked the murderer's mouth and he was dragged away. For a few minutes, Jake was left alone with Olivia.

'I'm sorry,' he gasped, tears streaming. 'I'm so sorry.'

But the girl was dead and she could neither forgive nor comfort him.

Jake used his finger to trace the inscription on the memorial. It was hard to believe that eight years had passed since that awful day. Five months after Olivia's death, he had learned from his father that ringmaster Sidney Tinsmouth had been tried and convicted for the murder. A jury had decided he was insane and the judge had sentenced him accordingly.

Insane. Jake guessed that *he* must have caught a whiff of Tinsmouth's madness that day. It was the only way he could explain the impossible things he had seen. As for the killer? He must still be locked away in a lunatic asylum somewhere, chained up just like Jupiter the Elephant . . .

A sudden instinct seized hold of Jake. He took the scarlet flower from the memorial and crushed it in his hand. He threw the petals into the wind and watched as they tumbled across the plaza and floated over the fence. Red teardrops disappearing into the night. Jake wondered what the Pale Man would think of this destruction.

He shivered slightly and walked on.

Chapter 3
Demon's Dance

Jake slumped into one of the chairs outside his mother's office. He hated this once-a-week visit to the cold, unfriendly Hobarron Institute. The only reason he was here was because his dad had the car on Thursdays, and his mum needed help carrying her files home. Jake had suggested they get a second car, but his mum said the weekly exercise did them both good. Maybe—but tonight, with his body bruised and aching, all Jake wanted was to get into a hot bath as soon as possible.

He took a horror comic from his bag and tried to lose himself in a story. It was no good. Pictures and speech bubbles swam before his eyes but his thoughts always turned back to Olivia Brown. Poor Olivia, who had died at the hands of a lunatic . . .

'Good evening, Jacob.'

Jake looked up into the faintly unpleasant face of

Dr Holmwood. The doctor gave one of his awkward smiles, showing a flash of nicotine-stained teeth. He caught sight of Jake's bruises and the smile changed into a frown.

'Well, my boy, and what has happened to you?'

Jake's swollen jaw clicked as he spoke. 'Sports accident. Footy practice.'

'Indeed? Rather violent football you play at that school.'

The doctor sat down. This close, Jake could smell a faint odour of tobacco and stale sweat coming off the man. Holmwood's fingers rapped against the arm of the chair. They looked like a pair of yellow claws.

'Your attacker,' Holmwood said, 'tell me about him.'

'I told you, it was an accident. I fell and . . . '

'Don't insult my intelligence, Jacob.'

Jake was surprised by the steely edge in the old man's voice.

'It was just a bully,' he admitted. 'Some kid who used to go to Masterson. He beat me up a bit, that's all.'

'This boy, do you know him well?'

'No. I mean, everyone *knows* Silas Jones. He was expelled last year for hitting a teacher. He's a bit of a psycho, I guess.'

'Does he pick on you especially?'

Jake hesitated. 'Maybe he *has* singled me out. A bit.'

'Why?'

Jake did not want to admit the reason, but Holmwood seemed to read it in his face.

'Because you're a loner? Yes, I suppose that would make you easier prey. But tell me, has Silas been seen around much since he was expelled? You haven't noticed him getting in with a new crowd or anything?' Holmwood leaned into Jake. 'Think carefully: have you picked up on any changes in the boy? His skin, for example.'

'His skin?'

'You may have noticed a certain paleness. Or have you seen any blemishes around his neck? Something like a tattoo, perhaps, or a scorch mark? Think before you answer.'

Jake could tell that Holmwood was no longer interested in the attack he had suffered. Perhaps he never had been. The Institute director seemed obsessed by Silas Jones's general state of health. Jake considered the work of the Hobarron Institute. Suddenly Silas's fears about what went on at this place seemed more reasonable. Perhaps an experiment had got out of hand and some dangerous substance had escaped the labs. Maybe a disease had become airborne. Was this Holmwood's way of asking Jake if the surrounding area had been infected? Did he think Silas had caught some kind of disease?

'I don't understand,' Jake said. 'Silas isn't ill. He's just mental.'

'Indeed?' Holmwood relaxed in his chair. 'Well, that's quite clear. Excellent.'

For the life of him, Jake couldn't see what was 'excellent' about being beaten up.

'Well, I must get back to work.' Holmwood's spindly legs crackled as he rose to his feet. 'If I don't see you before the holidays, Happy Christmas, Jacob.'

The old doctor stalked away down the corridor.

Minutes ticked by. Hobarron Institute employees in white

coats went to and fro between their offices and labs. Jake stared at the plaque on the door in front of him—**Dr Claire Harker, Senior Mechanical Engineer**—and willed his mother to appear. Another half an hour passed before the door flew open.

Jake's mum pulled off her lab coat and hooked it behind the door. Then she handed Jake a box stuffed with files and signalled for him to follow. They strode through the Institute, passing along one dull grey corridor after the next until they reached the lifts.

Squeezed into the lift, Jake caught sight of his mother's reflection in the mirrored walls. She looked tired, and almost as pale as Mr Quilp. His thoughts flew back to his encounter with the skeletal stranger. With his old-fashioned clothes and sinister style of speech, he would not have been out of place in one of Jake's horror comics. Coupled with his little companion crawling about behind the tinted windows of the limousine, Mr Quilp really could be the stuff of nightmares.

What kind of creature had that been? Jake wondered. Quilp had called it his 'guardian angel'. A pet dog, perhaps? This sinister man with a sinister pet suddenly reminded Jake of Sidney Tinsmouth and his pink-eyed rodent, Mr Smythe. The connection made Jake feel uneasy.

The lift reached the ground floor and Jake's mum signed them out.

'Careful with that box,' she said as they crossed the plaza, 'I don't want you dropping my papers all over the road again.'

'Yesss, Massster,' Jake hissed in his best Igor voice. 'By the

way, Mum, I was wondering, do we have Dr Saxby's home
phone number? I wanted to—'

Jake halted in front of the memorial. He couldn't believe
his eyes.

A single scarlet flower rested on the stone table.

'Jake? What's the matter?'

'N-nothing . . . I guess.'

'Hurry up, then, I want to get home.'

Brett waved them through the gate. The guard made a
gun of his fingers and mimed a shot. Jake returned fire.
Another of his and Brett's little rituals.

Situated just outside the town, the Harker home was a
short walk from the tower. They had gone a little way along
the road when Jake turned to his mum. He wanted to talk to
her about Quilp and the flower, but he saw by her distant
expression that now was not the time. She was thinking
about work.

Jake had heard only vague rumours about his mother's job
at the Institute. His dad had told him that she built top-secret
machines for the British government, and had once designed
a device for bringing water to people who lived in arid
deserts. However brilliant these machines were, Jake couldn't
help resenting them. They kept his mother's thoughts
far away from her family. So far away that it wasn't until they
reached the Closedown Canal that she looked at him properly
and noticed his injuries.

'Jake, your face is black and blue!'

He took a deep breath. There was no point in spinning
the footy practice story again. Holmwood knew the truth.

'I got beaten up. It's no big deal.'

'Who did this? Was it a stranger? What did they look like? Was there anything odd about their appearance?'

Jake reeled under the barrage of questions. Questions similar to those posed by Dr Holmwood. What was going on here?

'Well?'

'Mum, I don't . . . '

'I've told you before,' Claire snapped, 'you're too old for all that "Mum" stuff. My name is Claire.'

'It was just a boy who used to go to my school,' Jake muttered. He was surprised to see that his mother looked relieved. 'And I'm OK, in case you were wondering. I don't think anything's broken.'

'I can see you're OK, Jake. Well, we'll get this bullying issue sorted. Soon as your dad gets home, he'll be on the phone to your headmaster. There's no reason for you to be afraid.'

'I'm not afraid. And like I said, the kid doesn't go to school any more. There's nothing the head can do about it.'

'We'll contact the police then.'

'There's no need to go that far . . . '

'You know, I've told your father time and again—you should never walk from school alone. It's too dangerous. Not that *he* ever listens.'

'I don't need someone to walk with me, I'm fifteen years old!'

'And look what's happened to you.' She took Jake's hand in hers. Such a gesture from his mother was unusual. 'You're important, Jake. Important to your father and me. If you'd been seriously hurt . . . '

She released his hand and they walked on in silence.

The towpath beside the Closedown Canal was deserted. Sometimes they passed Simon Lydgate, a lad of seventeen who slept rough along the waterway. Jake scanned the banks on either side of the canal. He felt a twinge of disappointment. There was no sign of Simon's campfire.

Jake remembered that day about a year ago when he had been walking beside the canal, head stuck in a comic book. Cannoning into a wall of muscle, Jake had looked up. With his big frame and the scar splitting his upper lip, the boy standing before him looked like a gangster's bodyguard. Jake had taken a step back and blurted out an apology.

'No worries, mate,' Simon had grinned. 'Hey, is that *Tales From The Crypt*? Cool!'

They had struck up an immediate friendship based, to begin with, on their shared love of horror stories. Simon had been fascinated by Jake's encyclopaedic knowledge of all things monstrous, and had called this accumulated wisdom Jake's 'dark catalogue'. Over the next few months, their friendship had deepened. Simon had taught Jake how to build a fire, how to catch fish, and how to snare a rabbit. Although Simon spoke very little about himself, Jake had begun to identify strongly with this lonely boy. So much so that Simon had become almost like a brother to him.

Jake had wanted to show Simon the story he had found in the comic—the first horror tale he had ever read—but he guessed it would have to wait.

Moonlight ran in milky ripples across the dark canal water. A breeze whistled through the trees. Up ahead stood the tunnel through which they must pass to reach home. Jake looked into the mouth of the tunnel. A strange sensation, like the stroke of icy fingers, tingled at the back of his brain.

They were almost at the tunnel mouth when suddenly Jake dropped the box of files onto the path and reached out for his mother. His fingers locked around her arm.

'Ow! Jake, let go, you're hurting me.'

Jake stared into the tunnel.

'Don't go in there, Claire.'

Despite her continual requests, it was the first time that he had ever used his mother's name. Now it felt right on his lips. What Jake experienced as he looked into the darkness was a terror of the adult world.

And now his mother began to understand what was happening.

'What is it?' she asked. 'What do you sense?'

'Evil.'

As he spoke, the clock of the nearby St Swithin's church tolled the hour. Six o'clock and all is *not* well.

The wind picked up and moaned through the tunnel.

Claire slipped her hand into her bag.

'Someone in the tunnel?'

'Yes . . . '

'Who?'

'I've met him before. On the road. Mr Quilp.'

'Thank you for your introduction.'

Quilp's upper-class tones rang out hollowly from the arch-way.

Claire's hand searched inside her bag, probably seeking out the alarm she always carried with her.

Jake saw a pale smear in the darkness—the first hint of Mr Quilp's face as he wandered out of the tunnel. Soon a pair of china blue eyes found their form. He looked even taller and thinner than before, his legs and arms little more than bones wrapped up in an expensive suit. He stopped at the tunnel mouth.

'We meet again, Jacob. I told you it would not be long.'

'You know this . . . *man*?' Claire asked, disgust rippling through her voice.

'We met earlier today. He was the one who saved me from Silas Jones.'

'You see, my dear?' Quilp purred. 'I am not all bad.'

Claire used her body to shield Jake.

'Let my son go. Your quarrel is with me, not him.'

'Quarrel? Is that what you call it? There has been so much blood spilt on both sides that "quarrel" strikes me as a rather inadequate word. Shall we be honest with one another, Claire? This is, and always has been, a *war*. A war waged for over three hundred years between your side and ours. As you know, we are now entering the final battle. The last campaign before *our* new world is born. We had thought at this point that you were weak, that all your defences had been used up, but perhaps we were mistaken.'

'I don't know what you're talking about.'

'For a while now there has been a whisper in the wind,

the merest suggestion of a secret. It is now our belief that you, Claire Harker, have built a weapon for the Elders. With the Demontide so close at hand we must know of this . . . *miracle machine*,' Quilp sneered, but could not hide the trace of fear in his voice. '*You* must tell us what you know.'

'I'll never tell you.'

'Oh, I think you will.'

'You're wrong, witch. Kill me, do what you like, I won't talk.'

'Then the boy will die.' Quilp glanced up. 'Mr Pinch, will you come down and join us?'

High above the towpath stood Demon's Dance, an ancient oak tree that had grown out of the bank. Its thick branches reached all the way across the canal like fifty twisting snakes. Aware of his son's love of all things horrific, Jake's father had told him the tale of the tree. Even three hundred and fifty years ago, so the story went, this oak had been a giant, its trunk strong, its branches sturdy. So sturdy, in fact, that the tree had served well as a gallows for murderers, thieves, and outlaws.

The most famous person to ever dangle here had been a witch called Mother Grogan. Convicted of stealing babies and of eating their flesh, Grogan was strung by the neck from the highest branch. As the old woman kicked and struggled against her noose, she looked up and a curious expression settled across her features. Those who had gathered to witness the execution also lifted their eyes to that topmost branch. And there they saw *him*—her familiar, her demon helper—dancing a jig as one of his favourite witches died beneath him. Ever since that day, the huge, twisted oak tree had been known as Demon's Dance.

Now, as Jake followed Mr Quilp's gaze, it felt as if the pages of history had been turned back to an earlier time. The witch was no longer hanging from the highest branch, but her demon *was* there . . .

Jake covered his mouth with his hand.

'What is it?'

Claire's face turned as hard as flint. She looked both determined and disgusted.

'A demon.'

Small and hairless, it was about the size of a six-month-old baby. It scampered along the branches and swung between them with monkey-like agility. From this distance, it was impossible to make out the face. Jake was glad. He did not want to see it close up.

'Mr Pinch?' Quilp repeated.

The thing in the tree stopped dead. A pair of yellow eyes shone down.

'Your services are required.'

A strange sound, somewhere between the chunter of an ape and the howl of a wolf, burst from the creature's lips. Paw over paw, or hand over hand, it began to crawl down out of the tree. The demon was coming for them . . .

'This is your last chance,' said the Pale Man. 'What is the Elders' secret weapon? Tell me before Mr Pinch descends.'

'Never.' Claire reached for Jake's hand. 'Never.'

The tiny creature dropped to the ground. Grunting, its eyes fixed on Jake.

'Tell me before my demon tears your son to pieces.'

Pinch bounded down the canal bank. Again, Jake thought how monkey-like the thing appeared as it lumbered towards them, its shoulders raised and its little back arched. Face up, the demon snarled, displaying a mouth of needle-sharp teeth.

'Jake, do you have your phone with you?' Claire whispered urgently.

He shook his head. 'Left it at home.'

'Damn. Look, I need you to run to the phone box outside St Swithin's. Call your dad. Get him down here.'

'I won't leave you.'

'You must!'

Mr Pinch was within a few metres of them when Claire thrust her hand into her bag. She brought out a small glass ball, roughly the size of a pomegranate, and held it out towards Quilp and his demon. At the sight of this beautiful green sphere, Jake's mind filled with voices. Some were sweet and melodic while others howled out in pain and bitterness. One voice, rich and youthful, was raised above all others.

Welcome to your prison, Coven Master. Here you will endure throughout the Ages. Here you will rot unto the Ending of the World.

As the young man finished speaking an ugly cry rang out in protest. Even in his mind, Jake shrank from the hopelessness of that scream.

His mother's voice brought him back to reality.

'See now, Conjuror,' she said, her eyes flitting between

Quilp and the orb, 'here is the talisman and the sign of your weakness. Acknowledge it and cower.'

As soon as the ball had been revealed, the smug confidence had withered from the Pale Man's face. Now he shielded his eyes as if a powerful spotlight had been trained upon him. Close behind, Quilp's little demon had stopped in its tracks. It too seemed suddenly afraid.

'Here is the bane of your Master,' Claire continued. 'By the word and the faith of the witch ball, I bind you . . . ' She released Jake's hand and turned to him. 'Hurry, there isn't much time.'

'I won't leave you!'

'Jake, you have to. They can't hurt me now, I promise.'

'Who—what are they?'

'I'll explain everything when this is over. But please, I need you to get to the phone box and call your father. He'll know what to do.'

Jake gave a reluctant nod. 'OK, but I'm coming back.'

He kissed his mother. Then he began to climb the canal bank.

Jake's heart pounded so hard he thought that, at any minute, it might leap clean out of his throat. He had never felt fear like this before. The scene that he had left behind on the towpath seemed like a nightmare from one of his horror comics. From the roots that caught at his feet and the nettles that stung his hands, he knew that this was *not* a dream. Demons and witches, magic and monsters were real, though the rules by which they operated were unknown to him. All that knowledge he had accumulated over the years stood for nothing. Well, he would find out what it all meant soon enough. His mother had promised to explain everything.

Jake reached the top of the bank. Short of breath, he rested for a moment against the trunk of Demon's Dance. On the towpath below, the three figures were frozen as before—his mother, the witch, and the demon. Claire's voice rang out.

'I command you by this talisman of Hobarron, go now from here. Go before I destroy you and your familiar.'

As she spoke, the little demon crept towards Mr Quilp. Slowly, it climbed the body of the Pale Man until it reached his ear. Quilp listened to its whispers.

'The witch ball of Hobarron?' he asked; his voice carried to Jake on the breeze. 'A powerful talisman indeed. We thought it had been lost many years ago. Why would the Elders have given it to *you?*'

'Because . . . because . . . ' Claire stumbled.

'No, no, my dear.' Quilp lowered his hands and stared at the woman. 'The Elders would never have entrusted this most valued trinket to a mere employee. Someone who is not even directly related to the old families of the Hollow. That thing is not Hobarron's witch ball. It is a fake, a replica.'

Quilp pointed at the orb. He mouthed a few words and a dense, smoky vapour poured from his forefinger. It snaked a path towards Claire and wrapped itself around the ball. She cried out, as if burned, and the green glass shattered.

Her face long with horror, she glanced up at Jake and shouted:

'RUN!'

Then she turned and fled back along the canal path.

Quilp looked up to where Jake stood. He stroked Mr Pinch's bald head and gave his command.

'After him.'

The demon sprang from its master's shoulder and raced up the bank. Jake took to his heels and made for the canal bridge. The spire of St Swithin's church rose up in the near distance. Countless comic books and novels had told him that demons were afraid to enter holy places. Praying that this part of his dark catalogue was correct, Jake turned his body into a skid. Gravel spat up from his trainers. He began to run again, heading across the bridge and towards the safety of the church. He was halfway across when a startled cry made him glance down at the towpath. What he saw brought him to a screaming halt.

'Don't!' he cried. 'Leave her alone!'

Suspended five metres above the canal, his mother floated in midair. Her arms seemed to be locked to her sides, as if an invisible rope held them there. She turned in steady circles, her body reflected in the dark, swirling water below. Tears streaked her face and terror shimmered in her eyes. Her mouth widened into a scream—a cry of pain and horror—but Quilp's magic silenced her. The Pale Man stood on the towpath. His forefinger twirled as he conducted Claire's slow dance.

'One last chance,' he said. 'Tell me of this weapon that you have built for the Elders, and I shall release you and your son unharmed.'

'Tell him!' Jake shouted.

His mother shook her head. 'All I will tell you is this: the weapon is a mighty engine. A machine of ferocious power. Neither you nor your master can stop it.'

'Sad. So very, very sad,' Quilp sighed, 'but you've had your chance.'

Quilp's finger made a slashing motion across his throat. In the same instant, Claire Harker's head was severed from her shoulders. It tumbled through the air, hit the water and disappeared into the cold depths of the canal. A great gush of blood spouted from the stump of her neck.

With a snap of the witch's fingers, the headless corpse fell into the water. It floated there for a moment, turning in the swell. Jake dropped to his knees. It was as if all the air had been taken out of his body. He could feel nothing—not the wind on his face or the ground beneath him. For a few seconds there was no terror and no grief. The hideousness of what he had witnessed could not be processed by his brain. His mother had been butchered by a witch for the sake of a secret . . .

Claire's body drifted under the bridge and out of sight.

'Poor boy.'

Quilp and his demon had made their way up the bank and now stood at the end of the bridge. At the witch's words, Jake began to sense the first bright blade of emotion. His hands clenched at his sides.

The Pale Man turned to Mr Pinch.

'Kill him.'

Chapter 4
Stolen Memories

Jake could now see the demon fully. Its body was a mass of steely sinew, its arms roped with muscle. Six fingers sprouted from its hands, each ending in lethal talons. The thing did not possess a nose; instead a large hole, bubbling with green mucus, occupied the middle of its face. Mr Pinch's tongue flickered between his teeth and slurped across his fat lips. He was hungry.

The creature crawled towards him, and Jake knew that he *should* be desperately afraid. The thing was quick, agile; he had no hope of escaping it. Soon enough it would tear him to pieces. Whatever was left after the feasting had finished would probably be tipped over the side of the bridge. There, in the murky depths of the Closedown Canal, he would be reunited with his mother.

Yes, fear was the emotion that should be pumping through him right now. Instead, all Jake felt was a fiery anger. Anger at the witch and the demon. Anger at himself for not being able to save his mother.

He turned to face Mr Pinch . . .

Demonic Mr Pinch hesitated. The creature looked back at its master.

'He cannot harm you,' Quilp said. 'He's just a boy.'

'Hey, you there!' A voice boomed from the far side of the bridge. 'Stay away from him or you'll have me to answer to!'

It was Simon Lydgate. He pointed a finger at Quilp while, with his other hand, gestured for Jake to join him. Jake rose unsteadily to his feet and shuffled towards Simon. Now standing at either end of the bridge, only twenty metres of gravel walkway separated Jake and Simon from the witch and the demon.

'All right, kid?' Often when Simon spoke, his words came out in short, dry barks. Usually these were softened by his crooked smile. Not tonight. 'Come on, speak to me.'

Jake could not answer. The anger had faded, and now the pain of his mother's death hit home. Great, shuddering sobs tore through him. He felt Simon's arm wrap around his shoulders and draw him close.

'What have they done to you, Jake?' He switched back to Quilp. 'If you've hurt him, I'll . . .'

'I grow tired of this,' said Quilp. 'Kill them both.'

Mr Pinch pounced through the air. His powerful hind legs propelled him clean across the bridge. He landed at Simon Lydgate's throat. Talons pierced the boy's threadbare clothes and sank into the flesh beneath.

Both Simon and Jake tried to grab the ravenous demon,

but compared to Pinch's lightning reflexes their movements were slow and clumsy. Pinch lashed out with his paw and caught Jake a blow to the side of the head. Senses reeling, Jake stumbled back. He tripped and hit the ground with a dull crack. Flares of pain danced behind his eyes but he remained conscious. He glanced back to where his friend wrestled with the creature.

With Pinch's talons around his neck, Simon's words came out in a choked gurgle.

'Jake, get—get out of here!'

Jake hauled himself to his feet. He wasn't about to abandon his best friend, not after what had happened to his mother. He roared a cry of pain and frustration and rushed forward. He was within a few metres of Simon when a red light flashed from Quilp's hand and hit him in the stomach. Jake fell again. The wind had been knocked out of him and a dull pain throbbed in his gut. Simon was now writhing on the ground, his hands clutching at Mr Pinch.

Helpless, Jake watched as the demon opened its jaws and tore into Simon's neck.

'NO!'

Blood sprayed into the air. Simon twitched like a harpooned eel. After a few seconds, the blood eased to a trickle and the boy lay still upon the ground. Quilp walked over and nudged the unmoving body with his foot.

'Your friend is on his way to hobo heaven,' he laughed. 'And now, Master Harker, it's *your* turn.'

There was nothing more Jake could do.

He staggered to his feet and ran.

The woodland between the canal and St Swithin's passed in a silver blur. Jake's feet cracked against the frozen ground and his heart juddered in his chest. Winter birds, nesting in the icy branches of the trees, exploded into the night sky, their cries like a thousand screaming voices.

As he ran, Jake started to see faces between the trees—ghostly images of his mother and Simon Lydgate. Whether they were real or an illusion conjured by Quilp, it did not matter. In those spectral faces he saw the truth of his situation: no matter how hard he ran he could not hope to escape the jaws of the demon. Soon enough Mr Pinch would overtake him. He would be dragged to the ground and devoured. The ghosts nodded sadly, as if to confirm the hopelessness of these thoughts.

Just give up, they said. *It won't hurt for long, and then you can join us. You can be at peace . . .*

Jake heard a skitter of claws behind him. No longer running, he shuffled onwards. At any minute he expected to feel the sting of the monster's bite.

And then the bells of St Swithin's rang out.

A terrified scream cut through the woodland. Jake looked over his shoulder. It was Pinch. Hands clasped over his ears, the demon rolled in an agonized ball. Jake remembered a story from one of his horror comics in which a vampire had been tortured by the toll of a cathedral bell. Perhaps the sound of something sacred could ward off demonic forces as effectively as the sight of a crucifix or a splash of holy water. If so, that *must* mean that sanctified ground would provide a safe haven.

The bells stopped. It did not matter. Jake was now within a hundred metres of the church. He jumped over the grave-yard wall and dodged between the headstones. There was no light behind the stained glass windows. He prayed that the solid oak door was unlocked.

He reached the church steps, and was about to rush the door, when a hand caught at his leg and tripped him to the ground. Jake's head smacked against the stone step and his vision fractured into whirling shards. Through this kaleido-scope, he saw Mr Pinch's mouth stretch wide and lock down on his leg. His scream shattered the silence of the old churchyard.

The shadowy form of Mr Quilp appeared from between the trees.

'Your mother died trying to save you.'

The Pale Man stepped over the graveyard wall.

'Your friend choked to death on his own lifeblood. Again, an attempt to save your pitiful life.'

Wicked little teeth sank deeper into Jake's flesh, tearing muscle away from bone. His vision continued to reel in loops and spirals. He could see Quilp coming towards him. It appeared as if the man glided between the headstones.

'All that sacrifice for nothing. If only your mother had told me the Elders' secret, she might have saved you. Never mind, my boy, I'll tell Mr Pinch to make it quick.'

Quilp stood over him. Jake felt the witch's fingers rake through his hair. At his master's instruction, Pinch let go of the boy's leg and scampered up his body. Hot, meaty breath filled Jake's senses. He saw those jaws open once more. Soon they would close upon his throat.

'Please . . . ' Jake murmured.

'Goodnight, Jacob Harker.'

Light flooded through the church doors. Jake heard an exclamation of surprise and horror—then the sound of a gun being loaded with lightning speed. A second later, two shots rang out and grey gunsmoke billowed overhead. Pinch screeched and dropped to the ground. Quilp staggered back, his hand clamped on the bullet wound at his shoulder. The slightest movement hurt like hell, but Jake managed to twist his head around and look up at his saviour.

Through dimming eyes he saw Dr Saxby—Rachel's father—slip the revolver back into its holster.

Dr Saxby flipped his mobile phone shut.

'We've had word, sir. They've found Claire's body snagged in bramble under the canal bridge. The . . . um . . . the head was found further downstream.'

'Thank you, Malcolm.'

Dr Holmwood approached the examination table. Saxby joined him, his round, sweaty face a picture of concern. Jake stared up at the doctor and a small part of his brain wondered how someone so ordinary-looking could be the father of Rachel Saxby. The thought occupied a split second before grief and confusion overwhelmed it. His mother and his best friend were dead—murdered by a witch and a demon. He had almost suffered the same fate but had been rescued by Dr Saxby and brought . . . where exactly? The questions came thick and fast: how had he got here? Had Quilp and

Pinch been captured? Why was Dr Holmwood here? And, most puzzling of all, why did he seem unable to move or to speak? Jake knew the answer to only one of these questions. This was the Hobarron Institute. He would recognize these grey walls anywhere.

Apart from the surgical examination table on which he had been laid, the large, high-ceilinged room appeared to be featureless. People in white coats went in and out, checked their flipcharts and stole glances at Jake.

'Poor child,' Holmwood said.

'Can he hear us, sir?'

'Perhaps. Hypnotism is a tricky art, more magic than science.'

A faint look of disgust crossed Dr Saxby's features.

'Indeed. Well, I don't suppose it matters. For now.'

'Tell me again how you found him. Your earlier report was rather muddled.'

Saxby pressed a button on the far wall and a large video screen rose up out of the floor. *A Bond villain lair after all*, Jake thought. He watched the screen, aware that his eyes were the only part of his body still mobile. Perhaps that meant the hypnotic trance was wearing off. He strained to move the little finger of his right hand. Not a twitch.

'I was attending the weekly meeting of the Hobarron Institute Bell Ringers' Club . . . ' Saxby began.

Holmwood raised an eyebrow. 'We have a bell ringers' club now?'

'Afraid so. A few of us get together every Thursday night to . . . '

'Ring bells?'

'Yes, sir. Anyway, I heard a commotion outside and thought I'd better take a look. Luckily, I had my weapon with me.'

'Anyone outside the Institute see anything?'

'Only the old vicar of St Swithin's. We've worked our mojo on him. Now he thinks it was just a scuffle between a gang of louts.'

'Good work. But who was our mystery assailant?'

Saxby clicked a pen-like device and a photograph of the Pale Man appeared on-screen.

'Tobias Quilp. A witch of some considerable power. Fifty-three years of age, no living relatives. Since Tobias came to our attention in the early nineteen-eighties, we have inter-viewed most of the people connected with him. School friends described a malicious young boy, fond of tormenting animals. That aside, young Tobias was an excellent student. He attended the local grammar school and earned a place at Oxford University. He studied history, his special interest being the witchcraft trials of the seventeenth century. His book on Matthew Hopkins is still the most thorough history of the witchfinder . . . '

Jake's mind raced through his knowledge of horror, real and fictional. It did not take long to locate Matthew Hopkins within his dark catalogue. For a period of only two years, from 1645 to 1647, the self-appointed 'Witchfinder General' had tortured confessions from many suspected witches. Those convicted had been hanged by the neck until they were dead, after which Hopkins would claim his reward from the local community. He had been responsible for the murder of hundreds of innocent people.

Jake's attention returned to Saxby.

'It was while researching his book on Hopkins that Tobias met Esther Inglethorpe.'

Holmwood nodded grimly. 'Mother Inglethorpe. And through her Tobias was introduced to the Crowden Coven?'

'Yes. Inglethorpe was a professor at the Oxford college where Quilp studied. She saw that Tobias had a cruel mind, much like her own. Quilp was introduced to the mysteries of black magic and he never looked back. Within a few years he was third in command of the Crowden Coven, second only to Mother Inglethorpe herself.' The picture zoomed in to focus on Quilp's neck. An ugly black mark ran around his throat. 'Here's Quilp's brand, given to him when he joined the Coven.'

Jake thought that the mark looked like a rope burn. Perhaps that was how witches identified one another. And then he remembered that strange ritual Brett made him go through every time he arrived at the Hobarron Institute. The security guard had always paid special attention to Jake's neck.

'And Quilp's demon?'

Saxby pressed a button and the image on the screen switched to a pencil sketch of Mr Pinch.

'This is our only image of the demon, an illustration from a sorcerer's spell book from around the thirteenth century. He is a powerful creature that has been a familiar to many dark witches over the centuries. As you are aware, Quilp will have been assigned his demon when he was initiated into the Crowden Coven. We know that the witch has mastered many dark arts: levitation, hexes, voodoo enchantments . . . '

'And now we have them, this Mr Pinch and Mr Quilp. They are secured in the cells downstairs?'

'And separated. I'll be preparing a full report, of course, but my first impression is that Quilp and Mother Inglethorpe plotted this together. A kill-spell like the one performed tonight is very dark magic, difficult for even an experienced witch to pull off unaided.'

'It's all very strange,' Holmwood mused. 'Why would the Coven attack one of our employees?'

'That is surely obvious, sir,' Saxby said. 'The Demontide . . . '

'The Demontide is over six months away. Of course, we would expect an attack *then*, but what possible advantage is there in attacking *now*? We have fought the Coven once in every generation, but only ever at the time of the Demontide. Between those periods we do *not* engage with them. That is how it has been for over three hundred years, so why have they broken the pattern?'

'There can be only one reason. They have heard about the weapon.'

Holmwood gave a sharp nod. 'Yes . . . But they don't know what the weapon is. Quilp must have tortured Claire trying to find out. Then, when she wouldn't tell him, he turned on the boy.'

'Are you so sure Claire *didn't* tell him?'

'She was one of us.'

'She wasn't an Elder. Not one of the old Hobarron families.'

'She was Adam Harker's wife, and I trusted her,' Holmwood insisted. 'No, I am confident that the secret is still safe.'

'As to the weapon, sir . . . '

Holmwood raised an eyebrow. 'Go on.'

'Well, you know that I've voiced concerns before about this new plan.'

'Hardly "new", Dr Saxby—the weapon has been many years in the making.'

'My objection remains the same. It is unproven and untested, and the theory behind it is . . . '

'Rooted in good, honest science,' Holmwood cut in. 'The weapon was created using the most sophisticated machinery and engineering. And it is now our best hope of destroying the demon threat once and for all.'

'But can it be trusted? Are we sure that it will even work when the time comes? Remember, if we cannot stop the Demontide then the world is lost.'

'I am aware of that, doctor. We have faced the threat many times before and we have always triumphed.'

'This time it's different,' Saxby countered. 'This time there's a real danger that we *will* fail, especially if we place *all* our trust in the weapon . . . '

'Wrong.'

Adam Harker stood in the doorway, tears wet upon his cheeks. He strode towards the table and pulled Malcolm Saxby away from his son.

'Adam, I'm so sorry for your loss . . . ' Saxby began.

'I thank you for rescuing Jake,' Adam said, 'but don't pretend you're sorry that my wife is dead. You never liked Claire.'

Holmwood placed a hand on the bereaved man's shoulder. Adam brushed it off.

'As to your objections, you needn't fear,' he continued. 'I give you my word that in six months the weapon will be fully functional. Then three hundred years of horror will end and the threat of the Demontide will be no more. Now, leave me. I need to be alone with my son.'

Holmwood took Saxby by the arm and led him from the room.

Adam stood over Jake, the tears flowing freely now.

'I hope that one day you'll be able to forgive me, son. Forgive your mother, too. We tried to protect you.'

Adam took a silver coin from his pocket and began twirling it between his fingers.

'I'm sorry that I can't make this any easier for you, Jake.' The coin danced and dazzled. 'Look at the coin. Listen to my voice. Your head is heavy, your eyes are drooping. Your memories of tonight are fading. Your mother's death, what you saw, what you heard, everything is disappearing into darkness. When you wake up you will remember only what I have told you. Concentrate on my words.'

The coin spun in a silver blur.

'Jake, *this* is how your mother died . . . '

Chapter 5
Ten Minutes in the Nightmare Box

The old woman hurried out of Waterloo Station and into Leake Street. Anyone too slow to move out of her path was elbowed aside or swatted with her cane. Ignoring the yelps and complaints, Mother Inglethorpe's thoughts focused on her destination: Number 8 Yaga Passage. A phone call had summoned her to the Coven's London Headquarters. It seemed that Tobias Quilp's mission had not gone to plan.

Esther Inglethorpe shuddered at the thought of explaining their failure to the Coven Master. She needed to get her story in order, and so she went back to the beginning . . .

It had all started six months ago, with a rumour that the Hobarron Elders had devised a powerful new weapon. Mother Inglethorpe had not taken the story very seriously but the leader of the Coven had insisted on an investigation. The Coven numbered three Dark Seers among its thirteen members: Roland Grype, Ambrose Montague, and Felicity

Summers. Using the magic of their demons, these witches could see into people's homes, listen to their conversations, even eavesdrop on their thoughts. Together, they had been able to cut through the scientific and magical security cordon that the Hobarron Elders put up around themselves.

Almost as soon as they had bent their thoughts upon the weapon, Felicity Summers had been struck dead. Some form of magic employed by the Elders had felt her presence and lashed out across the miles. Even Esther's heart had trembled at the sight of the young woman's sudden death.

Then, almost immediately, another magical infection had struck, this time at Ambrose Montague. Well used to such attacks, the old man had escaped more or less unscathed. If you can call losing your left eye unscathed, Esther thought. An invisible hand had reached out for the witch and plucked the eye clean out of its socket.

Only that odious little man Roland Grype had pierced the Hobarron defences long enough to learn something. Esther remembered how he had crawled towards the head of their Coven, panting, exhausted, but obviously proud of his achievement.

'There *is* a weapon,' Grype hissed. 'I cannot be sure, but I believe the Elders have been developing it for many years. It is their last defence against the Demontide.'

'We must learn more,' the founder of the Coven had said. 'Tell me, did you see anyone closely connected to this weapon?'

'Claire Harker,' Grype nodded, delighted to have a ready answer.

'Adam Harker's wife,' Esther had sniffed. 'She's a mechanical engineer. Builds machines, computer systems, that sort of thing. Maybe the Elders have asked her to create a device that they can use against the Door. Some kind of machine that could destroy the entrance into the demon world.'

'A powerful device indeed,' the Coven Master whispered. 'Mrs Harker will pay dearly for her actions . . .'

He had then turned to Esther and Tobias Quilp. Their task was to learn all they could about the weapon. Esther knew that a secret operation was their only hope. The Hobarron Institute was a powerful organization, its wealth vast, its connections reaching into the highest levels of government. In the magical world, too, the Elders could not be underestimated.

A headstrong young witch called Sidney Tinsmouth had once tried to frighten the Elders by murdering a little girl within the grounds of the Institute. All agreed that it had been an amusing trick, but the Coven as a whole had paid very dearly for it. Tinsmouth himself was captured and, no doubt, executed. The Elders had been merciless in their revenge and had killed eight Coven witches in a single night. Although they had since recruited new members, the lesson was well learned. They could only attack the Institute when they were absolutely sure of their power.

And so Esther and Tobias had met at her cottage one warm August afternoon. There, in her garden of deadly nightshade, the two witches had devised their plan. It was obvious that, although Claire Harker was *not* an Elder, she was still unlikely to give up the secret easily.

'Maybe we could use the son,' Tobias had suggested.

'Son?' Mother Inglethorpe frowned. 'I was not aware the Harkers had a son.'

Quilp passed her an envelope. Inside she found three photographs, each showing a thin, lanky boy with brown hair falling over his eyes.

'Looks rather *soft*, doesn't he?' Quilp grinned. 'I'm sure that Mr Pinch could convince Claire to talk, especially if the boy was threatened.'

'My clever Tobias,' Inglethorpe chuckled. 'Yes, I think that will do very well.'

Of course, there had been *some* risk involved. Finding a time when Claire and Jake Harker were alone was the main difficulty. Using his Seer abilities, Grype had discovered that mother and son sometimes walked home together in the evenings. The other problem Esther foresaw was the chance that Claire or Jake might escape and tell Dr Holmwood what had happened. Tobias had reassured Esther on that score.

'After we learn all we can about the machine, Mr Pinch will kill them both—then we can dispose of the bodies. No one need ever know what really happened.'

It had seemed a foolproof plan. So what had gone wrong?

Mother Inglethorpe turned out of the noisy street and into an alleyway cloaked in silence. A sign bolted to the wall proclaimed this place:

YAGA Passage

The street was long and narrow, the pavement slick with ice. The soot-blackened walls either side leaned in at such an angle that it seemed only a matter of time before the buildings tumbled against each other. Mother Inglethorpe looked up once or twice. She caught sight of a parade of strange figures watching her from their windows. Creatures with the heads of animals and the bodies of men; shapes with long, spidery limbs and glowing eyes; ghostly forms that evaporated as soon as they were glimpsed. In one window she saw the silhouette of an eight-armed woman painting her forty fingernails.

Esther reached the door of a grubby-looking bookshop and rang the bell. Her eye slipped across the sign:

Crowden's
Emporium of Forgotten & Forbidden Books

A face appeared at the window. Mr Grype squinted. Almost amusing, Esther thought, that a Seer should have such bad eyesight. He ushered her in.

'Step in, step in, quickly now.' Grype glanced over her shoulder into the dark stretch of Yaga Passage. 'There are things living in this street I do not trust.'

'Your neighbours have always been somewhat strange,' Mother Inglethorpe admitted.

'Visitors from the borderland,' Grype sneered. 'Mangey

half-breeds. Still, a witch need not necessarily fear them, as long as she has her magic about her.'

Esther sniffed. Her fingers went to her breast and sought out the place in which Miss Creekley, her demon, nestled. Reassured, she followed Grype into the shop.

The air was musty with the smell of old paper. In every corner, upon every surface, floor to ceiling, wall to wall, books had been stacked and balanced and wedged until it appeared that the shop itself was constructed from old, leather-bound volumes. Mother Inglethorpe scanned a few of the titles: *A Practical Guide to Raising Demons*; *The Devil's Black Book—a Directory of the Damned*; *Hair, Skin and Fingernails—Their Use in Transformation Spells*; *Pyromancy—the Art of Reading the Future in Flames* (partly singed).

The only feature of the room, besides the creaking bookcases, was a big old fireplace. A few coals glowed in the grate, giving the room what little light and warmth it possessed. A dusty, ugly-looking bird perching upon the mantelpiece watched Mother Inglethorpe as she crossed the room. This was Mr Hegarty, Grype's familiar. It was a low-caste demon, its magic limited to the gift of Second Sight. In keeping with the bizarre humour of such creatures, it had managed to tear out its own eyes.

'Tell that hideous thing to stop watching me.'

Grype stroked the demon-bird's neck, ignoring the black beetles that fell from its plumage.

'Be nice to Mr Hegarty. He is a great favourite of Master Crowden's, and you need all the goodwill you can get after tonight's mess . . . Well, we better not keep him waiting. Follow me.'

'I know the way. You stay here and dust your books, *librarian*.'

Esther knew how much Grype hated that word. Librarian. It reflected his lowly position within the Coven. With his powers more or less limited to that of Second Sight, he had been given the job of cataloguing the Master's vast collection of supernatural tomes.

The witch left her enemy seething by the fire and went to Grype's small back office. This room was as crowded as the main shop, every surface cluttered with books. Mother Inglethorpe paused before a curtained doorway. The sign above the door:

THE MANAGEMENT—Entry strictly forbidden

The curtain fluttered. A breeze sighed out of the doorway and clutched Mother Inglethorpe around the throat. Summoning her courage, she stepped forward. The curtain flapped behind her and she left the world of the living and entered the Veil.

Her soul—what was left of it—quaked. It always did when she came here.

The Veil was not dark, and yet she struggled to see. It was not cold, and yet the atmosphere froze her to the marrow. Over the centuries mankind had given this place many names: the Passing Gate, the River Styx, the River of Three Crossings, Limbo, some even mistakenly thought that it was Hell. But Hell was filled with the hideous and the tormented—this was a realm of nothingness. It was the place through which the dead passed on their journey into the afterlife. As such, it was never supposed to be a home to anyone.

All the same, the black magician Marcus Crowden had made it *his* home.

'Mother Inglethorpe, welcome.'

Crowden came from out of the shadows, his strange cabinet floating behind him. The man—if he could still be called a man—was tall and broad. He wore the costume of a seventeeth century gentleman: a three-quarter length cloak, plain shirt and waistcoat. Buckles adorned his wide-brimmed hat and bucket boots. The hat sat low upon his brow and a dirty piece of cloth had been wound around the lower half of his face, so that only his eyes could be seen, hard and glinting.

Esther had been a witch for over forty years and had encountered many monstrous things. Even so, nothing chilled her quite as much as being in the presence of Master Crowden, the immortal leader of their Coven. From his own time of the 1600s to the present day, Crowden had straddled the centuries, never aging, never dying. *That* was powerful magic indeed. And yet Esther wondered—had the toll of those long years been scored upon his face? Is that why he kept it hidden?

She bowed. 'Please, what has happened to Tobias Quilp?'

'Tobias has been captured,' Crowden said. His voice was soft, almost musical. 'Both he and his demon are locked away in the vaults of the Institute.'

Esther stifled a sob. 'We must save him.'

'Pointless. We could not hope to take on the Elders within their own fortress. We must forget about Quilp, he is lost to us now.'

'No.'

'You naysay me, madam?'

Like a prowling lion, Crowden circled his favourite witch. Esther could feel his rancid breath upon her skin.

'It gives me no joy to tell you that your beloved is lost, yet it is so, and must be faced. And unfortunately his sacrifice appears to have achieved little. Claire Harker is dead but the weapon remains a secret.'

'She would not give it up?'

'From what I can gather, Quilp murdered her only after he was convinced that she would never betray the Elders.'

'Stupid woman.'

'Do not confuse stupidity and bravery, such ignorance does not become a member of my coven. We must now focus our efforts upon gathering all the information we can regarding this weapon. And from now on we must be discreet. Your clumsy attempts tonight have put the Elders on their guard. I do not believe they will launch an attack, but we have to be careful. Six months from now the Demontide will be at hand. It has been thwarted for over three hundred years—every generation of Elders has prevented it—but this time we shall prevail. The Door *will* be opened and demonkind will be set free. Imagine it, Mother Inglethorpe! Thousands of demons roaming the Earth, and all of them at *my* command!'

Esther's thin blood stirred at her master's words.

'And your part in our victory will be vital,' Crowden continued. 'I want you to watch Dr Harker, seek out clues as to the Elders' weapon. In the end, if your surveillance proves fruitless, we can always try your trick one last time.'

'Torture the boy.' Esther smiled.

'Indeed.'

'How *did* you first hear of the device, Master Crowden?' Esther asked.

'A little bird told of it. A spy from the Hobarron roost. And that was all that was told: the whisper of a weapon.'

'Who is the spy?'

'Ah, now that is *my* secret . . . One other thing that may interest you: Quilp managed one last act of cruelty before the Elders took him.'

Crowden waved a hand through the air. In the swirl of cloud that issued from his fingers, Esther could make out the form of a young man. Tattered clothes hung from his stocky frame. He looked frightened, his eyes darting in every direction. His hands had been bound together and there was a scarlet-stained bandage around his neck.

'His name is Simon Lydgate,' Crowden said. 'A friend of Jacob Harker. I had him picked up after I received the news of Quilp's failure. Mr Pinch had left the boy in a rather desperate state. It's remarkable he survived.'

'Why not kill him?'

'Bloodthirsty as always, my dear. But no, I think young Master Lydgate may prove useful to us. For the time being I will leave him in Grype's care. And now as to your punishment . . .'

Ten Minutes in the Nightmare Box

A shiver ran the length of Mother Inglethorpe's body. When Crowden had offered her the task of watching the Harkers, she had thought her failed plan had been forgiven. She ought to have known better. Forbidden knowledge and new spells awaited those that had served Crowden well. Witches that fell short of his expectations were not so lucky.

The Coven Master made a gesture with his forefinger and his black cabinet swept forward. Constructed entirely of wood, it was exactly like any stage magician's cabinet, except in one respect. This box was *alive*. The witches of the Coven had often wondered why their master did not appear to have a familiar of his own. Some speculated that, due to his vast experience of witchcraft, he had dispensed with the need for demonic power. Mother Inglethorpe had heard of such witches. In the old days, it was said that they could work spells through the natural magic of the world around them. The magic of the earth, of trees and streams, of the wind and the sea. Esther dismissed these tales as silly nonsense. Even Marcus Crowden needed his demon if he was to work magic.

A demon that took the shape of a wooden box filled with nightmares.

'Your punishment, madam. You must step inside my cabinet.'

'Please, Master, I am sorry . . . '

'No tears. Ten minutes in the box is all that I demand. Are you still my faithful servant?'

The door of the cabinet creaked open.

'Always,' she murmured.

Mother Inglethorpe stepped into the box.

The door slammed shut.

A moment later, the screams began.

Six Months Later

Chapter 6
Something Nasty in the Boathouse

Jake and Claire Harker stood before the canal tunnel.

Somewhere in the darkness a killer lurked.

'Come on, Jake,' Claire grinned, quickening her pace, 'let's get home. Your dad won't be too much longer and then we can eat. What would you like for tea?'

'Mum, wait . . . '

It didn't feel right—the brightly-lit canal, the chuckling water, the cheeriness of his mother. The whole scene was wrong. Jake held back, stared into the tunnel.

'Don't go in there.'

His mum laughed and marched on.

'NO!'

'Jake? Are you in there? Are you OK?'

The nightmare dissolved into the bathroom mirror. Jake's

reflection stared back at him. Another flashback. They were becoming rarer, as his therapist told him they would, but they still had the power to terrify him. He ran a basin of icy water and splashed his face. Still shivering, he opened the bathroom door.

Rachel stood outside. She looked at Jake for a moment and then dragged him into an embrace.

'I heard you were here,' she said. 'It's good to see you.'

Jake could only nod.

Downstairs, the Institute Summer Ball roared on. Glasses chinked, music played, and jokes were batted between friends. There had been an awkward lull when Adam Harker arrived with his son, but as soon as Jake slipped away the party atmosphere returned. The problem was that none of them had seen him since Claire's death. A death so sudden and terrible that they did not know how to console him. Only Rachel had bothered to seek him out.

'Fancy grabbing some fresh air?' she asked.

Jake followed her through the corridors of Green Gables, Dr Holmwood's huge manor house. By trying a dozen winding routes they found the back stairs and the door to the gardens. Once outside, Jake breathed a little easier.

'Bit much?' Rachel said, nodding towards the house.

'Yeah. Bit much.'

They walked on in silence. The grass crunched beneath their feet and the scent of jasmine hung heavy upon the night air. A hundred species of rose grew in the neatly tended beds that bordered the pathways. Sleepless insects droned around their heads. When they reached the riverbank, the sun was just dipping over the horizon, its last rays touching the water and dyeing it the colour of blood.

'We missed you at school,' Rachel said.

'We?'

'Sure. There's that kid in the year below you get on with. The one into zombies and stuff. And then there's Miss Bowles from biology, she asked after you. Even Killjoy Kilfoy misses you. Told me the other day that he hasn't read a decent horror story since you . . . ' Rachel took his hand. '*I've* missed you, Jake.'

Was that pity in her voice? Jake didn't want her pity. But if she'd genuinely missed him . . .

'Where have you been?'

The question was bound to be asked by someone, sometime. Jake had thought he wouldn't be able to answer it. Now he found the truth rushing out of him in a flood.

'After Mum died—after she was killed—my dad took six months off work. We travelled a lot; saw some amazing things—the pyramids, Niagara Falls, the ancient city of Petra. We stayed in the poshest hotels. Dr Holmwood paid for it all. It was . . . very nice of him. Everywhere we stayed, Dr Holmwood arranged for someone to see me, you know? Check that I was doing OK. I'm fine though.' Jake stole a glance at Rachel. 'Really, they said I'm fine now. I'm not mental or anything.'

Rachel squeezed Jake's hand.

'When we came home, I could've gone back to school but . . . '

'You weren't ready.'

'Dr Holmwood paid for private tuition. I'm behind, but I'll catch up. Probably have to take my GCSEs next year, though.'

'They were a nightmare!' Rachel said, rolling her eyes. 'But a brainbox like you shouldn't have any trouble.'

'The only thing I'm really behind with is biology. My mum used to help me out—she was a biologist before she switched to engineering. She used to...' A sob hitched in his throat. 'She . . .'

'It's all right, Jake. Let it out. You've been so brave . . .'

Jake's anger flared in an instant. He tore his hand from Rachel's.

'Brave?' he snarled. 'You think I'm brave? Are you some kind of idiot?'

Anger burned through his body. It spread out from his heart and engulfed his mind. All at once the world around him seemed to fade and he could hear a faint voice whisper deep within: *Welcome to your prison, Coven Master . . .*

'Jake? Can you hear me? Are you all right?'

The vision fell away. He saw Rachel, confused and hurt.

'I'm sorry. I don't know why I said that. It's just, I wasn't brave, Rachel. My mum and Simon were murdered right before my eyes, and I did nothing to save them.'

'The paper said it was a lunatic. He could've killed you too, Jake. He tried. I heard you'd been hurt.'

Jake pulled up his trouser leg. An ugly purple scar ran around his calf.

'My God, it looks like an animal bite.'

'I guess that's exactly what *he* was,' Jake said bitterly. 'An animal.'

'Do you remember much about him? What he looked like?'

'No. The police went on at me for days but the psychiatrists said I must have shut it out. They even tried to hypnotize me. Didn't work. But sometimes I still see bits of what happened. The bridge, my mum, somebody waiting in the dark. And something else . . . It's crazy, Rachel. Sometimes I see a monkey.'

'A monkey?'

'Or something like a monkey, clambering out of the tree. You know that big old oak by the canal? The one they used as a gallows years ago? They called it Demon's Dance . . . *Demons* . . .'

'Jake?'

'The memory of that night, Rachel—somehow it's not real.'

'I don't understand.'

'The bits I do remember—my mum asking me what I wanted for tea, even the moonlight on the water—it's as if it's a story I read in a book.'

'I guess it must seem like that. A dream, a nightmare.'

'No. I *know* my mother and Simon died. I know *they* killed them. But I also know that it was worse, so much worse than I remember it.'

'They? You think there were two of them?'

'A man,' Jake nodded, 'and something else. Something that came down out of the tree.'

The river burbled and grew darker as the sun slipped behind the trees. From the wood came the first stirrings of night creatures. Rachel took Jake's face in her hands and gazed into his eyes. The river, the forest, and the world fell away from Jake until all that was left was the angelic face before him. His heart throbbed, a deep and joyful beat.

'Do you know what I think?' she whispered. 'I think you're heartbroken. I think you're picking up the pieces of your life. It's hard, it hurts, it's taking a long time, and I think you need a friend to help you.'

She kissed him gently on the brow. With her touch, he felt the fire again in his veins, only this time it wasn't the flame of rage.

Rachel pulled away and the feeling was lost.

'Call me,' she said.

'Yeah. Yeah, I will . . . Are we going back to the house?'

'It's peaceful here. A good place to think; you should stay. We'll talk later.'

Jake watched until Rachel disappeared among the trees.

He took her advice and stayed by the riverbank for a while, thinking over the last six months.

After the murder, a passerby had found him in the woods that bordered the canal. An ambulance was called and he was taken to hospital. He had been unconscious and, at that time, it was not clear what had happened to his mother. When Jake woke up, and started screaming about a crazed killer, the murder hunt swung into action. Within a few hours, his mum's body had been found downstream of the canal tunnel. Despite the police not being able to trace Simon Lydgate, Jake continued to insist that his best friend had died trying to save him. He was interviewed many times in the weeks that followed but his memories of what had happened remained vague.

Weeks turned into months and no clue as to the identity of the killer could be found. Adam had taken time off work and father and son spent every moment together. Jake had always been close to his dad, and now the loss of his mum strengthened that bond. They had shared everything in these last months: their memories of Claire, their plans for the future . . .

Raised voices drew Jake out of his memories.

'What you're suggesting is evil, Saxby. Pure evil.'

It was his dad—there was an ugliness in his voice that Jake had never heard before.

'We've tried your way, Harker, and it hasn't worked. This is the only thing we can do now,' Rachel's father said, equally enraged.

Dr Holmwood broke in. 'Gentlemen, please . . . '

Jake crept through the trees, following the sound of the argument.

'I'm sorry, Adam,' Holmwood said, 'but I'm afraid Malcolm is right. Time is running out. We must consider other options.'

'Only two weeks remain,' Dr Saxby hissed. 'Two weeks before the Demontide. If we don't act soon then every demon in existence will be set free. They will kill every living thing and then they will claim this world as their own.

Do you understand what I'm saying, Harker? We are facing Armageddon!'

Jake stopped. He was standing on a raised bank. Below, in one of the sunken rose gardens, the three men huddled together. Adam tore the tie from his neck and jabbed a finger into Saxby's chest.

'I'm well aware of the Demontide, Malcolm. I have devoted every hour of every day to stopping it from happening. What have *you* been doing during all that time, eh? Pottering away in your lab, coming up with scientific defences against the Coven. Defences little better than guns and bullets . . . '

'My guns and bullets saved the life of your son!' Saxby bristled. 'The Institute took a big risk in allowing the weapon project to go ahead, Harker. If anyone found out—the government, the media—we could have been exposed. But we let Claire continue her work because what was promised to us was a miracle. *A weapon born of science that could destroy the demon threat once and for all.* I had my doubts but, believe me, I wanted this to work. And now it pains me to say it, it really does, but the weapon has failed.'

'You can't know that. Not yet.'

Dr Saxby sighed. 'I can, Adam. I can because your wife is dead.'

Adam Harker hit Dr Saxby square in the jaw. Jake knew that his father had always hated violence, and so he watched open-mouthed as Saxby staggered back into one of the rose bushes. Adam stalked away. Dr Holmwood helped Saxby to his feet.

'You know I'm right, Gordon,' Saxby wheezed. 'We have seen not one scrap of evidence that the weapon works.'

'True,' Holmwood mused, 'but given a *little* more time . . .'

'You said yourself, there is *no* more time. In a matter of weeks, this entire planet will stand upon the brink of Hell. If the weapon fails then we have to be prepared to take extreme measures.' Saxby grabbed hold of the old man. 'We must be prepared to kill.'

'I have committed such an act once before,' Holmwood said. 'Twenty-five years ago I took the life of an innocent child for the greater good. I'm not sure I could do it again.'

'We must,' Saxby insisted, 'or the world will fall to *them*. Crowden and his Coven of foul witches have waited for centuries. They will do anything to ensure that the Door is opened.'

'I must think,' Holmwood said. 'And I must speak to Joanna before I come to any decision. Come on, let's get back to the party.'

Jake wandered through the grounds. He hardly knew where he was going. The words 'Coven' and 'Demontide' reeled through his mind, tantalizing him with images that remained just out of reach. And then there was the name 'Joanna'. Jake knew only one person by that name. Surely Dr Holmwood didn't mean her . . .

A small boy darted out of the trees and cannoned into Jake. The child looked up, eyes filled with terror.

'I've seen it!'

Jake squatted down to the kid's level. 'Seen what?'

'Something *nasty* in the boathouse.'

'You're Sam Drake, aren't you? Your dad works with my dad at the Institute. I'm Jake. Come on, Sam, we'll find your parents. There's nothing to be scared of.'

Sam pulled away. 'There *is*. I went 'splorin' by myself and I saw it. There's a monster in the boathouse.'

With that, Sam Drake took off along the path. Jake watched until the kid disappeared into the house. Then he turned and walked towards the river.

Demons—monsters—his thoughts flew back to the night of his mother's murder. Something *nasty* in the tunnel. Perhaps the answers to all his questions waited in the boathouse . . .

He jogged down the path, his senses alert for any movement in the forest either side. At last, he came to the boathouse. The size and shape of a hay barn, it jutted out a few metres into the river. The open door creaked on its hinges. There was no light on and the only sound was the slap of water against wood. As Jake approached, he saw marks in the sandy soil in front of the boathouse. Footprints left by the terrified child.

'Anyone in there?' he called.

No answer.

Monsters. Demons.

He took a deep breath and stepped inside.

The place smelt of algae and motor oil. It was very dark. Jake ferreted in his pocket for his mobile phone and flipped it open. The illuminated screen acted as a kind of torch. By its light, he saw shelves crowded with old jam jars and tins of paint. Coils of rope, life jackets, canvas sails, fishing rods, and tackle boxes littered the floor. A raised walkway acted as a kind of jetty, a motor boat floating in the water below. The boat, a neat little vessel with a powerful outboard motor, had been covered over with a sheet of tarpaulin. Peeking out from under the sheet was the boat's name, painted around the prow:

Witchfinder

Again, something niggled at Jake's memory.

Witchfinder. Someone talking about a book written about Matthew Hopkins, the Witchfinder General. A brightly-lit room. A pencil sketch of a monster. A metal table. A silver coin, spinning before his eyes. '*This is how your mother di*—'

A voice interrupted his thoughts—

'*Jacob-sss.*'

It came from the rafters. Jake shone his makeshift torch upwards. Old spider webs wafted in the breeze. He swept the light across the roof—more spider webs, these ones fresh, the strands as thick as rope. With each new web the designs became ever more intricate and sturdy. The last, hanging above the boathouse's riverside door, shimmered like a silver cathedral. At the centre of this amazing construction sat the creator of the web, its two green eyes glowering.

The light failed. Jake flipped the phone shut and open again. It was no good: the battery had died.

'*Jacob-sss, I seee youuu.*'

The water lapped against the sides of the boat.

And then another sound came out of the darkness. The

click-click-click of insect legs. A monster was descending from the rafters.

Jake tried to run but his legs wouldn't move. This was impossible. Here he was, rooted to the spot, while something from another world closed in upon him. Surely he was dreaming. And yet this felt right—more real, in fact, than the memories of his mother's death.

Demons.

The black shape of the creature scuttled down the wall. It came closer, closer. Jake even thought he could see the dull gleam of its exoskeleton.

'*Ssshall I eat you, Jacob? Ssssecretly gobble you up? The Coven need never know. My misssstresss need never know.*'

Jake closed his eyes. Fear and memories raged inside his head.

'Miss Creekley! To me!'

The riverside doors burst open and moonlight flooded into the boathouse. Jake could hardly believe his eyes.

A woman was standing in the middle of the river—standing *on* the water! What happened next passed in a blur. Something small shot out of the boathouse and scuttled across the water. Jake saw it climb up the woman's body and into the folds of her dress. Then the stranger swept backwards across the river and disappeared into the trees on the far bank. This strange spectacle was over in the space of ten seconds.

Jake ran to the boathouse doors. He scanned the bank and the river. There was nothing to be seen.

The witch and her demon had vanished.

Chapter 7
Dreams of the witchfinder

Jake tried to concentrate on his maths homework. He had already missed several months of school and, although the private tuition organized by Dr Holmwood was excellent, he had been forced to postpone his GCSE exams until the following year. He couldn't afford to fall further behind.

OK then, he thought, here goes: *Triangle ABC is isosceles. AB = AC = 12 cm. Angle ABC is . . .* Jake groaned and pushed the question book aside.

It was no good, he couldn't concentrate. Fresh air—that was what he needed. He headed for the door.

It was warm outside, the promise of a glorious summer on the late May air. Turning left out of his street, Jake strode through the park and playing fields. For what felt like the millionth time, he went over in his head what had happened at Dr Holmwood's party. The scene in the boathouse with the spider-monster and the woman on the water seemed too crazy to have been real but, coupled with the argument he had overheard in the garden, it all made a twisted kind of sense.

From what Jake could make out, a coven of witches was determined to bring about the 'Demontide', during which demonic forces would break free and take over the world. The Hobarron Institute had developed a weapon to stop them, but Dr Saxby doubted that it would work. He was trying to persuade Dr Holmwood into another, more deadly course of action.

Jake took these revelations in his stride. The idea that the stuffy Hobarron Institute was not only a scientific community, but an organization dedicated to fighting witches and demons, should have shocked him to the core. Yet it was as if he already knew this story.

'Of course you do,' Jake murmured, 'it all has something to do with Mum's death. She worked on the weapon: that's why she was murdered. It wasn't a psychopath, it was one of them. The Coven . . . '

'Harker?'

Silas Jones crossed the playing field and made his way towards Jake. The bully seemed to have lost weight and it looked as if he hadn't slept in weeks.

'Harker,' Silas repeated. His eyes were everywhere at once, staring into the trees that bordered the playing fields, flitting back to Jake, then out to the main road. 'How've you been?'

'Fine,' Jake said, surprised at Silas's concern.

'Good.' Silas's left eye twitched nervously. 'I'm good, too.

Stopped messing around and got myself a plumbing appren-
ticeship. Not been in trouble for months.'

'Really?' Jake couldn't hide his amazement.

'Yeah . . . Listen, I was . . . er . . . sorry to hear about your
mum. Her being killed and stuff—that really . . . sucked . . .
So, I've been looking out for you for a while now. Where've
you been?'

'Abroad. Me and my dad . . . '

'I wanted to know if you'd seen *him* again.'

'Who?'

'That freak. That skinny, pale-assed freak.'

'I don't know who you mean.'

'That day—the day your mum was done in—we saw him.
Don't you remember?' There was a kind of pleading in
Silas's voice. 'I went to the police afterwards. Told 'em I'd
seen this nutcase with you that afternoon. I've been in trou-
ble a lot of times, yeah? I know all the cops at the station.
But the guy who interviewed me, I'd never seen him before.
An old guy, big head, yellow teeth, smelt of fags.'

Dr Holmwood. So the Institute's power even extended
into the police, Jake thought.

'He told me to forget what I'd seen. Said it wasn't important. But the thing is, Jake, I can't get that guy out of my
head. You do remember him, don't you? He told me to be
good or he would come and find me. The Pale Man . . . '

Jake froze. He felt memories crumbling, walls of lies frac-
turing apart. Blades of light appeared between the cracks
and Jake cried out. The truth burned inside his mind. The
Pale Man. The man on the road. Mr Culp? Mr Kilp? No . . .

Mr Quilp.

Quilp and his demon.

'Hey, Harker, you OK?'

Jake stared into the haunted eyes of Silas Jones.

'I remember him,' he murmured. 'I remember every-thing . . .'

'Are you sure you're all right, Jake? You look . . .'

'How do I look?' Jake said, eyeing his father.

'I don't know. Tired. A bit upset . . .'

'I am "a bit upset", I suppose.' His laugh had a bitter sting to it. 'I guess I just don't like being manipulated and lied to.'

Jake caught sight of his reflection in the kitchen window. The pale boy with the haggard face and hollow eyes looked like a stranger. In the hours after his meeting with Silas Jones, Jake had wandered the town, piecing together the past and growing angrier as each memory fell into place. As soon as his dad got home from the Institute, Jake had cornered him in the kitchen.

'Lied to?' Adam frowned. 'Who's lied to you?'

'Everyone. For example, the night Mum died—*you* were there.'

'I beg your pardon?'

Soap suds from the washing up dripped from Adam's hands. The bubbles shimmered . . .

'I remember—something shiny in your hand.' Jake got up from the kitchen table and stood in front of his father. 'A coin. You told me you were sorry.'

'That was at the hospital, after you'd regained conscious-ness, I was sorry because your mum had died and . . . '

'The room was clinical,' Jake snapped. 'Sterile. I was lying on a bed.'

'That's right, the hospital bed. Jake, I don't underst—'

'Didn't seem like a hospital bed. It was metal. An exami-nation table, like the ones you see in alien abduction movies.'

'Don't be ridiculous.' Adam managed a small, dry chuckle.

'I was strapped down.'

'You weren't strapped down, Jake.'

'I was. And it wasn't a hospital.'

'It was New Town Accident and Emergency.'

'Stop lying to me!' Jake roared. 'It was the Institute. I was held prisoner by the Hobarron bloody Institute!'

'Jake, please . . . '

'I was strapped down to a table and hypnotized!'

'Just calm down. We can talk this out...'

'You were there. So was Dr Saxby and Dr Holmwood. You were arguing about magic and demons. And a weapon.' Jake smashed his fist against the kitchen door. 'Tell me the truth, Dad! Tell me about the witch and the demon that killed my mum. Tell me about the machine she built. Tell me about what will happen at the Demontide!'

Adam gaped at his son. He looked frightened, guilty, and careworn—all at the same time. Suddenly, he reached out and drew Jake into a hug. Jake could feel his father shaking. In that moment, his fury vanished.

'It's all right, Dad. We're going to be OK.'

Adam gave a shivery laugh. 'I should be the one telling you that. The truth is, I don't think we *are* going to be OK, son. Not any more. Not unless . . . '

Adam released Jake and rushed into the hall. He pulled on his coat and grabbed his car keys from the pocket.

'Stay here,' he instructed. 'Don't move from this house until you hear from me. There are some things I have to take care of at the Institute. Then we're leaving. Pack some clothes, just a small bag. We travel light.'

'Where are we going?'

'I don't know yet. Somewhere far away. The States maybe, or the Far East.'

'But the Demontide,' Jake said. 'You have to be here to stop it. The weapon—'

'It's too late for that. Saxby was right—the weapon will never work. And if we stay . . . '

Dread washed across Adam Harker's face.

'What is it, Dad? What does Dr Saxby want to do? I heard you arguing at the party last night. He said something about being prepared to kill.'

'That's enough. Get packed.'

Adam dashed down the corridor. The front door slammed shut.

Nine o'clock, and there was still no sign of his dad. Jake heated up some takeaway pizza and sat nibbling pepperoni slices in front of the TV. He stared at the phone, willing it to ring. Maybe he could call his dad's mobile or try his private line at work. He managed to resist. An instinct told him that, at this stage, the mighty Hobarron Institute might be as dangerous to him as the mysterious Coven.

Eleven o'clock. An hour of wearing a hole in the lounge carpet and midnight arrived. Jake swore as the first chime rang out from the clock in the hall. He could cycle over to Hobarron; tell Brett at the gate that he was dropping something off for his dad. He'd give Adam another hour and then he'd have to do something.

He picked up an old comic from the bookcase and dropped into an armchair. He hadn't read any horror since his mother's death. He didn't need to.

'I'm living my own horror story now,' he murmured.

Maybe he'd just dip into this one, for old time's sake . . .

The sand was soft beneath his boots, the air damp on his face. He moved with stealthy, catlike strides, always alert for signs that he was being watched. His gaze swept the clifftops. Content that only the moon tracked his progress, he continued across the bay. The wind had died and the night birds stayed songless in their nests. The sea, as tranquil as a millpond, did no more than whisper against the shore. It was as if the world was holding its breath, waiting to see if he would fail. If he did, then the Age of Man was over. In a few hours, a new and terrible dawn would break across this land—across all lands. From the mouth of this little bay, the Demontide would begin.

As if in response to this vision, a blue flame crackled between his fingers. It was not enough. Digging deep into himself he tried to summon the full extent of his powers. Thoughts of Eleanor filled his mind. Pretty Eleanor, his childhood sweetheart, who had promised to be his when all this was over. They would be married in his father's church in the village of Starfall. Ever proud of his son, the old preacher himself would conduct the ceremony.

He went on imagining, conjuring pictures of his and Eleanor's life together—their first home, the birth of their children, birthdays and Christmases. God willing, these things would come to pass. But if he faltered now then there was no future for him and Eleanor. No future for his father and mother, or for anyone else in this beautiful and miserable world.

Power surged into his arm. The flame roared.

He began to climb the rocks on the far side of the bay. The large cavern loomed overhead. There was a superstition in the village that this cave had a voice. Lying awake in his room at the tavern, he had heard it himself: a low moan that called out from the bay. He was steeped in superstition and believed many impossible things. Within the pages of his diary, he had recorded his encounters with dozens of unholy creatures and, upon his body, the story of his magical life could be read in a hundred scars and burns. However, as an occult expert, he was convinced that the so-called 'Voice of the Cave' was nothing more than the echo of the wind. In fact, this was one of the few natural phenomena that he had observed since coming to this accursed place. Every other strange thing had been the result of magic . . .

The darkest he had ever known.

He stood now in the mouth of the cave, the flame dancing between his fingers. Blue light licked up the cavern walls and shimmered across the stalactites. It was not cold but still he drew his cloak close about him. Hairs on the back of his neck bristled to attention. Every fibre of his being felt it, thick upon the air: Evil. He had been aware of it all his life. Evil like an icy hand upon his cheek, like a freezing fist clasped around his heart. To feel the presence of true, demonic Evil was a gift, his father had said, and he must *use it wisely. He must seek evil out and, with the help of God, put an end to it.*

As a boy, his ability had been a curse, and he had done all he could to ignore it. Only in this last year had he truly used his gift. He had seen the cruelty and the injustice meted out to the poor folk by people like Matthew Hopkins and the other witchfinders. Men who saw witches everywhere and lined their purses with blood money. His father had encouraged him to follow these men wherever they went and to challenge their work. The irony was that he had been confused with them, and labelled a witchfinder, too.

The latest outbreak of witch-hunting had started in a little village by the sea. From the moment he had stepped into the community, he had felt Evil everywhere. In the streets and houses, in the river, even in the church. It had choked the air and poured out of every doorway.

Here was a place where real witches thrived.

Now, standing in this cave, he felt it stronger than ever. Pure Evil. He touched the enchanted glass ball that hung around his neck . . .

A man came forward out of the darkness. Behind him floated a tall black box.

The Coven Master smiled.

'Welcome, Witchfinder.'

Jake woke with a start. He looked down at his hands, half-expecting to find the blue flame flickering between his fingers. He had never had a dream so vivid, so *real*. It felt as if the dream had come to him in the same way the memories of his mother's murder had returned. A sudden flash emerging from a hidden part of his mind, but what did it mean . . . ?

The front door slammed shut. His father's voice rang out—

'Where are you?'

Jake ran out into the hall. Adam, his face drawn with fear, his clothes muddied and torn, raced to meet his son. Thick files stuffed with paper spilled out from under his arms. His words came in panicked snatches.

'They're—almost here—go upstairs—now!'

'Who's almost here?' Jake could hear panic in his own voice.

'Holmwood—Saxby—*her*. Go. If I can, I'll explain later.'

A thunderous crack sounded from the front of the house. Splinters appeared in the door. Adam pushed Jake down the hall and towards the stairs.

'Get into bed,' he hissed. 'If they start questioning you, play dumb. Don't try to call the police. They have eyes everywhere. Whatever you hear now, whatever you see, stay upstairs. Promise me.'

'But, Dad . . . '

'Promise!'

Jake gave a reluctant nod.

'OK. Now, go . . . '

The door gave way.

Jake caught a glimpse of Dr Holmwood and a dozen white-coated men on the lawn. He didn't think Holmwood had seen *him*. Obeying his father, he ran to the stairs.

A torn sheet of blue paper caught Jake's eye as he hit the first step. It must have fallen out of his dad's files. He scooped it up, stuffed it in his pocket and bounded upstairs.

Noise—clamour—swearing. The sound of Adam Harker being dragged to his knees. Questions—*What have I done? Where are you taking me?* No answers. Adam's heels kicked against the floor and he was bundled out of the house. Sick with fear, Jake crossed the landing and slipped into his bedroom. From the window, he watched the white-coated men force his father into a waiting ambulance. The doors closed, the engine started and the ambulance drove out of the street. Adam's abduction was over in the space of three minutes.

Footsteps on the stairs. Jake scooted under the duvet and closed his eyes. The door eased open. A few seconds later it clicked shut again. Muffled voices throbbed through the floor. As quietly as he could, Jake left his bedroom and crept downstairs. A crack of light shone through the living room door. Jake tiptoed to the door and peered into the room.

Dr Saxby paced up and down. Dr Holmwood sat on the sofa and smoked a cigarette. There was a third person in the room but Jake could only see the top of her head poking over a chair back.

' . . . sound asleep,' Dr Holmwood said.

'So, where have you taken Adam?' Saxby asked. 'Back to the Institute?'

'Surely even *you* wouldn't want Adam to be held in the Institute cells like some common conjuror!' Holmwood snapped. 'Dr Harker is not our enemy—his only crime was to love his son. For now, I will keep him at Green Gables. My house is comfortable, but it is as secure as any prison.'

The woman coughed. The eyes of the men turned to her. 'What about the boy?'

There was something familiar about that deep, raspy voice. Jake had heard it before, many years ago.

'Surely he *must* go to Hobarron's Hollow,' Saxby said.

Holmwood hesitated. 'I—I can see no other solution. Yes, the boy must go. I will notify all Hollow residents to expect him. We don't want anyone talking about the Demontide and frightening the child away. Not when a sacrifice is our only hope.'

'We are sure then, that the weapon will not work?' the woman asked.

'It has been tested and does appear to be useless.' Holmwood sounded defeated.

'A grand scheme that came to nothing,' Saxby sighed. 'It was always a foolish dream . . . '

'My brother is not a fool!'

The woman turned her face to Saxby. Jake almost cried out in surprise. He ought to have known! He had heard her name mentioned the night of Dr Holmwood's party. He had not seen her for almost ten years, but now he recognized Aunt Joanna, his father's sister.

'I was there that night in Hobarron Bay,' she said, spitting the words at Saxby. 'I saw what was done to Luke.' Her eyes flickered towards Dr Holmwood. 'My brother and I stood on the clifftops and watched as the boy's throat was cut from ear to ear. You may be an Elder, Saxby, but have *you* ever witnessed the murder of a child?'

'No,' the doctor admitted.

'Then keep your mouth shut about my brother. Adam grew up reliving that sight, night after night in his dreams. And he swore that he would never allow such a thing to happen again. He would find another way. His "grand scheme", as you call it, his great weapon, could have saved us all. Instead we cart him off like a madman and prepare, once again, to kill an innocent child.' She turned to Holmwood. 'I will bring Jacob to Hobarron's Hollow. To my home . . .'

Joanna Harker got to her feet.

'We *will* stop the Demontide, gentlemen, as we always have. But mark my words: one day we will burn in Hell for these things we do.'

Chapter 8
Attack of the Hellhounds

Jake tiptoed across to his desk and turned on the reading lamp. By its light, he studied the paper his father had dropped in the hall. A fragment of an engineer's blueprint, it looked as if it had been torn from a larger sheet. The central design was of a box, a metre in length and fifty-three centimetres in width and depth. Cables snaked out from the base while the casing itself seemed to be transparent. The title of this strange contraption had been stamped above it, although the last word had been partially torn away:

HOBARRON WEAPON:INCU

Project Leaders: Dr Claire Harker,
Dr Adam Harker
Overseen by: Dr Gordon Holmwood

So *this* was the weapon his mother had created! The machine she had devised to stop the Demontide! But what did it do? After ten minutes or so staring at the drawing, Jake gave up trying to work it out. He turned off the light and went to the window.

The moon blinked between the clouds. Silver shadows danced across the garden.

Jake eased open his bedroom window and climbed out onto the sill. Teeth gritted, he slid down the clattering drain-pipe. With one eye on the dark windows of the house, he crossed the garden and took his BMX from behind the shed. The squeal of the gate sounded unnaturally loud in the early morning stillness.

Jake checked his watch—3:30 a.m. He had about two hours until dawn. He mounted the bike, flipped the torch on the crossbar and pedalled along the lane. His legs pumped as he hit the main road and swept the bike in a wide circle. While he focused on the road ahead, fresh mysteries raced through his mind.

After Holmwood and Saxby left, he had waited until he heard Aunt Joanna climb the stairs. Half an hour later, her snores signalled that it was safe to leave. Before setting out, he had placed a can of spray paint and a wire coat hanger in his rucksack.

What did Joanna Harker have to do with all this?

Jake hadn't seen his aunt for a long time. In fact, he was pretty sure he'd only met her once. An untidy hulk of a woman, she'd turned up unannounced at his sixth birthday party. When she bent down to give him a kiss, Jake had smelt whisky on her breath. His father had whispered a few stern words in her ear and she'd left pretty sharpish. After that, Jake only ever heard her mentioned in passing between his mum and dad. There had never been any talk of her being connected to the Hobarron Institute. And yet, in her conversation with Holmwood and Saxby, it sounded as if she had some authority within the organization. What possible role could she play?

Jake turned off the main road and into the woodlands. The forest path ran down to the river. All along the bank, he could hear the stir of wetland creatures in their hollows.

Hobarron's Hollow. The place that Aunt Joanna planned to take him. He whispered the name over and over. Why should this place share the same name as a scientific institute? An institute whose real work was the destruction of demonkind. More troubling still was the fact that, due to the weapon's failure, it looked as if a sacrifice was needed to stop the Demontide. Jake grimaced—it was pretty obvious who that sacrifice was going to be . . .

Twenty minutes of furious pedalling brought Jake to a huge iron gate. The rear entrance to Green Gables, Dr Holmwood's manor house. The black eye of a security camera glinted down at him. In a flash, he snatched the spray paint from his rucksack and blinded the lens. Then he straightened out the wire coat hanger and threw it at the gate. Sparks crackled between the bars. As he suspected: electrified. He picked up the scorched wire and tucked it back into his rucksack.

Jake hid his bike in the undergrowth and slipped down

the bank. Attached to the gate was a chain-link fence, about four metres high and topped with barbed wire. Jake followed it all the way through the forest. He had expected the fence to end at the river's edge, but it plunged into the water and stretched out quite a distance from the shore. He took off his shoes and tied the laces around the straps of his backpack. Then he stepped into the icy water. Hissing through his teeth, he waded forward. Reeds caught at his legs as if they were another part of Dr Holmwood's security cordon. When the water had reached his chin, he kicked off from the bottom and swam the last few metres around the end of the fence.

He had begun to make his way back to the shore when he saw a light track across the water. A man in uniform appeared from between the trees and spoke into his fist.

'I'm at the south perimeter, no sign of an intruder. I'll go and check the camera. Probably just short-circuited or something.'

A voice crackled through the walkie-talkie.

'Come back to the hut first. I'll walk down to the gate with you and we'll take one of the dogs. If there *is* someone in the grounds, it could be dangerous. Remember what Dr Holmwood says about the enemies of the Institute.'

'Spook stories,' the guard laughed. 'You know, for a clever guy, I think the doc's got a few bats in the belfry. But OK, I'm on my way. Shuck needs a run anyway.'

Shuck. In the ancient legends of the eastern counties of England, Black Shuck was the name of a hellhound. That didn't sound good.

Jake swam quickly to the shore and scrambled up the bank. Teeth chattering, he pulled on his soggy trainers. The backpack had half filled with river water which Jake now emptied out onto the ground. Green Gables was a ten minute walk through the woods. Jake set off, and was under the shadow of the house before three minutes had elapsed. The run helped him warm up.

Silhouettes moved across the window of the security guard's hut. The small wooden building stood by itself, a stone's throw from the main house. Two dirt bikes with helmets on their saddles rested against the hut wall. A fenced-in dog run was attached to the hut, kennels at the rear. Leashes with empty collars hung from the kennel roofs. Jake gulped. There was no sign of the dogs.

The hut door swung open and Brett, the guard from the Institute, strode out.

'Come on, Shuck.'

A large, elegant Doberman trotted out of the hut. Brett fitted a leash around its neck and its ears pricked up on either side of its head like two demonic horns. Jake waited until the men and the dog had disappeared from view. Then he made a dash for the hut.

Brett had locked the door behind him. It appeared to be a simple catch. Jake took the wire coat hanger from his bag and slotted it between the door and the jamb. With a little jiggling, the catch flipped and he was inside.

A bank of monitors marked *Driveway*, *Forecourt*, *Rose Garden*, *Main Hall*, *Cellar*, *Woodland Path* stood along one wall. The screen labelled *Rear Gate* was blank. Jake watched as Brett, Shuck, and the other guard crossed the rose garden. At that pace, it would take them maybe seven minutes to reach the gate—another ten or so to check the area and alert the house. At best, he had twenty minutes to get into the house and rescue his father. That was *if* he could get into the house.

Jake had visited Green Gables many times. The place was a high-tech fortress, the doors electronically secured. With one eye on the monitors, he searched the coats that hung behind the door. Nothing but sweet wrappers and pocket fluff. He turned his attention to the filing cabinet. Papers, bills, receipts, old security tapes . . .

The minutes ticked by and his search became frantic. No longer caring about the evidence he would leave behind, he tore open files and ransacked drawers. His gaze shifted to the screen marked *Woodland Path*. The guards and the dog flashed across the monitor. Soon they would be at the gate.

He spun around and, in his panic, knocked a mug of cold tea from the desk. Jake cursed. Then, seeing what lay beneath the cup, his heart leapt. His luck was holding— Brett had been using his keycard as a coaster. Jake grabbed the card and checked the house monitors. Each showed an empty room. An idea popped into his head. If this was the *only* monitoring station, he might be able to buy himself a little more time. He grabbed a hammer from a toolbox under the desk and set to work. Within seconds he had smashed every one of the monitor screens.

The silent fortress waited.

Jake went to the back door. A card swipe device was bolted

to the wall. He tried the keycard. The LED flashed red. Maybe the card was faulty. Maybe that was why Brett had been using it as a coaster. If he ran back to the hut . . .

A low growl came from the bushes directly behind Jake.

'Oh crap,' he muttered.

There was no hope of running back to the hut now. Any sudden movement and the dog would be on him. He tried the card again. *Red.*

'Good doggy,' he said, frantically swiping the card. 'Good pooch.'

The LED flashed: *red, red, red, red . . .*

The growl deepened. Paws padded onto the path.

'Good Rex. Good Rover.'

. . . red, red, red, red . . .

Wet jaws slapped together. The hound came closer, closer.

'Come on, come on!'

Swipe. *Red.* Swipe, swipe, swipe. *Red, red, red.*

Claws clicked across the paving. Saliva slopped onto the ground.

Jake felt hot breath against the back of his legs.

'Don't eat me,' he pleaded.

Swipe.

Green.

The door swung open.

Jake moved just in time. He heard the snap of the dog's jaws followed by a yelp of frustration. The beast pounced as Jake closed the door. A thrashing head with spittle-flecked jowls caught against the door jamb. Jake fell back into the hall while his foot kicked out at the door. For a moment, he thought that the massive hound would succeed in forcing its way into the house. He could hear the scrabble of its hind legs, could feel the power of those heavy-muscled limbs. The battle of wills between Jake and the dog lasted less than a minute. To Jake, it felt like hours. Finally, the dog let out an exhausted pant and pulled its head back. Its collar caught against the jamb and slipped from its neck. The door slammed shut.

The silver name tag twinkled up at Jake, and identified his attacker as 'Cerberus'. A dark catalogue reference told him that, in Greek and Roman mythology, Cerberus was the ancient guardian of the underworld—a monstrous beast with three heads.

'Cerberus.' Jake nodded. 'Figures.'

Despite the rumpus, the household remained undisturbed. Jake got to his feet and crept along the corridor. His plan had been hazy at best and now that he was inside Green Gables he wondered how he would find his father. There must be over a hundred rooms, most of which he had never seen.

The corridor opened out into a huge entrance hall. Like the rest of the house, it was a scene of luxurious splendour. Beautifully woven tapestries hung from the walls. A staircase made of iron and glass swept down from the floor above. The marble floor, polished to perfection, gleamed . . . Except that wasn't quite true. No, not polished to perfection. From the door to the stairs, two parallel tracks tarnished the marble.

Jake imagined his father being dragged from the ambulance and across the wet ground outside. Perhaps the muddy heels of his dad's shoes had made those tracks. Jake followed them up the glass staircase and onto the landing. There the tracks skirted right and into the west wing of the house. In the thick pile carpet of the corridor they became furrows. It was as if Adam Harker had laid out a trail for his son to follow, like a man in a labyrinth dropping pebbles behind him.

Jake now entered a part of Green Gables he had never seen before. The corridor, decorated with crimson wallpaper, stretched out before him like a long, red throat. The walls were high and, above a rail four metres or so overhead, the faces of men stared down at him. Jake's gaze skipped between the portraits. The costumes were Jacobean, Georgian, Victorian, Edwardian, but the men all possessed similar features. It was not hard to work out that these were ancestors of Dr Gordon Holmwood. Beneath each was a golden name plaque. Jake reached the last—a stern-looking character with a short beard and heavy-lidded eyes. His plaque read:

TIBERIUS HOLMWOOD
FIRST OF THE HOBARRON ELDERS, 1645

The tracks ended at the door beneath Tiberius's portrait.

There was no swipe card device outside.

'Open bloody Sesame,' Jake growled.

He rattled and pushed at the handle. To his surprise, the door swung back to reveal a big, well-furnished bedroom.

That the door to Adam Harker's cell should open so easily was not difficult to understand. Not when Jake saw the state of his father. He rushed to the bed and lifted Adam's head from the pillow.

The man had been heavily drugged.

'Dad? Can you hear me?'

Jake slapped his father's face. He tried to pull Adam into a sitting position but the dead weight was too much for him. The man flopped back onto the bed. Then his eyes fluttered and Adam focused on his son.

'Go,' he said, his words slurred. 'Don't st-stay here. Dangerous. Can't help me.'

'I'll bring the police.'

'Told you. No pol-eeese. Wouldn't believe you. Elders too powerful.'

Jake thought of Silas Jones being interviewed by Dr Holmwood and knew that his dad was right.

'I can't leave you here,' he said.

'Must. Go.'

'Listen, Dad, I overheard Dr Holmwood and Aunt Joanna talking—they want to take me to a place called "Hobarron's Hollow" . . . '

Adam nodded. 'The Demontide will start in the Hollow. The D-Door will open and demonkind will be s-set free.'

'But what about the weapon you and Mum worked on? I've seen a blueprint—a diagram of a box with wires coming out of it.'

'We created the weapon to f-fight the darkness. But it never worked. Never functioned. Wi-without the weapon, the Elders will need a sacrifice to stop the Demontide. They wi-will kill a child . . . '

'But there must be another way of stopping it.'

'Muh-maybe. The answer is in the Hollow, Jake. Fr-frozen in Time.'

'I don't understand.'

Adam's eyes glazed over. 'Ab-ra-cad-abra . . . '

'Dad?'

Adam struggled to focus. 'To understand you must find Tinsmouth. He—he lives inside the lion's head now.'

Tinsmouth. The man who had murdered little Olivia Brown at the Hobarron Fete. Why would his father want him to seek out a man like that? Anyway, surely Tinsmouth was still locked up somewhere.

Loud, angry voices echoed from downstairs.

Jake tried again to lift his father. Adam pushed him away.

'Go. Run. Stay—stay away from the Hollow. Only death waits for you there . . . '

For a moment, Adam appeared to come out of his trance. He fixed Jake with a sad stare.

'I love you, Jake. My son. *My son* . . . '

His eyes rolled white and he fell back onto the bed.

Footsteps thundered along the corridor.

'The door's open!' Holmwood's voice raised in anger. 'Someone's in there!'

Jake raced across the room, slammed the door and jammed a chair under the handle. Then he returned to the bed. He leaned over and put his lips to the unconscious man's ear.

'I'm sorry, Dad, but I'm going to Hobarron's Hollow. Weapon or no weapon, I'll find a way to stop the Demontide.

No one is going to be sacrificed—enough people have died already.' He bent down and kissed his dad's forehead. 'Then I'm coming back for you.'

Jake crossed to the window and raised the sash. Shoulders thudded against the door. Jake took one last look at his father and slipped through the window.

His memory of the house had served him well. A trail of ivy ran along this side of the building. Jake grasped the trellis frame beneath and used it as a ladder. He was halfway down when he heard the door splinter and the guards rush into the room.

'No one here.'

'The window, you fools!'

Jake jumped to the ground. His ankle twisted beneath him but he had no time to feel the pain. A shot rang out. The bullet kicked up the gravel a few inches from his foot. Bloody hell, did they want to kill him? No time to think. He ran.

Jake sped through the deep, velvety shadows of the rose garden. As he ran, he could hear the chaos of a house shocked from its slumbers. Windows whistled open and a confusion of voices bellowed across each other. The whole household had been roused and was now on the lookout for the intruder. Engines spluttered into life. Jake remembered the dirt bikes he had seen resting against the guard's hut.

Reaching the woods, he heard a sound even more frightening than the roar of the bikes.

The dogs' howls echoed between the trees.

Shuck and Cerberus had joined the hunt.

Three more shots cut through the air. The bark of the birch tree near Jake's head exploded into splinters. Glancing back, he saw Brett and the other security guard standing astride the dirt bikes. They had stopped for a moment to take aim. Now they holstered the rifles behind them, stomped down on the kick-start and resumed their pursuit. Jake remembered all those silly conversations he had had with Brett over the years. All the jokes and playful backchat—would their friendship count for anything if he was caught?

Bounding ahead of the bikes, the hellhounds had not slowed *their* pursuit. Their great heads nodded as they ran, as if to say—*Oh yes, we'll catch you soon, my friend. Then it's chow time!*

Jake raced on. His legs ached down to the bone and tears stung his eyes. Up ahead, he could see the shimmer of the river. All at once, the morning sun blazed across the tops of the trees. The forest came alive with shadows, the river burned with a fiery light, and Jake was blinded. He tripped down the bank and hit the water with a flat smack. The cold knocked the wind out of him. He had just managed to get to his feet again when he heard the scamper of paws on the bank.

Cerberus was the first to arrive on the shore. The dog's lip curled back to reveal a mouth stuffed with vicious teeth. The hackles on its back rose as it fixed its gaze on its prey. From somewhere nearby, Jake could hear the whine of the bikes. He was either going to be gunned down or torn to pieces. Maybe both.

Attack of the Hellhounds

The dog fired off a few short barks that hit Jake like bullets in the chest. He held out a trembling hand and staggered back into the water. Cerberus padded forward, face low to the ground, spine arched, hind legs poised to pounce. Thick strands of drool slipped between his black lips and foamed around his muzzle.

Chow time.

Chapter 9
Strange Rain

Cerberus yelped and collapsed to the ground.

A more timid creature than his partner, Shuck had been scrambling on the bank above, trying to find a safe route down. His weight had been too much for the loose earth and it had crumbled beneath him. The dog had fallen through the air and landed heavily on Cerberus's back. Now they rolled over, legs entangled, mouths snapping.

Jake took his chance. He shrugged the backpack from his shoulders and tossed it away into the river. Then he filled his lungs and dived. Blades of frosty water stung his body. Swimming with his trainers on was difficult, but the adrenalin made sure he kept up a frantic pace. He had reached the end of the chain-link fence when the bullets started cutting through the water. It was no good—he couldn't hope to get back to the shore before the guards had made it through the gate. He would have to abandon his bike. Turning his body, he started to swim across to the opposite bank.

In the middle of the river, the underwater currents strengthened. However hard he swam, he could not fight them. He felt himself being turned this way and that, the currents flipping him like a plastic bag caught in a breeze. They swept him downriver and kept him pinned beneath the surface. His lungs burned and his blood screamed for oxygen. He kicked hard, pushed with his hands, but the pressure was too strong. Reeds rose up like silky green tentacles and locked Jake in a deadly embrace. Bubbles erupted from his mouth, his eyes bulged and his vision darkened.

Then, in the darkness, he heard his father's voice—

Remember the power. Feel it . . .

It came in a rush—power unbound. The fire exploded from his hands and the underwater world boiled like a cauldron. The reeds snapped away from his legs and Jake felt himself flying backwards through the water. With the speed of a torpedo, he broke the surface. The river raged beneath him, as if a whirlpool had awakened in its depths. At the base of this vortex fish lay flapping on the dry ground of the riverbed.

Jake soared into the air. The men and the guard dogs on the bank, no larger than toy soldiers now, did not seem to notice his flight. Their eyes stayed fixed on the river while Jake hurtled higher and higher. He could see the bend of the river as it curled around the woods. The trees themselves appeared tiny, a green tapestry woven around the doll's house that was Green Gables.

Higher. Higher.

Below him, the cluster of houses that made up Hobarron Fields. Beyond, the grey sprawl of New Town and the grid of black streets that sliced through it. Masterson High, the canal and the fields. And there, glinting like a new pin, the great Institute itself. A place of science, magic, and mystery. All of it falling away from Jake as he flew into the cold, blue sky.

Voices.

' . . . washed up on the riverbank. Just a few scratches and bruises . . . '

'Damn lucky he wasn't killed. Those men of yours ought to be better trained.'

'Brave though, to try to rescue his father.'

'What now?'

'The plan remains the same. Soon as he recovers, I'll take him to Hobarron's Hollow.'

Only death waits for you there . . .

Darkness.

Mother Inglethorpe stood once more inside the Veil. That realm of nothingness was as chilling as ever. If the witch concentrated on the horizon, she could see a host of white shapes passing like mist between the worlds of the living and the dead.

Esther came to the end of her report.

'As to why Dr Holmwood has imprisoned Adam Harker, I cannot guess.'

'Surely that is obvious,' Crowden said. 'There has been a disagreement between Dr Harker and the other Elders. It must be something to do with the weapon.'

Crowden stood back from his favourite witch and eyed her carefully. As ever, his demonic black cabinet swirled behind him. Mother Inglethorpe tried not to think about those ten minutes she had spent inside the nightmare box.

'And you say something else happened last night?' Crowden asked.

'Yes, just before dawn.'

'You saw it?'

'No. I was at home, sleeping.'

'And your familiar?'

'Miss Creekley was with me. I have been following the boy and his father twenty-four hours a day for the last six months. I have crossed continents with them.' Mother Inglethorpe panicked. 'I am not like you. I-I must sleep sometimes.'

'Do I detect a disrespectful tone, madam?'

'No. It's just, I've tried my best.'

'Tut-tut. You know the price of failure.'

The door of the nightmare box opened a crack. Hungry for Esther Inglethorpe, its voice called out. The witch shivered.

'I will spare you,' Crowden said, 'this time.' He snapped his fingers and the cabinet slammed shut. 'Now, tell me what little you *do* know.'

'Something to do with the boy,' the witch gasped. 'I spoke to a wood sprite that lives in one of the trees surrounding

Green Gables. His story was rather nonsensical, you know what these forest imps are like. He told me that the boy had attempted to rescue his father and had been chased from the house. He'd tried to swim the river but got into trouble. That's where the story breaks down. Something frightened the imp and he hid in the trunk of his tree.'

'What frightened him?'

'"Oldcraft". That was all he would say.'

'*Oldcraft . . .* '

The Coven Master's face darkened. Mother Inglethorpe waited, her hands twisted together, her eye on the cabinet.

'Where is Jacob Harker now?' Crowden muttered.

'They left for Hobarron's Hollow this morning.'

'Stay with him, Mother—watch him.'

Crowden waved his hand and conjured a grey mist into the air. Inside the vapour, a picture started to take shape. Mother Inglethorpe could make out the short steeple of a church and a road running down to the sea. She recognized the place immediately.

'They will flock there soon enough,' Crowden purred. 'All the old families, every one a descendant of traitors. They will go in the hope of denying us the Demontide yet again. But we shall be waiting, my Coven and I. This time, demonkind *will* be set free . . . '

The rumble of the road brought him round.

'Are you awake?'

Jake groaned. A steady current from the car's air conditioning cooled his hot skin. He blinked the world into a kind of focus. He saw yellow cornfields—shreds of violet cloud— a speckle of birds dusting the sky.

'Don't worry,' the driver said, 'we're nearly home.'

Jake's head rolled to the right. He could just make out the red hair of the driver and her big hands on the steering wheel.

'Home?'

'That's right.' The hair bobbed. 'Then we'll get you straight to bed. You're still very poorly. Now, go back to sleep.'

'Dad. W-where?'

'Shhh. Be a good boy and close your eyes.'

Exhaustion sapped Jake's resistance. His eyes drooped. Before sleep reclaimed him he saw a sign growing larger, larger, larger—

Welcome to
HOBARRON'S HOLLOW
'A Village With A History'

The squabble of the chaffinches in the chestnut tree outside his window roused Jake early. Blinking the sleep from his eyes, he gazed around the unfamiliar bedroom. It was comfortable but poorly furnished, with only the bed, a chair, an old wardrobe, and a full length mirror that leaned against one wall. Jake threw back the bedclothes and stood before the mirror. He flushed red. Aunt Joanna must have undressed him. At least she had stopped short of stripping his underpants.

Fresh underwear, a pair of jeans, a T-shirt, and trainers sat on the chair. As he pulled on the clothes, his stomach gurgled. It felt as if he hadn't eaten in weeks. He opened the bedroom door and stepped out onto the landing. Mouthwatering aromas—crisp, salty bacon and hot, fresh bread—wafted up the stairs. They led him down to the kitchen.

Aunt Joanna stood at the oven, an apron wrapped around her ample stomach.

'Morning, sleepyhead, you look famished. Bacon sarnie and a cup of tea, I think. Sit down—it won't be a jiffy.'

The kitchen was like the rest of the house: small, homely, a little untidy. Pots and pans were stacked in a tottering pile beside the sink; bills and letters had been pinned to the sideboard with a large bowie knife. On the windowsill, a fat ginger tomcat dozed in the early morning sunshine.

Aunt Joanna placed two doorstep sandwiches in front of Jake. Now that he came to look at her, he could see the similarities between this woman and his father. They had the same deep brown eyes and coppery red hair. She also possessed her brother's big frame.

'My name's Joanna, in case you were wondering. I'm your dad's sis—'

'I know who you are.'

'Clever lad. Thought you'd have forgotten me. We only met the once.'

'My sixth birthday,' Jake said, remembering his aunt's whisky-flavoured breath.

'That's right. Well, it's good to see you've got an appetite. A fever like that can . . . '

'How long have I been ill?'

'A week. I kept you at home until you were stronger. Had your GP pop in now and then to make sure the fever was under control. Yesterday he gave me the OK to bring you down here. Glad to have you.'

'Where's "here"?'

'Stonycroft Cottage. My home. Home to your father, too, when he was a boy. Been Harkers at Stonycroft since—well, heaven knows when.'

'I can't remember much about getting ill.'

'Just a freak fever. Maybe you stayed out too long in the rain.'

Aunt and nephew held each other's gaze. Jake decided to play along, for now. Against his father's wishes, he had come to Hobarron's Hollow to find a way to stop the Demontide. If he was going to be able to move about the village freely then he would have to keep his aunt's trust.

While he sipped his sugary tea, a question niggled. How *had* he escaped the river? There was really only one answer. Half-drowned, he must have been dragged out by Brett and the other guard, then taken back home. His exposure to the freezing water had resulted in a fever. And his memory of flying above the river? A hallucination caused by lack of oxygen to the brain.

'So, where's my dad then?' he smiled.

'Called away on business. Didn't have time to say goodbye. Asked me to look after you. I've got my work here, and so

I'm afraid you'll have to spend your summer holiday with me.'

'Can I call him?'

Joanna shook her head. 'He's somewhere in the wilds of South America. No satellite phone.'

Again, a lie that could not be challenged.

'I'd like to get a breath of fresh air.'

'But you haven't finished your sandwich.'

'I've lost my appetite.'

'All right. Don't go too far, you're still weak. Lunch at one.'

Jake left the table and ducked into the low corridor. He was at the cottage door when Joanna called out.

'Welcome to the Hollow!'

Stonycroft Cottage, thatched and whitewashed, stood by itself at the end of a wooded lane. Jake stepped back and breathed in the atmosphere of the place. This was where his father had grown up. Years ago, Adam Harker had played in the cottage garden, climbed these trees and cycled this pathway. Jake found it hard to imagine his dad as a boy. All he knew of Adam's past were the few things his dad had let slip—he had grown up in a village on the east coast of England; he'd had one sister, Joanna, who had teased him about the gap between his front teeth; his mother and father had died in a car accident. Apart from his love of horror comics, that was about it.

Jake walked slowly up the lane. Bedridden for a week, the muscles in his legs ached like hell. By the time he reached the main road his head felt light. He took a few deep breaths and wandered on.

Strange Rain

Hobarron's Hollow was little more than a group of cottages built on a steep hillside. From its position on the crest of the hill, an ugly church of weather-beaten stone overlooked the village. Jake decided against a trek uphill, and instead walked down the road towards what looked like a small town square with a war memorial at its centre. Further on, he saw the road plummet down to the cliffs. These pale red rocks curved out from the mainland to form a kind of natural harbour or bay.

Entering the square, he saw the few shops that served the Hollow: a butcher's, post office, off licence, corner shop, and a pub called The Voice of the Cave. Fishermen smoking briar pipes shared a joke on the steps of the pub. Cheery old folks waited at the bus stop. Mothers with babies dressed in knitwear called out greetings to one another. A perfect picture postcard of an English seaside village, Jake thought . . . Too perfect perhaps. Were those smiles a little strained? Were the jokes a little forced? And was it his imagination, or did the eyes of these people keep flickering in his direction?

Jake crossed the square and entered the post office. The bell above the door jangled. He grabbed a notebook and a biro from the shelves and went to the counter. A man in his early forties with thinning hair and a warm smile punched the keys of an antique till.

'One pound and fifty new pence, sir.'

Jake swore under his breath.

'I'm sorry, I've come out without any money.'

'You're Jacob Harker, aren't you? Joanna's nephew?' The postmaster dropped Jake's purchases into a brown paper bag.

'No need to look so puzzled—I'm afraid we've all been gossiping about you. A new face is always a five-day-wonder in the village. I'm Eric, by the way. Eric Drake.'

Drake. The same name as the boy who'd been spooked by 'something nasty' in Dr Holmwood's boathouse. Eric must have caught the look on Jake's face.

'I know your father, of course. We all grew up together—Joanna, Adam, my brother and me. Walter went on to work at the Institute. I wasn't brainy enough, I'm afraid.'

'Funny,' Jake said.

'Hmm?'

'How so many people from this village ended up at the Institute.'

'Well, Dr Holmwood is a Hollow man, too. He has a great sense of family; likes to keep people together. And we have an excellent school here, so it's no wonder we turn out so many bright kids. I don't believe the Institute only employs people from the Hollow though,' Eric laughed. 'Your mother wasn't from here, was she?'

'No,' Jake conceded.

It was true that many of the top people at the Institute came from all over the world. Still, it was equally true that Jake's father, Dr Saxby, and Eric Drake's brother held some of the highest positions within the organization.

Eric handed over the bag.

'No charge. Call it a "welcome to the Hollow gift". Drop by again and I'll tell you some tales about your old man!'

Jake smiled and left the shop.

He sat down on the steps of the memorial. Print covered

all four sides of the obelisk, but this was not a traditional monument to the war dead. There was no mention of any particular conflict. Instead, it was just a list of names, each of which began with the title 'Elder'. Jake found several Harkers, Saxbys, Drakes, and Holmwoods on the list, dates beside each. The earliest death was recorded as 1645.

Comfortable with a pen in hand, Jake looked down at the notepad. He had not written since his mother's death. Stories would not come to him. But this was not a story, it was real life, and he had to make sense of it. He wrote:

HOBARRON ELDERS	THE COVEN
Dr Holmwood	Coven leader (someone named
Dad	Crowden?)
Dr Saxby	Mother Inglethorpe (and demon—
Aunt Joanna	one I saw in the boathouse?)
Walter Drake	Mr Quilp (and Pinch)

A coven traditionally consists of thirteen members. If this is true there are at least ten other witches in the Coven. As for the Elders—who knows? Maybe the whole village! Remember Dr Holmwood saying that he would have to notify them that I was coming so that they didn't frighten me away.

Each Elder belongs to one of the old families that have lived in the Hollow for generations—right back to when Tiberius Holmwood founded the Elders in 1645. The Institute was established by Dr Holmwood some time in the last thirty years in order, I guess, to study, monitor, and defend against witchcraft. The Elders only ever become really active at the time of THE DEMONTIDE—a time of Evil and, possibly, the end of mankind. The Coven has worked for centuries to bring this about but the Elders have stopped them every time. The next Demontide will take place here, in Hobarron's Hollow, in a few days . . .

QUESTIONS:

1. The machine in the blueprint was called the 'HOBARRON WEAPON: INCU'—a high-tech box with cables & wires—but what does the weapon do? Mum called it 'a machine of ferocious power'. Is it a bomb? Aunt Joanna must have found the blueprint in my room—no hope of seeing it again now.

2. Why did my dad ask me to find Sidney Tinsmouth? Does he really hold the secret to what's going on here?

3. As the weapon doesn't work, Saxby says there is only one other way to stop the Demontide: the Elders must be prepared to kill—a child sacrifice. Dr Holmwood said he had 'committed such an act once before'. A boy called Luke was murdered . . .

4. I have dreamed of someone called the Witchfinder. Why?—and who is this man?

Jake chewed the end of the biro. He scanned what he had written and, although there were many questions unanswered, what he should do next seemed pretty clear.

He should take his dad's advice and RUN.

After all, it was obvious that *he* was the intended child sacrifice. Why else had it been so important that Aunt Joanna should bring him here? If he was smart, he would start running now and not stop until he was far away from Hobarron's Hollow and its creepy inhabitants.

There was only one problem with this plan: his dad had said that *the answer was in the Hollow*. By finding this answer, Jake felt that he might be able to make things right. He had watched helplessly as his mother was murdered, he had failed to save his friend Simon Lydgate. Whatever the cost, he could not now abandon his father. He would stay in Hobarron's Hollow until the truth was known. And he would find a way to stop the Demontide.

Jake reread what he had written. Sidney Tinsmouth was the obvious starting point, but all his dad had said was that Tinsmouth lived 'in the lion's head'. For the moment, Jake could make no sense of that cryptic statement, and so he decided to begin his investigations here in the Hollow.

Jake glanced up from the notebook. Mouth open, he stared across the square.

'Rachel?'

Her name had barely left his lips when Rachel Saxby disappeared down a side street. Jake thrust pen and notebook into his pocket and raced across the square. Spots of rain spat into his eyes. The sky darkened and the breeze strengthened. There were a few startled murmurs from the OAPs at the bus stop. The mothers looked up fretfully and pushed their prams under shop awnings. One of the fishermen let loose a string of swear words. Quite an overreaction for a bit of drizzle, Jake thought.

A toad exploded at his feet.

Jake skidded to a stop. *Slap, slap, slap.* A dozen more toads hit the pavement and vanished in a blur of blood. The murmurs turned into gasps. A scream broke out. The fishermen, burbling in their thick accents, hurried back into the pub. The OAPs tottered off in the direction of the post office. As

Jake watched, something large and green hit one old girl directly on the head. In an instant, her plastic shower hood turned a disgusting shade of red. Thick strands of toad guts hung from her shoulders like party streamers.

The perfect picture postcard was gone.

Chaos reigned.

Chapter 10
The First Omen

Jake closed the post office door behind him.

Thirty or forty people had crammed their way into the little shop. Now they jostled for space, fear and anger in their eyes. Tins of food, packets of washing powder, newspapers and dozens of other goods were knocked off their shelves in the panic. Roller blinds, a shade greener than the amphibians falling from the sky, had been lowered to shut off the view of the square. Above the hubbub, Jake could hear a steady *thump-thump-thump* against the windows.

The mothers and the OAPs tried their best to clean the gore from their coats, hats, and faces. A baby sitting in its pushchair sucked happily on a severed toad's leg. There was a general wailing and chirrup of frightened voices—*Mind your arm, Jonas Sykes!—Now look what you've done, Roger! I'll have to pay for that jar of peanut butter!—Raining toads! It's happening again, ain't it, Maggie?* Jake tore a page from his notebook and used it to clean bits of toad off his trainers.

'Toads—then the mist—then the monsters.' One of the young mothers shivered and held her baby to her chest. 'That was what my grandfather told me. First came the toads . . .'

'She's right!' This woman was in her forties and very glamorous. Her long red nails pointed at the blinds just as another toad smashed against the glass. 'I remember the last time very well. I was about seventeen. Ross McDale and I were parked in his car on the clifftops. We were . . . Well, we were young.'

Despite the weirdness of the situation, a few titters greeted this remark.

'We saw it coming in from the sea,' Long Nails continued. 'The mist. The second day and the Second Omen. Each day a fresh sign. Four in all. Four signs before the Demonti—'

'Miss Daniels!'

The entire crowd turned to Mr Drake, the postmaster. He was staring at the glamorous woman with daggers in his eyes.

'Let's not talk nonsense in front of our new friend.' Drake glanced over to where Jake stood in the doorway. 'I'm sure you've *all* heard about young Mr Harker here. Adam's son— Joanna's nephew. He's come to spend his summer holiday in the Hollow. This is Jake.'

Forty faces—young and old, plain and beautiful, smooth and weather-beaten—made an effort to relax into easy smiles. Most didn't manage it.

The First Omen

'You—you must forgive us,' Miss Daniels flustered. 'We are a superstitious people here in the Hollow. We get excitable over such silly nonsense.'

They all murmured in agreement.

'Welcome, Jake!' a voice shouted from the back. This greeting was soon taken up, and the chant almost managed to drown out the thunder of toads on glass.

'We tend to get ourselves a little worked up when this sort of thing happens. It's almost like a ritual of ours,' Mr Drake chuckled. His gaze swept the crowd, looking for support. 'You see, Jake, this sort of thing isn't that unusual.'

'Raining toads?' Jake said, disbelieving. 'Not unusual?'

A middle-aged woman with jet-black hair and a beaky, birdlike face spoke up.

'Not in these parts. It's all to do with atmospheric pressure, you see. We have lots of hot air currents streaming in at this time of year. They pass over cold seawater and that causes fish, frogs, any smaller form of sea life, to be drawn into the air. Later they are deposited on the mainland like rain. A very natural phenomenon.'

'You seemed scared enough a few minutes ago,' Jake observed.

The woman gave a cool shrug of the shoulders.

'I think it's stopping,' said Mr Drake.

The postmaster went to the window and raised the blind.

Jake jumped as a single toad smacked the glass. This one hit without any force and dropped groggily to the ground. A gruesome mess of red and green, the post office window looked as if an ogre had been slaughtered right outside.

The shop started to empty. Most of the people filing past Jake held out their hands and wished him a 'pleasant holiday in the Hollow'. Jake did his best to nod and smile. The bell jingled one last time and he was alone again with the postmaster. Mr Drake took a broom from behind the counter and started sweeping up the mess.

'Old-fashioned broom, that,' Jake observed. 'Looks a bit like a witch's.'

Mr Drake blinked twice and went on sweeping.

'So, do you believe all that stuff about Omens?' Jake said lightly. 'Or was that woman just a bit mental?'

Drake paused. He rested a forearm on the broom and fixed Jake with a hard stare.

'You don't know this village, Mr Harker. It's not your home. We have our own beliefs and customs here, and I won't have them made fun of, understand? Now, unless there's anything else I can help you with?'

Jake was halfway out of the shop when he turned back.

'Mr Drake?'

The postmaster beamed at Jake, as bright and friendly as ever.

'Does Dr Saxby have a house in the Hollow? I'd like to pop by and say hello.'

'What a nice idea. Yes, Dr Saxby's family home is at the top of the village. Just take the road to the right of St Meredith's church and you'll come to it.'

Jake closed the door behind him.

'Weirdo,' he muttered.

The clouds had vanished and the sun shone down on a

bizarre scene. A carpet of tiny green corpses covered the town square. The Elders' memorial was now so smattered with slime that it was impossible to read the names. Jake picked his way between the toads, careful not to step in any fresh goo. A couple of the fishermen stood on the steps of the pub and surveyed the amphibian graveyard from beneath bushy brows. They raised their pipes in greeting as Jake passed.

He had reached the road that led back uphill when a deep croak brought him to a halt. The only toad left unexploded sat on the pavement in front of him. Jake sank to his knee and examined the creature. Except for its milky white belly, warts covered every inch of its skin. Orange eyes with black slit pupils shone in the glare of the sun. The toad waddled towards Jake.

'*Bufo bufo.*'

Jake blinked. It took a moment for him to realize that it was *not* the toad that had spoken. He looked up at the beaky-faced woman from the post office.

'I'm sorry?'

'*Bufo bufo.* The Latin name for the common toad. Ugly brute, isn't he? I'm Alice Splane, by the way.' She gave Jake a stiff nod. 'I'm an ornithologist by profession—that's a fancy word for someone who knows a lot about birds—but I dabble in herpetology, too: the study of reptiles and amphibians. The common toad is identifiable by his webbed hind feet, his broad body, and his rounded snout.'

Alice pointed out these details, all the while keeping her hand a good distance from '*Bufo bufo*'.

'What about that?'

Jake indicated a dark blemish on the toad's back. It was so well-defined that it seemed as if someone had drawn it with a black felt-tipped pen.

'Just the usual markings,' Alice shrugged.

Jake shook his head. 'It's crazy, but I think I've seen that symbol somewhere before . . . '

'"Symbol"? It can hardly be called a symbol, Jake. Such a word would suggest that the toad had been *deliberately* marked by someone. Like a toad tattoo!'

Alice Splane tittered. It struck Jake as an uneasy laugh.

'No, no,' Alice continued, 'it's just Nature's blemish. We all have them: beauty spots, moles, acne scars.'

'I guess.'

'Honestly, I would suggest that you're seeing patterns in things that aren't there. Like noticing a face in the clouds or pictures in the flames of a fire. Our brains are programmed to seek out these things.' She glanced at her watch. 'Goodness, is that the hour? I must be going.'

And with that, the woman turned and strode away.

'Weirder and weirder,' Jake said.

The whole village seemed to be in on the conspiracy to keep him in the dark about the Demontide and the sacrifice that was needed to stop it. Despite the horror of it, Jake couldn't help smiling at their bumbling attempts to keep the secret.

Rrrurrrp.

The toad hopped across the pavement. Jake dropped to his knees again and lowered his head to get a better look at the toad's tattoo. He *had* seen it before. Think . . .

The toad's tongue lashed out.

'Ow! Bloody hell!'

The shock was twofold. First, there was the horror of seeing that hideously long tongue shoot out from the toad's throat. Black and dripping, the thing sprang towards Jake and latched onto his right hand. The tip stuck there, pulsating as the toad's poison pumped into his bloodstream.

The second shock was the pain—a thousand times brighter than a paper cut, and growing worse by the second. Tentacles of agony lashed along his arm, into his chest, up to his throat and clawed behind his eyes. They cut across his brain like a razor blade and sliced down the length of his spine. Any minute now, he was going to lose consciousness.

There was only one thing he could do. The thought of it made his stomach flip.

He pinched the monstrous tongue between thumb and forefinger.

Another agonized cry escaped his lips. The toad's tongue was as spiky as a porcupine's back. Tears filled Jake's eyes, but he did not let go. Bit by bit, he peeled the tongue away from his hand.

Jake gasped in surprise. Unlike the tongue of a human being, it didn't end with a tip but with a circular sucker, like the pads on an octopus's leg. A set of tiny teeth ran all around the sucker, each one covered in Jake's blood. The teeth gnashed angrily while a thick green substance oozed from the tube of the tongue.

Jake tore the last tooth from his flesh. He shot to his feet and kicked out at the toad. The creature sailed through the air, hit the glass wall of the bus stop and, like its brothers before it, exploded in a murky haze.

The pain began to ease as Jake sucked the poison from the wound and spat it out. The stuff tasted like rotten eggs. He should probably go straight to hospital, get himself checked out. Exhaustion washed through him. All he wanted to do now was to sleep. He staggered back towards Stonycroft Cottage.

'*Bufo bufo*,' he panted. 'Common toad. Yeah, right!'

A bolt of blue light shot out from the Witchfinder's palm. It hit the other man square in the chest and sent him reeling back towards the portal. A smoky oval of shimmering shadows, the portal waited, ready to consume the witch.

'Welcome to your prison, Coven Master.' The Witchfinder's rich tones echoed around the cavern chamber. 'Here you will endure throughout the Ages. Here you will rot unto the Ending of the World.'

The witch teetered on the brink of the Veil. His hands reached out and tried to grasp the edges of the portal—his fingers sank through the smoke. The deep well of his horror could be seen in his eyes and heard in the hopelessness of his scream. The Witchfinder showed no pity. A fresh surge of magical energy pulsed along his arm and he released it through his fingers. The second burst struck the Coven Master and sent him screaming into the Veil. His other hand outstretched, the Witchfinder concentrated on maintaining the portal. He held on until he was sure that his enemy had been captured, then he closed his fist. The portal fizzled—shrank . . .

The Coven Master struggled towards the closing window.

'I will find a way out,' he screeched. 'If it takes me centuries, I will open the Door and demonkind *will* sweep across this wretched planet. I promise you . . .'

'Try to escape and you will be dragged back. The Veil is now your home and your evil is at an end. Farewell, witch.'

'NO!'

The portal crackled and closed.

The Witchfinder now turned to the Door.

He raised his hand again and gathered together the last shreds of his magic. The swirls, pentagrams, and pictures that had been etched into the Door shone with a fiery light. Huge cracks started to appear all across the stone slab. Any minute now, demonkind would break through this doorway and flood across the world. The Witchfinder pointed towards the symbol at the centre of the Door—

—and released the freezing spell.

'Please . . .' he hissed through gritted teeth.

A deathly chill spread out from his heart and into his hands. His breath billowed white before his eyes. The Witchfinder continued to direct his magic at the Door, even as his fingers turned blue and little ice crystals crackled across his skin . . .

Finally, he turned away from the Door and staggered towards the cavern entrance. His heart slowed with every step, the chambers clogging with icy blood. The enchanted ball around his neck became too heavy for the frozen string. It fell to the ground and rolled away into the shadows. The Witchfinder hardly noticed. He concentrated on the path ahead. If only he could make it into the bay, the sun's first rays would warm his cold body.

The name of his beloved creaked through his lips for the last time—

'El-ea-nor . . .'

Chapter 11
The Ghost in the Graveyard

Mr Grype draped a copy of *Elementary Hexes: Blackheads to Boils* across his face and closed his eyes. It had been a long day and his nerves were raw. The Demontide was fast approaching and he had done nothing in recent months to win his master's approval. He needed to think of something that would bring him to Crowden's attention, and quickly. After the Coven's victory—when the Door had been opened and demonkind set free—the Master would hand out rewards to his most loyal witches. Come what may, Grype was determined to be among them.

It was no good—the witch could not sleep. He rose from his chair and stretched. His poor old back creaked. Mr Hegarty, Grype's vulture-like familiar, was sound asleep on his perch above the fireplace. A beetle dropped from the bird's plumage and, without waking, Hegarty snapped it out of the air. The demon swallowed. A second later, the beetle burrowed out of the bird's skull and reappeared between its dirty feathers. A neat trick, Mr Grype had always thought.

Footsteps echoed along Yaga Passage. There were always footsteps, day and night, never ceasing, never giving Grype a moment's peace. A strange shadow with eight writhing arms stopped at the filthy window of Crowden's Emporium. The door handle rattled.

'Will you come out and play, little librarian?' It was a woman's voice, purring in the deep, velvety tones of the American South.

Mr Grype shuddered. He plucked a few defensive spells from his store of knowledge and held out his hand, ready to cast the magic. It was a useless gesture. Deep down he knew that, if this creature broke into the shop, his magic could not save him.

Eight hands tapped at the window and fear surged through Mr Grype. The creature rattled the handle again.

'Oh, honey, you're no fun!' it crowed.

The shadow moved on.

Grype took a pile of old books from his desk and started returning them to their shelves. Nine times out of ten this task calmed his nerves. Not tonight. He would never admit it to Mother Inglethorpe and the others, but he felt his inadequacy very deeply. Dark witches were chosen by a coven for two reasons: they had a talent for magic and they revered the power of Evil. Someone like Tobias Quilp ticked both boxes—his mind was as black as ink and he was clever when it came to picking up spells. Sometimes, however, a witch had more going for them in one department than the other.

Although Grype was spiteful and vindictive, his magic was second-rate. How he hated people like Quilp and Inglethorpe, with their dark souls and extraordinary powers.

And then there was the late Sidney Tinsmouth, of course.

Yes, Sidney had been a very rare case indeed . . .

If only Grype could learn a new skill or discover a new secret. Something that would be of use to the Coven. Then he could show all those doubters and name-callers . . .

A thunderous crash made the librarian cry out. Mr Hegarty's eyes snapped open and he shot off his perch.

'What is it, my love?' Grype said in a panicky voice.

The demon flapped around the shop. Terrified, it didn't even pause to collect the beetles that fell from its plumage. Ten minutes or so passed before Mr Grype could calm the creature.

Another crash. Perhaps the many-armed monster had returned? But there was no shadow at the window and the sound did not come from Yaga Passage. It came from *inside* the shop. From the storeroom at the back.

'Impossible,' Grype murmured.

With his demon squawking in his ear, he walked slowly between the shelves. The dust from the books knocked over by Mr Hegarty still swirled in the air. As Grype approached the storeroom, another pounding crash made the dust shiver. Cracks started to appear in the wood of the storeroom door.

'Impossible,' Grype repeated.

Apart from books and old papers only one thing was kept in the storeroom. The boy. Simon Lydgate had been locked up in there ever since the night of Quilp's capture. For the last six months, Grype had used the same sleeping spell to keep Simon under control. He had checked in on him every night, fed him a little, cast the spell . . .

'Oh dear!'

This was the first night he had forgotten to work the magic! All that fretting about his place in the Coven had driven Simon clean out of his mind. Yet even without the spell, the boy was so weak and malnourished it was difficult to see how he had the strength to batter his cell door.

'*Grrraaaggghhhh!*'

The cry made Mr Grype whimper. The little man gathered up what courage he possessed and bent down to the keyhole. At first, he could see nothing but shredded paper and torn bindings. Great heavy books, some thousands of pages thick, had been torn through, as if by powerful claws. The only light came from a bare bulb, which swung to and fro. It flashed across a dirty old bearskin rug in the centre of the room . . .

The 'rug' twitched.

And now Grype began to make out the features of a strange body. Legs covered in coarse hair pawed at the ground. A long snout snuffled the air. Intense green eyes with slit-shaped pupils stared through the keyhole. The thing saw Grype and drool dripped from its jaws. The witch staggered back as it launched itself at the door. He mumbled a half-forgotten strengthening spell and the cracks started to repair themselves.

Grype headed straight for his office. He dashed through the curtained doorway and into the Veil. The grey mist pressed in on him from all sides. Where was his master?

'Librarian, what can I do for you at this ungodly hour?'

Marcus Crowden, his eyes hidden beneath the shadow of his wide-brimmed hat, stepped out of the mist.

'Forgive my intrusion, Master.'

Crowden motioned with his fingers. His black cabinet emerged from the mist and began to swirl around Grype.

'There is nothing to forgive. But let us hope your news is worthy of my time. Otherwise . . . '

The door of the nightmare box opened a fraction. Ugly voices called out to Grype.

'It's the boy,' Grype squeaked. 'Simon Lydgate.'

'What of him?'

'He has woken.'

'You forgot the sleeping spell?'

The cabinet inched towards Grype. Its mouth yawned . . .

'Yes, but perhaps I did right by forgetting.'

Crowden held out his hand and the cabinet stopped an inch short of its prey.

'How so?'

'The boy. He is . . . changing . . . '

Crowden's eyes dazzled.

'Pray tell me, Mr Grype—into what?'

'ELEANOR!'

Jake's eyes snapped open and he dragged himself from his dream of the Witchfinder. He just about managed to make it across the bedroom and open the window before vomiting. A pile of brilliant green puke splattered across the front step of Stonycroft Cottage. It was exactly the same colour as the toad's poison.

Jake breathed deeply and looked out across the rooftops of Hobarron's Hollow. The sky in the east was growing lighter by the second. He checked his watch—5:30 a.m. He had been asleep for over fifteen hours! He remembered coming back to the cottage after being bitten by the toad and managing to eat some lunch. Then he had gone upstairs for a lie down. Aunt Joanna had called after him.

'Sure you're all right, Jake?'

''M fine. Just feel a bit tired.'

'You're probably still weak from the fever. You get some sleep. Don't let the bed bugs bite.'

'Or the mutant toads,' Jake had said under his breath.

Now he glanced down at his hand. A bandage had been wrapped around the wound. It looked like a professional job—Aunt Joanna must have called in a doctor. Jake peeked under the dressing to find the bite mark clean and smelling of disinfectant. He drew a few deep breaths of morning air, and his thoughts returned to the dream.

Where had these sights and sounds, these images and emotions come from? They unnerved him, and yet he had also felt a strange comfort while walking in the mysterious Witchfinder's skin. A man who had been frozen in ice . . . Is that what his father had meant by saying that the answer to the Demontide was 'frozen in time'? Without the weapon, and with his sacrifice looming, maybe this long-dead Witchfinder held the key? But how could that be?

Jake could make no sense of it. He pulled on some clothes and headed downstairs.

The kitchen was in darkness. Without turning on the light, Jake poured himself a glass of water. The pipes clanked and gurgled. Lollygag, the ginger tomcat, gave him a filthy look and sprang from the windowsill. He curled up under the table and was soon asleep again. Jake was swallowing down another glass of water when he saw the shadowy figure in the corner of the kitchen. The shock made him choke.

It was Aunt Joanna, slumped in an armchair. Her head was thrown back and her mouth was open. She didn't appear to be breathing.

Jake shot across the room. He took his aunt by the shoulders and shook her.

'Joanna? Are you OK?'

No response. Her lips had turned a pale shade of blue. There was no rise and fall of her chest. Jake shook her again.

'Wake up! Come on!'

He had raised his hand, and was about to slap her face, when the woman grunted. Her eyes opened a fraction.

'M'uh? That you, Adam? Or is it my darling Luke?' She let out a heartbreaking sob and tears ran down her cheeks. 'No, Luke's dead. My sweet boy. They killed him, you know. They took his blood, every last drop . . . For the greater good, they said. Tragedy is, they were right. My poor, poor boy . . . '

A photograph album lay open in her lap. There was only one picture on the page. It showed three children standing on the clifftops, arm-in-arm. They were smiling as only children can. Rusty red hair identified Adam and Joanna Harker. The name of the third child—a boy with pale skin and wide, dark eyes—was written beneath the photograph.

Luke Seward.

The boy who was sacrificed to stop the last Demontide, Jake thought.

He reached for the photograph. An empty bottle that had been resting beneath the album fell to the floor and shattered. Jake leaned in and smelt his aunt's breath. It reeked of whisky. Her eyes closed again and she started snoring. Jake swept up the glass and covered her with an old blanket brought down from his bedroom. He wanted to look at the photograph more closely but his head began to pound. He needed some fresh air.

He strode along the lane and up to the main road. He wanted to see Rachel. Why was she in the village? Maybe she knew something about what was going on here. It was much too early to call at the Saxby house but he headed uphill anyway.

Despite the road being very steep he kept up a quick pace. Birds flitted between the trees, busy with a bit of early-morning nest building. A milk float rattled by. A boy delivering newspapers freewheeled down the hill at a suicidal speed. Jake jogged along the road and drank in the atmosphere of the slow-waking village.

Before he knew it, he was at the gate of St Meredith's.

The church was a hideous block of a building. Built out of large, crudely carved stones, it was not cross-shaped, like most churches, but a simple rectangle. Slates were missing from the roof and the short steeple leaned drunkenly to one side. Small, undecorated windows and a plain archway entrance only added to its ugliness. Still, it wasn't doing *too* badly for its age—a plaque above the door dated the church from AD 785!

A far more impressive structure stood nearby.

The grand mausoleum dominated the graveyard. It was a kind of over-ground crypt, about four metres in height with big Roman pillars supporting the roof and marble steps leading up to a large oak door. Although clearly very old, there were no cracks in its sandy stonework and its pillars were free of moss and vines. Often these mausoleums had the names of those buried within written on the walls. There were no such markings here. Instead, dozens of paintings had been etched all the way round. The colours of the frescoes had faded and yet the scenes were still dramatic and forceful. Jake saw faces, terrifying and sublime; bodies, broken and beautiful; eyes filled with compassion and loathing. Each picture showed a great battle raging between angels and demons.

Jake's breath caught in his throat. His heart pounded. Slowly, almost reverently, he climbed the mausoleum steps. He had reached the great door, and was stretching out a hand to touch the frescoes, when a shadow fell over him.

'You can't go inside,' a voice whispered. 'The door's locked. It won't open again until the end of the world.'

Jake turned.

A boy with pale skin and dark eyes stood at the bottom of the mausoleum steps. Jake recognized him immediately.

It was Luke Seward.

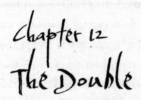

Chapter 12
The Double

Shafts of golden light shone against the spectre's pale skin.

The ghost and Jake stared at one another.

Meanwhile, the world beyond the graveyard plodded on as normal—the birds' dawn chorus came to an end; the milk float rumbled past; aeroplanes left trails in the sky—all as if ghosts and witches and demons did not exist.

The ghost held out his hand.

'Hello, Jake.'

'Luke . . .'

The boy frowned. 'What did you call me?'

Jake stepped forward. Seen from a slightly different angle, the spirit appeared more solid, more lifelike.

'You're real.'

'I think so,' the boy laughed.

Now that Jake had emerged from between the pillars of the mausoleum, the kid's voice no longer echoed. The hollow, spectral tone was gone and he sounded exactly like what he was—a boy of about ten years old.

'I'm sorry,' Jake smiled, 'I thought for a moment you were a ghost.'

'Cool!'

'You'd like to be a ghost?'

The boy considered. 'I guess it would be fun, maybe for just a day. Spying on people and scaring them stupid, that'd be a laugh. I dunno though. I think it would be pretty lonely. Not like vampires—they're dead, too, but in lots of stories they hang out together in gangs. Being a vampire would be wicked.'

'Do you read many vampire stories?'

'Yeah, I've got books and books at home. They're my favourite monsters.'

'Mine too,' Jake laughed.

'But they're pretty weak, really. There's loads of ways you can kill a vampire: put a stake through its heart, cut off its head, drown it in holy water . . . '

'Ah, but not *all* the legends are the same. Did you know that, in many stories, you would have to stake a vamp, then cut off its head *and* stuff its mouth with garlic to make sure it didn't come back?'

'Wow.' The boy looked genuinely impressed. 'Someone told me you knew loads of stuff about monsters, and you really do!'

'Who told you?'

'Might've been your Aunt Joanna.' The kid shrugged. 'Or your dad. He comes to the Hollow sometimes to visit my mum. I like your dad a lot. Sometimes he brings me comics, horror comics like the ones you've got.'

'You've met my dad?'

'Course. But he's not been around much lately. Where is he?'

'Abroad, so they say . . . ' Jake realized that the boy was still waiting for his outstretched hand to be shaken. 'Sorry, mate, didn't mean to leave you hanging. So, what's your name?'

'Eddie Rice.'

'What are you doing up this early, Eddie?'

'I'm always up early. I'm like a backwards vampire.'

Jake laughed again.

'Anyway, I saw you passing my house a few minutes ago and I thought I'd come and say hi. Sorry if I scared you. Though I am pretty psyched that I managed it, you being a hardcore horror fan and all. Which reminds me, will you come and have a look at my comic collection? I don't think I've got as many as you—your dad told me you've got, like, millions—but maybe I've got a few you haven't.'

'Sure, why not?'

Eddie Rice grinned from ear to ear and led the way down the path.

The boys turned right out of the churchyard gate and onto a country lane. Leaving the village behind, they walked into open countryside. Cattle grazed in the fields while crows pecked at the blackberry bushes on either side of the lane.

'I know why you called me Luke,' Eddie said. 'You know about my uncle, don't you?'

'Your uncle?'

'Luke Seward. He was my mum's brother. My mum says I have to call him "uncle" when I speak about him. Which feels strange, because I never met the guy. He died years and years ago.'

Jake nodded. 'I saw a picture of him in my aunt's photo album. You really look like him.'

'Your dad says I'm Luke's "double". They were best friends, your dad and my Uncle Luke. I reckon that's why Adam comes and sees me whenever he's in the Hollow. I remind him of the friend he lost.'

'How did your uncle die, Eddie?'

'He was murdered.' The kid's voice was calm, even. 'He was thirteen years old on the night they came for him . . . '

'They?'

'The killers. My grandparents were away for the night and the housekeeper didn't hear a thing. They dragged him from his bed and took him down to the bay. The police said, from the footprints, it looked like there were three of them. They took Uncle Luke to Crowden's Sorrow.'

'Crowden's . . . ?'

'Yeah. It's a huge cave in the bay. The killers dragged Luke into the cave and cut his throat. There was a big investigation, but they never found out who did it or why.'

He was a sacrifice, Jake thought, *butchered by Dr Holmwood and the Elders to prevent the Demontide*. But how could the death of an innocent boy have stopped the Crowden Coven from achieving their victory? Having said that, how was the 'Incu' weapon supposed to have stopped them?

'I never knew Luke but his death makes me sad,' Eddie continued. 'It makes me sad because it makes other people sad. My mum's never got over it. I think that's why my dad left us. And your dad, he really loved Luke.'

It was so strange, this secret life Jake's father had led. There had never been any mention of Hobarron's Hollow or Eddie Rice, and yet it was obvious that Adam Harker had often visited the boy here. He had even brought Eddie comic books, treating him like a second son. Maybe Jake should be jealous but he couldn't help liking the kid.

'Here we are,' Eddie said, bringing Jake out of his day-dream.

The Rice house stood at the end of a dusty track. It was a big old building made out of the same kind of irregular grey bricks as the church. On the roof, a weathervane in the shape of a cow turned in the breeze. As Jake and Eddie approached, a woman emerged from the house.

Mrs Rice wore a tatty black dress. Fearful eyes stared out from her gaunt face.

'Who is your friend, Edward?' she asked.

'This is Jake,' Eddie said, brushing past his mother. 'Dr Harker's son.'

Mrs Rice focused on Jake. Trembling hands covered her heart.

'May God preserve and keep you, Jacob Harker,' she murmured.

* * *

Dr Holmwood blew cigarette smoke down the receiver. The phone rang three times before someone picked up.

'Saxby residence.'

'Malcolm? Gordon here. You've reached the Hollow safely. Good. Now, we're sure this is a secure line?'

'Absolutely. There's only Rachel in the house and she's still asleep. No risk of anyone overhearing us.'

'Excellent. Have you had a chance to assess the situation?'

'Yes, and I'm afraid the initial reports were accurate, sir. The first Omen *has* arrived.'

'Toads,' Holmwood grumbled. 'I hate the bloody toads! Almost as bad as the monsters, but at least *their* activities are restricted to the cavern. So, anyone outside the village see the beastly things?'

'No one other than Jacob Harker—if you can call *him* an outsider. Apparently Susan Daniels and a few others made a bit of a scene in the post office, talking about omens and portents . . .'

'Oh God,' Holmwood groaned.

'Drake tried to cover it up as best he could. I don't suppose it really matters: the boy must have guessed a lot of the story by now.'

'I heard he was injured.'

'One of the toads bit him,' Saxby confirmed. 'He managed to make it back to Joanna's cottage. Alice Splane removed the poison and dressed the wound while he was sleeping. He won't suffer any further effects. Must have had a few unpleasant dreams, though.'

'Hmm. He's damn lucky that a magical infection expert was on the scene.'

'It was lucky for all of us. If his blood had been contaminated . . .'

'There is still hope that we may not need his blood, Dr Saxby.'

'A *very* slim hope, sir—and growing slimmer by the hour. We're expecting the second omen some time today; the third possibly tomorrow. This means we have only about three days until the Demontide.'

'And with that in mind, I am bringing Adam Harker to the Hollow.'

'What? Sir, I would strongly urge you to reconsider. Adam is not stable. What if he escaped and found the boy? What if they disappeared together? Then all would be lost.'

'Adam *must* be there,' Holmwood insisted. 'He is the second-in-rank Elder. Whenever the Demontide falls, all of the Elders have to be present. You know the rules.'

Saxby grunted. 'Very well. But he must be kept drugged and out of the way. Especially if we need to . . . take desperate measures. How will you bring him?'

'In a convoy of three armour-plated vehicles. We'll have standard issue weapons as well as magical protection and . . .' Holmwood stopped. He thought he had heard the faintest of clicks on the line. 'Saxby, you're sure no one is listening in?'

'Positive.'

'Hmph. Probably just my nerves. Anyway, we'll bring Adam across country via back roads. There is only one place on the route vulnerable to attack. Wykely Woods. I want several Elders to meet us at Steerpike Bridge and escort the convoy through the forest.'

'When will you bring him?'

'Midnight, the day after tomorrow. Be ready. Oh, and one last thing: you'd better spread the word about the second omen. Although its effects will be limited to the Hollow, we must make sure the villagers have taken the traditional precaution. God help anyone still outside when the mist rolls in.'

Holmwood hung up.

The doctor stubbed out his cigarette. He left his office and took the lift down into the bowels of Hobarron Tower. Leaving the lift, he walked along a long, grey corridor with fluorescent strip lights buzzing overhead. At the end of the corridor he stopped, took the keycard from his pocket and pressed it against the panel on the wall. A cobwebbed door marked—

—groaned open.

The doctor paced around the old laboratory. Floor to ceiling, the room was filled with scientific equipment, all of it switched off, shut down, and covered in plastic sheets. The doctor thought to himself: *this place is full of ghosts.* He could remember Claire and Adam Harker as young scientists, working happily here. In those days they had loved each other very deeply, but the gradual pressure of their work had destroyed that love.

Holmwood turned and faced the box.

It stood on a metal table in the centre of the room, numerous cables and wires snaking out of its back. The doctor approached and ran his fingers over the transparent lid. This machine had once contained their only hope of defeating the Demontide. Now Holmwood saw that it had always been a false hope. The weapon had failed, and so only one option remained.

'Saxby's right,' Holmwood said aloud. 'There is no other way. *Jacob has to die.*'

Chapter 13
Eclipse

Eddie led Jake into a large hall decorated with faded portraits and tatty old tapestries. The floor had been pieced together from a jigsaw of roughhewn stone. A wooden staircase made a rickety path up to the first floor. There was something familiar about the layout of the place.

As if answering an unasked question, Eddie said, 'Years ago, this was the Holmwood manor house.'

Of course. Although the construction materials were far more traditional and ancient than those used in Dr Holmwood's luxurious house, this place had obviously been the blueprint for Green Gables.

'Dr Holmwood's family home,' Jake said, as if speaking to himself.

'He still comes here sometimes,' Eddie nodded. 'Says he likes to remember his roots, where he came from.'

Holmwood, Dr Saxby, Walter Drake, my dad—they all

visited this place regularly, Jake thought. *The old families coming home. I wonder if the Institute organized bus trips!*

'That's the man who built the house. Tiberius Holmwood.'

Eddie pointed to a portrait at the head of the stairs. Jake immediately recognized the cropped beard and hooded eyes of the first of the Hobarron Elders. At that moment, sunlight dazzled through the windows that overlooked the great hall and shone on the dusty painting. Fascinated, Jake climbed the stairs.

'After my dad left us, Dr Holmwood let me and my mum stay here rent free,' Eddie said, following Jake up the stairs. 'He's been very kind to us. But . . . ' Eddie blushed. 'But I don't . . . '

'You don't trust him.'

'How did you know?'

Jake didn't answer. He had reached the top of the stairs, his eyes rooted on the portrait.

The trill of a telephone echoed around the great hall.

'I'm just going to see if mum's OK,' Eddie said. 'She's a bit uncomfortable around strangers.'

He trotted down the stairs. From somewhere far away, Jake heard Mrs Rice's voice.

'Holmwood Manor . . . Oh, it's you. What do you want . . . ? Yes, I'm fully aware of what happened in the square yesterday . . . '

A door slammed and Mrs Rice could no longer be heard. Had Jake been less obsessed with the portrait, he might have sneaked within earshot of the conversation. As it was, he could not tear himself from the picture.

The painting appeared to be an exact match for the one hanging in the corridor at Green Gables. The expression on Tiberius Holmwood's face—prim and haughty—was the same, as was the period costume. The colours may have faded a bit, making the scene significantly darker, but that was only natural considering the painting's age. Jake figured that this was the original from which the Green Gables version had been copied. However, there was one major difference.

This had once been a portrait of *two* people.

The second figure stood to the left of Tiberius Holmwood. He wore a wide-brimmed hat, a plain shirt, and a three-quarter length jacket. Behind the man stood a tall box, like a magician's cabinet. That was all Jake could make out. Someone had vandalized the portrait, using black paint to mask the stranger's face.

Eddie bounded up the stairs.

'Mum's cool. So, you want to see my room?'

'Eddie, who was this man?' Jake pointed to the ruined face.

'Beats me. I've asked Mum and Dr Holmwood, no one knows. Least, they say they don't. Anyway, history's dead boring. Come on!'

Eddie's room was in the attic where the servants had once slept. There was a skylight in the roof and, on a glorious summer day like this, the bedroom was warm and cosy. Jake could only imagine what it was like in the winter, with a cold wind howling off the sea and rattling the roof tiles. Apart from a bed, an old wardrobe, and a wash basin there was a plasma TV, a DVD player, and a stack of films in one corner. The modern appliances looked very out of place in this musty, cobwebbed room.

Jake sat on the bed while Eddie dragged boxes of comics from the wardrobe. A few movie posters tacked to the wall caught his eye.

'*Nightmare on Slaughter Avenue, Psycho Town, All Hallow's Eve*,' Jake said. 'Your mum lets you watch this stuff?'

'Sure,' Eddie grinned. 'Well, to be honest, she doesn't know I watch 'em. She doesn't take much interest in what I do.'

'They're a bit scary for a ten year old.'

'Hey, I'm twelve.'

'Sorry. But even so.'

'I bet you've seen them.'

'Well, yes, but I'm fifteen.'

'And those movies are eighteen certificate. So we're both too young.'

'Touché,' Jake smiled. 'So, your mum. Has she always been . . .'

'Strange?'

'I wasn't going to say that.'

'It's cool. It's like I said, she never got over Luke being murdered. She was only eight when it happened. They were inseparable, her and her brother, and then, one day, he wasn't there any more. And he didn't just disappear. He was killed in just about the most horrible way you can imagine.'

'And you say they never found out who did it?'

'I think my mum knows.'

'What?'

'I think it was someone close to the family. Sometimes I even think Dr Holmwood might have had something to do with it.'

This kid's as sharp as a tack, Jake thought. *No wonder he doesn't trust Holmwood ... Must be scary for him, all alone in this house, surrounded by memories of his uncle.*

Jake imagined himself as a young kid, curled up in that bed, alert to all the strange noises of the old house. He wondered if Eddie stayed awake at night, watching the bedroom door, waiting to see if the handle would turn. One night *they* might come for him—the killers who had abducted and sacrificed his Uncle Luke. It struck Jake as a lonely, fearful kind of existence.

'Look at these! Pretty wicked, right?'

Eyes agleam, Eddie displayed his comics like a pirate showing off his treasure trove. Jake was quite impressed. There were a few nice reprints of *Chamber of Darkness*, a couple of *House of Mystery* editions wrapped in plastic, and a full boxed set of the *Haunt of Fear*. For the next hour, the boys chatted about their shared passion.

'It's a great collection,' Jake said, picking up a copy of *Haunt of Fear*.

'Thanks,' Eddie beamed.

'Are your mates into comics too?'

'Don't have many friends.' Eddie's smile died. He concentrated hard on packing his comics back into their boxes. 'Kids at school don't seem to like me very much. They call me names—think I'm creepy because I like horror stuff.'

No friends. A distant, emotionally detached mother. Even an absent father. The likeness was not lost on Jake.

The clock of St Meredith's church struck noon. Jake swore under his breath. He had allowed himself the luxury of believing, just for a moment, that he was a normal kid again. In truth, his life was no longer normal, and he couldn't waste time pretending that it was. He had to focus on stopping the Demontide.

'Sorry, Ed, I've gotta make a move.'

The boy's face fell. 'Really? I thought we could get some lunch and then go down to the bay. I could show you Crowden's Sorrow.'

'That's not a bad idea. What about tomorrow?'

Eddie's grin flashed back into place. 'Sure. Where are you off to now?'

'The Saxbys.'

'Are you going to see Rachel?'

'You know Rachel?'

'Course. She's my cousin.'

Eddie explained as they climbed down out of the attic. Rachel's mother, who had died giving birth to her, had been Eddie's aunt. They weren't all that close, but Rachel always popped in to see the Rices whenever she visited the Hollow.

The boys left the dingy chill of Holmwood Manor and strode out into the sunshine.

'How often does Rachel come here?' Jake asked.

'Once every three months maybe. I don't think she likes the Hollow much. I guess it *is* a bit boring here . . . '

'Eddie, this place is anything *but* boring.'

They came to the end of the dirt track and headed along the road. The sun tingled pleasantly on the back of Jake's neck. Looking down over the little white cottages, the pinkish-red cliffs and the sparkling sea beyond, it was difficult to imagine that anything bad could happen in such a place. Jake only had to turn west, in the direction of two dark stone structures, to feel that certainty slip away. Like a pair of evil eyes, Holmwood Manor and St Meredith's church glowered over the village.

A short walk through an apple orchard brought Jake and Eddie to a modern house surrounded by a large terraced garden. Sitting alone on a bench beside a tropical fish pond was Rachel Saxby.

Jake stopped. Even with her back turned, she had the power to render him speechless. Immune to the girl's magic, Eddie ran on ahead.

'Hello, cuz! What are you . . . Oh, Rach, that's disgusting!'

Rachel was wearing a light summer dress. With one leg propped up on the bench, the hem of the dress had fallen back to reveal a shapely calf and a well-toned thigh. Jake tried not to gawp. It was a valiant effort but not an entirely successful one. The girl raised an eyebrow. She snipped a pair of toenail scissors through the air to get his attention.

'Earth calling Jake Harker.'

'Sorry, Rachel. I was . . . Nothing. Sorry.'

'Cute. He's blushing.'

'Don't make fun of my friend,' Eddie ordered. 'Anyway, you're the one who should be embarrassed. Cutting your toe-nails in public, it's gross.'

Eddie brushed the nails aside and took a seat next to his cousin.

'I didn't know you guys were friends.' Rachel smiled.

'We met this morning,' Eddie grinned, 'but I think we're going to be best ma—'

A frightened cry cut the boy short.

'Edward! Get back into the house this instant!'

A figure came darting through the orchard. If Eddie had looked like a ghost in the graveyard, then Jake figured that his mother resembled a banshee. The shrieking spectre hur-tled through the trees, her black dress flying behind her. She reached her son and snatched hold of his hand.

'I'm sorry, Jacob,' she gasped, 'but Edward must come back to the house.'

'Mum, I was talking to Rachel and . . .'

'Not now. The weather report has warned of a storm com-ing in off the sea. A terrible storm.' Her gaze caught hold of Jake like a fish hook and reeled him in. 'It will break at any moment. I don't want you caught out in it. Please, Jake, run along home. Your aunt will be worried.'

'But, Mum . . .' Eddie protested.

'Back to the house,' Mrs Rice warned. 'I shan't tell you again.'

'Don't worry, mate,' Jake said, 'I'll catch up with you tomorrow.'

Eddie's shoulders sagged. He shambled away in the direction of Holmwood Manor. Mrs Rice was about to leave too when Jake caught hold of her arm.

'Can I have a word? Will you excuse us, Rachel?'

Rachel gave a half curious, half amused nod.

Jake led Mildred Rice to a crab-apple tree a little distance away.

'This storm,' he said, 'it came here once before, didn't it?'

'I have to go. My son . . . '

'A generation ago, a dark storm threatened Hobarron's Hollow. Your brother Luke was at the centre of it. If the storm had broken here, then it would have spread like a tide across the world. A Demontide . . . '

Mrs Rice trembled. Tears rolled down her cheeks. Jake guessed that she was no more than thirty-five years old, and yet the burden of her life in the Hollow had given her the bent back and rounded shoulders of an old woman.

'But something held back the storm,' Jake continued. 'A great evil that cancelled out the evil to come. A sacrifice. The Elders—they murdered your brother.'

Mrs Rice wiped her eyes. Her thin hand caught at Jake and drew him close.

'You are no child of God, Jacob Harker,' she whispered, 'but He loves you just the same. A storm *is* coming, and its Second Omen is near at hand. Run home. Wait it out. Then flee Hobarron's Hollow. Flee while there's still time.'

The woman strode away.

Rachel wrapped her arm around Jake's shoulder.

'I've never seen Mildred Rice so upset,' she said. 'What did you say to the old witch?'

'You'd never heard of the Hollow . . . ?' Rachel asked.

They walked through the Saxby orchard, back towards the road.

'I don't understand how that's possible, everyone knows about this place.'

'So it seems. Have you always come here, Rachel?'

'Uh-huh—there's never been a summer we haven't come back. The Drakes holiday here too. Must say, though, I've never met anyone connected with the Institute who didn't know about the village. Why would your dad keep it secret . . . ? Jake, where are we going?'

'Just a little further.'

Rachel gave him a curious glance. 'Something's going on with you, Jake Harker. Come on, out with it.'

'I'd tell you, but I think you'd have me committed.'

'Remember that night in Dr Holmwood's rose garden?' she said, slipping her hand into his. 'I said I was your friend. I said I'd help you. You can tell me anything.'

'I'm sorry, Rachel. The time isn't right.'

'I'll be here when it is,' she promised.

They walked on.

Rachel started asking questions about what had happened after the party at Green Gables. Why hadn't he called her? How had he got to the Hollow? Jake found himself spinning the same lies that he had been told: he'd been ill with a fever; Aunt Joanna had taken up the parental reins after his father had been called away on business. By the time all the lies had been repeated, they had reached St Meredith's graveyard and the strange mausoleum.

The paintings of angels and demons stood out from the shadows. Jake laid a hand against one of the frescoes.

'What do you know about this place?'

'Only that it used to scare me stupid.'

'Huh?'

'We'd sneak up here in the middle of the night, me and some of the village kids. Those paintings in the moonlight.' Rachel shuddered. 'We'd dare each other to run to the door and knock. Don't laugh, but we even chanted the Hobarron Poem—that made it extra creepy!'

'A poem?'

'An old nursery rhyme the Hollow people sing to their children. One of the verses went something like this: *Witchfinder, Witchfinder—Evil he saw—and used all his power—to seal up the Door.*'

'Witchfinder?'

'It's the Witchfinder's tomb. Jake, are you all right? You look like you've seen a ghost.'

'Rachel . . . who is the Witchfinder?'

'It's just a local legend. I heard bits of it when I was a kid.'

'Tell me.'

'Not much to tell. Sometime in the sixteen hundreds, a stranger came to the village. It wasn't called Hobarron's Hollow then, I'm not even sure it had a name. Anyway, there had been rumours of witchcraft in the area and this guy turned up to investigate. I guess he was like that awful man they've made movies about. The one who hanged all those poor women for being witches and then collected his reward. What was his name? Hopkirk?'

'Matthew Hopkins. The Witchfinder General.'

'That's it. I think *our* witchfinder even knew Hopkins.'

'What was his name?'

Rachel shrugged. 'I've only ever heard him called "the Witchfinder". He came to the village and, sure enough, he found black magic being practised around every corner. He started this whole campaign against a coven of local witches. Accused them of summoning demons and all kinds of crazy stuff. The story gets a bit muddled from this point. Some versions even say that he had dark powers of his own. Anyway, he fought this coven and saved the village from sin. What a hero!'

'Maybe he genuinely believed in what he was doing,' Jake said.

'From what I've heard, these witchfinders just went around condemning people who fitted the bill,' Rachel said. Her gaze ran over the paintings. 'He might've comforted himself by thinking he was an angel ridding the world of demons, but the Hobarron Witchfinder was a monster. And the really horrible thing is, the people of this village thanked him for it! When he died they built this tomb for him.'

Historically, Jake knew that Rachel's description of 'the witchfinder' was correct. Whether or not they had genuinely believed that they were doing God's work, men like

Eclipse

Matthew Hopkins had been responsible for the slaughter of hundreds of innocent people. And yet the man Jake had seen in his dreams—the Witchfinder whose skin he had worn—had not seemed evil. Battered and careworn, he had been like the faded figures on these walls. An avenging angel standing alone against the forces of darkness.

A Land Rover roared up to the church gate. The horn wailed.

'It's my dad,' Rachel said, her forehead pinched. 'Just a minute.'

She dashed between the gravestones. When she reached the Land Rover, the driver's window whirred down and Jake heard the barking voice of Dr Saxby. A few minutes later, Rachel ran back.

'Sorry, Jake. My dad's flipping out for some reason. He says I have to come home now.'

'Can't you tell him . . . ?'

'I've never seen him like this.' She looked back towards the 4x4. 'He said to tell you that your aunt has called and wants you home pronto. Look, call me later, OK?'

Rachel gave an awkward smile and headed back to the car. She jumped in and the Land Rover bounded down the lane.

No sooner had the car disappeared, than an inhuman shriek rang across the Hollow. Jake looked up. At first he couldn't understand what he was seeing. It was like a total eclipse—the sun blotted out of the sky and a cold shadow cast across the earth. As a little boy, Jake remembered seeing a solar eclipse. The moon had moved slowly across the sun until only a thin halo of light remained.

This sudden gloom was nothing to do with the moon.

It was only when breaks started to appear in the darkness that Jake understood what was happening. The cries should have alerted him earlier. As the blanket of birds swept across the sky, they called out in panicked unison. The flock was frightened. Made up of all kinds of seabirds—gulls and terns, gannets and guillemots—it flew west, away from Hobarron's Hollow. Jake looked down the hill, towards the sea, and his mouth dropped open in surprise.

In the streets, another kind of swarm had started to flee the village. Thousands of rats raced and bumped and tumbled up the hill, all in a desperate bid to escape some unseen menace. The road had turned into an undulating mass of black bodies.

'Rats abandoning a sinking ship,' Jake said.

With a final rustle of wings, the last of the birds passed overhead. Reaching the brow of the hill, the tidal wave of rats broke up into streams and spread out into the fields. Within minutes, the rodents had also vanished.

An eerie silence settled over Hobarron's Hollow. Jake walked down to the graveyard gate. Despite the heat of the day, he felt the need to rub warmth into his arms.

A foghorn blared across the bay. Jake scanned the coast.

'Oh . . . my . . . God . . . '

It rose out of the sea—a mist, thick and green . . .

'The Second Omen,' Jake murmured.

He started to run.

Chapter 14
Mistery

The sea had vanished. Its calm blue surface now lay beneath the unearthly mist. Many shades of green ran through the fog: fern and forest, olive and lime, moss and shamrock. The bulk of it was a sickly grey-green vapour—the colour of poison gas. It crept across the bay and ate away at the shore. It banked behind the cliffs and sent out tendrils into the streets of Hobarron's Hollow. Slither by slither it invaded the sleepy village.

Dogs howled and children cried. A foghorn moaned, its lonely voice lost in the mist. As Jake ran downhill, engines started and cars tore out of driveways. Families had been packed in, grannies and grandads huddled together on the back seat, children stacked on their laps. Wild-eyed mothers and fathers sat behind steering wheels. If the car in front hesitated, horns sang out in protest and bumper nudged bumper.

Jake skidded to a halt. What on earth was he doing, running back to Stonycroft Cottage? Although there were no fleeing crowds, many people appeared to be leaving Hobarron's Hollow. They knew what was coming. If it was worse than the toads, then Jake ought to join them. He started back up the hill.

He had run a few paces when an old man called out from the window of his house.

'Where are you going, you idiot? Get home now!'

'But the people,' Jake said, pointing to the cars. 'There's this mist coming in from the bay and . . . '

'A few morons always run,' the old man nodded, 'but there's no need. Get home, lock your door, and make sure you've a sprig of holly in your window. Don't dare venture outside until the mist clears.'

Jake looked down into the bay. The mist had now reached the first houses, its smoky fingers locking them in a tight fist. It wouldn't be long before it reached Stonycroft Cottage.

'Will you let me in?' he called to the old man.

'I don't know you. You're not a Hollow man . . . No. No, I'm sorry . . . Look, there's a bicycle down the side of the house—take it and go!'

The window slammed shut and the curtains swished together.

Jake had no time to think. A quick glance told him that the mist had devoured the town square. Only the tip of the war memorial stood above it, like the peak of a mountain breaking through an evil cloud. The cars loaded with their nervous passengers had now roared out of the village. The dogs quit their barking and the foghorn sent out its final wail. That eerie stillness returned to the Hollow.

Jake vaulted the garden fence. He grabbed the bicycle, and the window above his head shot open.

'Put it on!' the old man called.

A long coat made of coarse material and patched with leather landed at Jake's feet. The window slammed shut again. Without pausing, Jake pulled on the coat and wheeled the bike to the road.

The mist was within a few metres of the lane leading to Joanna's cottage. Soon it would snuffle its way into every corner of the Hollow. *And then what?* Jake thought. Clearly, it wasn't any ordinary mist—the colour alone told him that. The thicker it became the more it resembled those poisonous gas clouds he had seen in old war movies. Maybe that was precisely what it was: a deadly, choking vapour.

Jake pushed off. The hill was so steep that he could find no traction in the bike chain. Instead, he freewheeled down the deserted pavement. His speed increased and his hand hovered over the brake. The old man had kept the machine in good repair, tyres pumped, gears oiled. Even so, at this breakneck pace, Jake found the bike difficult to control. He dodged a few obstacles—a wooden bench, an abandoned skateboard, a broken umbrella—each swerve threatening to tip him over the handlebars.

Lumbering, lurching, the mist made its way into the lane. Jake reached the junction a second or two later. He turned into a skid. The rear wheel slipped on a patch of loose stones and the bike shot out from under him. It flipped over and clattered into the mist. Arms outstretched, Jake tumbled helplessly after the bike.

Instinct, and the old man's coat, saved him. He pulled it over his head and drew his hands into the sleeves. A few deep breaths steadied his nerves. He peeked out from under the collar. Just the sight of that weird green smoke all around was enough to re-energize him. He darted forward.

He was almost clear when the last lick of mist caught him around the throat. A sting of acid burned into his flesh and Jake screamed. Blood began to trickle down his neck. There was no time to worry about the wound—he staggered on down the lane. A voice deep inside told him to run but he could not bring himself to turn his back on the mist. It crept towards him at a lazy pace, almost like a predator toying with its prey.

Suddenly, the mist reared up, its fingers scorching the topmost branches of the trees. Leaves burst into flame and fell in a crackling rain of fire. Like a wave about to break, the acid fog towered over Jake . . .

He bolted for the cottage door. Rattled the handle.

It was locked.

'Aunt Joanna!'

No answer.

Green tentacles locked around Jake's ankles. His trousers started to smoulder.

'Hey! Let me in!'

He glanced over his shoulder and his blood turned to ice.

The mist had swallowed the lane. There was nothing to be seen except billows of swirling, burning green. The front garden was gone, as was the path. Again, Jake thought that the mist must have some kind of consciousness because it seemed to be playing with him. Only the step on which he stood had been left untouched.

But now those lethal fingers began to tease him. They struck twice across his face.

'Arrgghhh!'

Another finger scarred his forehead. Another slashed his hands. The pain was as bright as if he had plunged his hand into scalding water.

Jake pounded on the door.

'LET ME IN!'

The mist pressed against his back and smoke rose from the old man's coat. The scorched leather smelt like a roasting animal. It wouldn't be long before the coat was stripped from him. His T-shirt and trousers would burn up in an instant. Then, layer by layer, the skin would be boiled off his bones . . .

There was nothing else he could do.

Jake filled his lungs and stepped back *into* the mist.

It felt as if he had been thrown headlong into a blazing inferno. The vapour's fiery touch scorched his face and hands. A scream worked its way along his throat but he managed to keep his mouth clamped shut. If he breathed in, the mist would burn his insides to an ashy cinder. Eyes closed, Jake took the short run up and threw himself at the door.

Wood splintered. The lock snapped. Jake staggered into the cottage, turned and slammed the door behind him.

Through the letter box he heard the sigh of the mist. It sounded like a disappointed child.

The phone in the hall rang. Jake snatched up the receiver.

'Is that you?' Joanna's voice—booming, frightened. 'Are you safe?'

'I'm fine.'

He looked at himself in the mirror that hung above the phone table. 'Fine' was a white lie. His neck was still bleeding and blisters were forming across his face and hands.

'Where are you, Aunt Joanna?'

'I'm staying the night at Alice Splane's—she's an old friend of mine.'

Jake remembered the bird-like woman who had lectured him about the poisonous toad.

'Thought I'd better check in. This awful mist.' Joanna gave a boisterous laugh. 'It's quite treacherous.'

'No kidding.' Much as he needed to play along, Jake was getting a little sick of his aunt's games.

'I think you should stay inside until the mist has passed,' Joanna continued. 'Could be dangerous, walking through the streets—you might get run down or something. I'll be home in the morning. Have you seen Lollygag?'

'I'll find him, don't worry.'

Jake hung up. He dug out the scrap of paper on which Eddie had written his mobile number. He wanted to check that the kid was OK. Eddie answered after the first ring.

'Jake! Hey! What's the deal with this mist?'

'Ed, listen to me: stay indoors, don't even think about going out.'

'Couldn't even if I wanted to,' Eddie said ruefully. 'Mum's locked all the doors and windows. What d'you think's going on?'

'I don't know. Listen, if the mist has cleared up in the morning, can you meet me down in the bay? Say about nine a.m.?'

'No probs.'

'Thanks. Gotta go.'

Jake dialled Rachel's number. A robotic voice cut in.

'Sorry, there is a fault. Please try later. Sorry, there is a fault . . . '

He slammed down the receiver and went in search of the ginger tomcat.

Lollygag was not in his usual position on the kitchen windowsill. The mist sweated at the window and left liquid green streaks on the pane. Jake wondered why the powerful acid did not eat through the glass. Then he saw the little branch with its sharp green leaves and red berries hanging above the sink, and remembered what the old man had said: *make sure you've a sprig of holly in your window.* A quick dark catalogue reference reminded Jake that holly had once been used as protection against witches and demons, storms and tempests.

Jake was about to head upstairs when he saw something poking through the catflap.

'Lollygag?'

The fleshy animal was stuck in the opening. Its front paws rested on the ground while its head lolled forward.

'Come on, shake a leg,' Jake smiled.

He went over to the flap and dropped to one knee. His smile fell away. Lollygag's eyes were fixed in a terrified stare. Jake reached out for the cat's collar—the name tag jingled as he slipped a finger beneath it. Taking a deep breath, he pulled.

The front half of the cat fell forward.

There was *no* back half.

It was as if the animal had been cut in two. Guts and entrails flopped out of the severed section and splashed across the kitchen floor. At the place where Lollygag had been lopped in half the hair was burnt to a crisp. Jake thought he was going to puke but held it down. He imagined what must have happened: caught outside, the fat cat had been too slow to escape the oncoming mist. It had managed to wriggle partway through the flap before the acid tentacles had caught hold of it. In his death, Lollygag had paid the price for his overeating and lack of exercise.

'Poor Lolls, you should have chased the rats,' Jake sighed.

'I should have seen it!' Crowden cried. 'The moment he was dragged in here, I should have read it in his face. This is wonderful!'

Three figures stood in the nothingness of the Veil: Master Crowden, Mother Inglethorpe, and Mr Grype. The toady librarian was grinning like a Cheshire cat. Crowden was also smiling—at least, Esther Inglethorpe believed he was. There was no mistaking the glee in his eyes, although with the dirty cloth wound around his face one could never be sure.

Mistery

Simon Lydgate lay unconscious at the Master's feet.

'I don't understand what's so important about this pathetic creature,' Esther Inglethorpe sniffed.

Grype's face twisted with rage.

'She is trying to undermine me, Master!'

'Hush, Grype,' Crowden said soothingly. 'No one can take this momentous discovery away from you. Least of all those who, in recent times, have failed me.' Eyes as hard as flint bored into Esther. 'You shall have your reward, my faithful librarian.'

Grype flinched at the hated word. It came as something of a relief to Esther that the Master had laced his praise with a pinch of cruelty. To build a man up and cut him down in the same sentence was an art Crowden had perfected over many centuries.

'Forgive my stupidity,' Esther said, 'but if Grype could describe once more what happened last night, I might begin to make sense of it.'

'Willingly.' Exaggerating both his courage and his magical ability, Grype made a four-course meal of the simple story . . . 'A binding spell held the door while I ran to inform Master Crowden of the boy's metamorphosis. Ambrose Montague and Georgina Fleck arrived within minutes and aided me in pacifying the . . . creature. It was a difficult task.'

'Really?' Mother Inglethorpe shrugged. 'From what you've described, I can't imagine why three witches should have had any trouble with a simple werewolf.'

'You show your ignorance, Mother!' Crowden sneered.

Grype's grin spread further across his ugly face. Esther could do nothing except bow her head.

Crowden sank to his knees, like a man worshipping at an altar. He ran his gloved hands through the sleeping boy's hair.

'No, Simon Lydgate is much more than a mere werewolf.'

Esther forgot about her fear and embarrassment. She knelt beside her Master.

'What *is* he?'

'Can you not guess?'

'A magical being—something that wears human skin as a disguise?'

'More than that. This thing does not even remember its true nature. It thinks it *is* human.'

'But how?'

'I believe someone has fooled it. Erased its memories, hidden its past.'

'Why would someone demean it so?' There was something like pity in Esther's voice. 'To deceive it into thinking it is a mere human being. *That* is cruelty.'

'Perhaps it was done out of misguided love.'

'Even so, this makes no sense,' Esther protested. 'Simon Lydgate lived close by the Hobarron Institute. He was practically sleeping on their doorstep. The Elders would have brought him in, questioned him.'

Grype chipped in. 'Perhaps they didn't see him as a threat.'

Crowden turned a withering look on his librarian.

'You have seen the true nature of this thing. How can you

doubt its power? No, the Elders would not have tolerated its existence. If they had known, Simon would certainly have been locked away.'

'Then why didn't they act?'

'They can't have known about him,' Grype said.

'They must have,' Esther insisted. 'They have Seers of their own. Their magic protects everything within a five mile radius of the tower. Quilp and I had to work powerful charms before he could enter the town without being detected.'

'Someone knew,' Crowden said. 'An Elder, an employee of the Institute, someone was protecting the boy. But why?'

Several minutes passed in silence. The utter and chilling silence of the Veil.

'I have a question,' Esther said at last. 'The green mist has settled over the Hollow—the Second Omen has come. As intriguing as this mystery is, how does it have any relevance to the Demontide?'

'It has no relevance,' Crowden laughed. 'Not yet, at least. But this poor "boy" has been sent to us as a blessing. Surely you see that?'

'I confess, I do not. How can he be used?'

Grype's chest puffed out. 'At Master Crowden's request, I have looked into his future. It is . . . hazy.'

Esther rolled her eyes.

'But—but I have seen—he will play a vital role in the Demontide.'

'As our ally or our enemy?'

'He cannot be our enemy,' Crowden purred.

'Why not?'

'Because of what he is.'

'Not a werewolf,' Esther said. 'Not a vampire. What then?'

'He is Evil, Mother Inglethorpe.' Crowden grabbed a handful of hair and raised Simon's face to the light. 'Evil incarnate.'

The door of the nightmare box swung open. A grey mist poured out of the cabinet and banked up in front of Marcus Crowden. It formed into a kind of oval screen or mirror. Magical energy crackled across the surface.

'Ah, excellent,' the Coven Master crowed. 'My spy from the Hollow is coming through.' He turned to Mother Inglethorpe. 'Perhaps you would like to meet her?'

Chapter 15
Whispers in the Dark

The picture in the smoky mirror began to take shape.

Crowden waved a hand at Grype. 'Take the creature back to its cell.'

'I wonder if I might stay,' the librarian squeaked. 'Perhaps I can be of service.'

'Mother Inglethorpe will render me any service I deem necessary. Now hurry along.'

Grype flushed red. 'But I have earned my place here. My discovery—my . . . '

'Do not be foolish. Go now before my patience runs dry.'

Grype avoided the laughing eyes of Esther Inglethorpe. He took hold of Simon Lydgate under the arms and dragged him roughly towards the curtained doorway.

'Take care with my prize, little librarian,' Crowden snapped. 'Very soon, I shall be sending him out into the world. To use a modern phrase, it is time to shake things up.'

The witch and the boy disappeared and Crowden turned back to the mirror.

'My spy arrives.'

Feature by feature, a face formed out of the shadows. Long, blonde hair—fair complexion—cupid's bow lips—sea-green eyes. The image of the girl haunted the mirror.

'I am here, Master Crowden.'

'And what have you to tell me?'

The spy's gaze flickered between Crowden and Esther Inglethorpe.

'You can speak freely,' Crowden said. 'Come now, your time in my mirror is short. What have you learned of the Elders' plans?'

A pained expression gripped those beautiful features.

'If you wish to avoid the fate the Elders have plotted for you, then tell me what you know.'

'It's difficult. Jake's my friend. I haven't known him long, but I . . . '

'What do you mean, you haven't known him for long?' Esther cut in. 'You go to school with the boy, don't you?'

'Yes . . . but I . . . I care about him. I need to know—will you hurt him?'

Crowden smiled. 'Oh yes. I plan to torture him.'

The figure in the mirror gasped. Tears swam in her eyes.

'I will torture him with every shred of dark magic at my disposal,' Crowden continued. 'And, as Master Harker writhes in agony, I will make his father watch. For only then will Adam Harker reveal the secret of the Hobarron Weapon. There are but a few days remaining before the

Demontide. I *must* know what hidden device the Elders have at their command.'

'If you plan to hurt him, I won't tell you what I know.'

'Oh, I think you will. Remember how you came to me, desperate and afraid? How you pleaded for me to save you from the sacrificial knife? I will honour the promise I made to you, my dear. I will protect you from the evil of the Elders. But only if you tell me everything. You have five seconds in which to speak. Tick-tock, tick-tock . . . '

'All right, I'll tell you!'

The girl crumpled under the weight of her betrayal. She took a moment to compose herself.

'I overheard them speaking on the phone,' she said. 'Dr Holmwood is bringing Adam Harker to the Hollow. They'll come through Wykely Woods at around midnight the day after tomorrow.'

'This is excellent news. And now I have a task for you, my child.' Crowden gestured with his hand and the smoke mirror drifted towards him. The girl shrank back as the Master's eyes bored into her. 'You must arrange for Jake Harker to be present when his father is driven through the woods.'

'How?'

'I leave that to you, but know this: if you fail me, you need no longer fear the Hobarron Elders. I will cut your pretty throat myself.'

A beautiful summer morning had broken across Hobarron Bay. The sun sparkled on the sand, waves wrinkled the sea.

The gulls, flying in circles overhead, had returned to their nests. It was as if the madness of the green mist had never happened.

Walking down to the beach, Jake had noticed that the trees and bushes showed no sign of the vapour's acid touch. Even the burns he had suffered had healed overnight. Only an old bicycle dumped in the lane and a tiny grave in the back garden told him that his recent experience had been real. Last night, the second Omen had come to Hobarron's Hollow.

How long now until the Demontide? How long until the Elders made *him* their sacrifice?

Eddie Rice raced across the beach. He reached Jake and doubled over, hands on his knees, panting.

'Hey, Jake! I've brought Rachel with me. Hope that's OK.'

The girl walked across the shingle. Her expression unnerved Jake. Was she angry with him?

'I tried calling you last night,' he said.

'My battery was dead. Can I have a word? Eddie, stay here a minute.'

Rachel led Jake a little way up the beach. Out of earshot, she turned and said:

'What the hell do you think you're doing?'

''M sorry?'

'Eddie told me you wanted to meet him down here. Why?'

'I wanted him to show me a cavern in the bay. A place called Crowden's Sorrow.'

'Have you heard the story of what happened in that cave?'

Jake nodded. Rachel made a disgusted sound.

'So let me get this straight: you want a twelve-year-old

boy to show you the place where his uncle was murdered? How insensitive can you get?'

'I don't want him to go *into* the cave, Rachel. If he could just point out where it is, that's all I need.'

'It's still a hideous idea. Why do you want to see the place at all?'

Because it was here that the Witchfinder was frozen in time, Jake thought. Because inside that cave might lie the secret to holding back the Demontide.

'If I thought you'd understand, I'd explain it,' he said.

'Try me.'

'I wouldn't know where to begin.'

'Then I'm coming too.'

'What?'

Rachel stalked back across the beach.

'Eddie!' she shouted. 'Jake wants you to show us where this cave is. Crowden's Sorrow. You OK with that?'

'Sure,' Eddie said. 'Why wouldn't I be? Come on.'

Something in Rachel's face told Jake that a smug smile would not be wise. He shrugged instead, and jogged alongside Eddie. The boy headed to the far side of the bay, making for a line of large, jagged rocks.

It was cooler here, in the shadow of the cliffs. Darker, too. Coming out of the brilliant sunshine, Jake had to blink the beach back into focus. The jumbled line of rocks started halfway up the shore, ran alongside the cliffs and plunged into the sea. It was obvious where the boulders had come from. Over hundreds of years, the wind and the rain had quarried the great red stones from the cliff face.

Eddie climbed up onto one of the boulders. He pointed to a spot roughly halfway along the mouth of the bay.

'Crowden's Sorrow,' he announced.

Jutting out from the cliffs, the entrance to Crowden's Sorrow reminded Jake of a wolf's gaping jaws. The impression was strengthened by the fang-like rocks ranged across the cavern roof. Otherwise tranquil, the sea lashed before the cave, leaving foam around its lips. This wolf was hungry.

For a while, no one said a word. They just stared into the darkness, each imagining the terror of being dragged into the cave. Of dying there . . .

'Eddie, I want you to stay here,' Jake said.

'What? No way!'

'Listen to me. We need a lookout, right?'

Eddie didn't look convinced.

'OK, buddy, I'm gonna level with you. There's a good chance we're being watched right now.'

'Who by?'

Jake hesitated. 'Can I trust you?'

'Course.'

'OK. There's stuff I haven't told you, either of you. Before I came to the Hollow I had some . . . *weird* experiences. Things I can't explain. Not yet. But I can tell you this—something evil is coming to this village. Maybe it's already here. The mist last night was an omen of its presence. Anyway, it's possible that there are answers to be found in that cave. This force—this evil—it has people working for it, Eddie. Bad people. I need you to keep watch while me and Rachel check out the cavern. We can't do this without you, mate.'

Eddie's eyes glistened with excitement. 'Cool.'

'Keep your eyes on the clifftops,' Jake instructed.

'What am I looking for?'

'Anything strange.'

Jake and Rachel started across the boulders.

'Good work with the James Bond stuff,' she whispered. 'That ought to keep him occupied.'

'I meant every word.'

The girl paused. 'Jake, what's going on here?'

'I wish I knew.'

It was a tricky climb. The rocks leading to Crowden's Sorrow were jagged and seaweed-slick. The further out they got the more the waves pounded against the cliffs. The spray rained down on Jake and Rachel and they were soon soaked to the skin. On the other side of the bay, the sun blazed. Here, under the shadow of the mountainous cliffs, an autumn-like chill sank into their bones. It took almost a quarter of an hour of clambering to reach the cavern.

This was it—the place he had seen in his dreams.

'You shouldn't have come,' Jake said.

'Don't be so melodramatic. It's just a cave. A big, creepy, scary-ass cave.'

Rachel attempted a carefree laugh. It came out as a nervous titter.

Every instinct in his body screamed at Jake. He felt that same foreboding sensation he had experienced on the night of his mother's death. They ought to turn back. Run. He took a final look back at Eddie—the kid was dutifully scanning the cliffs—and stepped inside Crowden's Sorrow.

It felt like a punch to the gut. Jake reeled backwards. The wet walls, the dripping rock, the moss covered stalactites: everything spun in a sickening haze. He heard Rachel's voice, felt her hands, but reality seemed to fall away from him. The inner fabric of the cliff had been infected by it—evil. Evil pouring from every porous rock and pooling in every limpid pond. Its voice, made up of a thousand tongues, reached into Jake's mind.

We see you, Jacob Harker.

Jake struggled to speak. *What are you?*

Master of all, servant to none. We are the multitude that wait behind the Door. We are the Ageless and the Unending. The voice cackled. *Our time draws near.*

I won't let you into this world, Jake cried.

Foolish boy, how can you stand against us? True, you stopped us once before but this time . . .

I stopped you before? What do you mean?

He does not know. He does not see. Mortal eyes are so bound by Time and Space. We shall say no more. In our silence, his failure is assured . . .

'Jake, answer me. Are you all right?'

Rachel's face—beautiful as the dawn—came out of the darkness. With her help, Jake got to his feet. He tried his best to hide his fear. The demons had reached out and identified *him* as their opponent. Perhaps in some way they had already known that he had set himself the task of standing against the Demontide.

'What happened?' Rachel asked.

'It was nothing. Come on.'

Jake slipped the rucksack from his back and took out two torches. He handed one to Rachel.

'Fainting like that isn't nothing, Jake. What's going on?'

Jake sighed. 'Before the end of today, you'll know everything.'

'You promise?'

He made a cross over his heart. 'Hope to die.'

'Don't say that.' Rachel shivered. 'Not here . . . So, what now?'

Jake swept his torch around the cave. The finger of light stretched into unending darkness.

'We go forward,' he said, and reached for her hand.

The echo of the waves rustled through the cavern. After about twenty metres the rocky ground beneath their feet began to slope gently upwards. With each step, the ceiling dropped and the space between the cavern walls became ever narrower. Eventually their torches played over a craggy wall.

'End of the line,' Rachel said.

Jake held out his hand, palm forward, like a man pushing against an invisible door.

'I can feel a breeze.'

He stepped sideways and pressed his shoulder against the cave wall. A smile spread across his face. He reached for Rachel and drew her close.

'Do you see?'

'It's just a dead end. Jake, I don't underst—' And then her eyes picked the illusion apart. 'Amazing!'

What had looked like the back wall of the cave was, in

fact, a screen of rock. It reached out from the left wall and cut across the path. There was a gap of about a metre through which a cold breeze whistled. The colouration of the rock, even the streaks of iron embedded in it, matched perfectly with the right-hand wall, giving the impression of a solid barrier.

'It's like one of those magic eye pictures,' Rachel said. 'Stare at it long enough and you see through the trick.'

'It's not a trick of Nature,' said Jake, 'it's deliberate.' He shone his torch on the craggy screen. The light followed the iron streaks. 'These veins have been painted in to match up with the natural iron veins on the right-hand wall.'

'Why would anyone do that?'

'To fool people like us. Anyone exploring the cave would think they could go no further.'

Jake started forward. Rachel caught the strap of his rucksack.

'Do you have any idea what we might be walking into?'

'Honestly, I don't. Rachel, if you want to go back . . . '

'Not on your life. I feel like Alice jumping down the rabbit hole.'

'Whatever lies ahead, I can guarantee you one thing,' Jake said. 'It ain't Wonderland.'

Together, they stepped into the heart of Crowden's Sorrow.

The mouth of the cavern had been the size of a cathedral doorway. This inner space carried on that theme. Any cathedral on Earth could fit easily within this vast natural chamber. Walls of red rock soared upwards and came together to form a colossal arched ceiling. All across the ceiling, hundreds of stalactites hung down like an army of watchful gargoyles. Stalagmites rose out of the floor, a mirror image of their roof-dwelling brothers.

Water, dripping from the roof, had somehow managed to mould the stalagmites into twisted, human-shaped forms. Perhaps it was just that instinct that Alice Splane had talked about—the tendency to see faces in clouds or in the flames of a fire—but those giant stone formations looked uncannily *human.* Here was one with a hunched back and long, gangly arms. Over there, a rock figure with the face of an old man. The stalagmite nearest Jake seemed to have a hood covering its head. A kind of three-fingered hand reached out from the folds of its cloak. Dozens of these strange statues covered the cavern floor.

Jake and Rachel turned off their torches. There was no need for them. A bright green moss or lichen grew in patches all around the cavern and gave off an eerie phosphorous light.

'This must reach right under Hobarron's Hollow. The entire cliff is a shell!' Jake's whisper boomed in the empty space. 'Oh my God—Rachel, look at this!'

He took her hand and raced her between the stone figures.

A towering staircase stood at the centre of the cavern. Unlike the stalagmites there was no question of this being a natural feature. Each step, smooth and regular, had been deliberately carved. Jake craned his neck upwards. His eyes strained. It was no good. The staircase soared into the gloom and beyond his line of sight.

'I think it reaches into the ceiling,' Jake said. 'Someone has carved right through the cliff!'

'But why?'

'Only one way to find out. I hope you're good with heights.'

They started the ascent.

'This even out-weirds that green mist yesterday,' Rachel said. 'You won't believe this, Jake, but I saw it eat through the swing in our garden!'

'You're just lucky you don't have any pets.'

'What?'

'Doesn't matter.'

'My dad said it was like acid rain. Said there had been a spill of toxic material just up the coast and the wind had blown it in. I checked on the internet—there was no mention of anything on the news. And I've never heard of acid rain so powerful it could eat through solid wood! Anyway, why didn't it eat right into the houses?'

'I think they were protected,' Jake said.

'How?'

'By magic.'

Rachel stopped and turned. 'Are you making fun of me?'

'Never. But, Rachel, think. An acid mist that comes out of nowhere. A rain of toads . . . '

'It's weird,' she admitted, 'but there must be rational explanations.'

'Sure, climatic pressures can account for the toads. Maybe your dad's toxic spill story can explain the mist. But put them together, and maybe we need to look beyond the rational world for answers.'

By the time they reached the midpoint of the staircase sweat was running down their faces. They were now about fifty metres up. Rachel looked over the edge. The colour drained from her face and she swallowed hard.

It was strange—the higher they climbed the colder the air became. Their breath began to snake before them in grey twists. Legs aching, lungs burning, they reached the cavern ceiling. Those huge stalactites loomed all around them. Up close, Jake saw the similarities between these figures and the ones below. Each was unique and yet they shared the same human-like features: faces and limbs hewn from the rock by the constant drip of water. Another weird aspect of these gargoyles was the fact that their faces seemed to be turned towards the staircase.

Turned towards Jake and Rachel.

The staircase continued through a large hole carved out of the ceiling. The luminous lichen did not spread beyond the cavity. Torches in hand, Jake and Rachel climbed into the darkness.

That was when the whispers began.

Chapter 16
Golems

'*Hear him—his footstep in the dark—his tread upon the stair.*'

'*He returns at the End of All Things. At the Dawn of the Demontide . . .*'

Rachel shuddered. The voices were as sharp as knives. The torch in her hand flickered twice and went out.

'*He is not alone. I sense another. Her fear is like the sweetest symphony . . .*'

'*A girl. But it is not HER.*'

'*No, no, no,*' the voices gabbled together. '*SHE has not returned with him. She is long gone, and cannot re-emerge from the dust of death. The mortals cannot pluck HER from the pages of history.*'

A single voice, rich and slurping rose up. '*But deep down, he* will *remember her. His sweet Eleanor . . .*'

'Eleanor . . .' It was Jake's voice, hollow and sad.

Rachel's torch sparked back into life.

They were standing in a small chamber, roughly five metres in height and width. It was horribly cold, the steps and the walls coated with ice. The staircase continued right up to the roof. Jake was kneeling near the top of the steps, his hand hovering an inch below the grey stone ceiling. Elaborate designs—moons and stars, pentagrams and triangles, figures and faces—were carved all over the stone. At the centre was a symbol in the rough shape of a trident. Reddish-brown stains had been smeared all across this marking.

'What is it?' Rachel asked.

'It's a doorway,' said Jake. '*The* Doorway.'

'To what?'

He shook his head. Rachel joined him beneath the Door.

'Those voices?'

'Them. They are waiting to break through. It won't be long now.' He sounded distant, as if his soul had flown far away from Crowden's Sorrow. 'We can't stop it, Rachel. The Demontide is coming . . .'

'*He admits defeat!*' the voices echoed gleefully.

Jake put his hands over his ears. Tears coursed down his cheeks.

'*What would his beloved think if she saw him now? His*

sweet Eleanor. His long-dead maiden. She would weep for him . . .'

'DO NOT SPEAK OF HER!'

Jake roared the command. His eyes blazed. He pressed his palms against the stone door. All at once, the swirls and triangles, the moons and pentagrams shone with a fiery blue light. Screams of surprise and fear rang out from beyond the Doorway.

'Now cease your wicked prattle,' Jake said. He took his hands from the stone. 'I shall meet you soon enough. Then shall our reckoning commence.'

A single, dark voice broke out. '*We shall look forward to it, old friend. In the meantime, the Third Omen is come.*'

The sound of stone breaking against stone rose up from the cavern. It echoed like thunder in the little chamber.

'What is it?' Rachel cried.

'Gargoyles,' Jake said, his voice normal again. 'They're waking up.'

Hand in hand, they raced down the steps and out of the chamber.

Rachel halted at the stop of the staircase. She had tried not to look down as they climbed. Now, standing at this dizzy height, it was impossible not to stare at the cavern floor hundreds of metres below. She could feel Jake gently pulling at her arm. As the sound of splitting stone rang out on all sides, she tried to move. She could not.

'We have to get out of here.' Jake stood before her, blocking her view. 'Keep your eyes on me. Don't look down. We have to move fast.'

She allowed herself a stray sideways glance. Her gaze fell on one of the stalactites. Growing out of the roof, its weathered skin resembled that of an old woman, her arms thrown over her head. One of the arms flinched—creaked— and reached out for the stairs.

'Let's go,' Rachel nodded.

They plunged headlong down the staircase, taking the steps three at a time. From all around came the sound of stone monsters awakening. The air filled with dust. Within seconds the floor of the cavern had been coated in a grainy mist. The dust roiled and began to climb the stairs. It reached Jake and Rachel and obscured all but the step in front of them.

'I can't see the edge of the staircase,' Rachel said. 'We could fall.'

'Have to—to keep going,' Jake choked.

They tore a path through the dust. Occasionally, as they ran, Jake would look down and his eye would catch movement in the mist. A misshapen head, a giant fist, a twisted red back loomed out of the shadows. Glancing up, he could see the stalactites clamber across the cavern roof and down the walls. Soon they would join their brothers below. The walls quaked as dozens of craggy hands and feet descended.

Jake hit the floor with a jolt. He turned to Rachel. Hair and skin dusted white, the girl looked ghostly.

'The gap in the wall's straight ahead,' Jake shouted. 'Don't stop for anything!'

They ran.

As they dodged across the wet, uneven ground, Jake tried

to keep his thoughts on the path ahead. It was not easy. His mind kept slipping back to that moment at the Door. It had felt as if another soul had taken possession of his body; that another voice had been speaking through him. And yet, in some sense, he had been comfortable with that strange presence. As comfortable as he had been in his dreams of the Witchfinder.

ELEANOR.

The name made his heart ache . . .

The bone-shattering arm of a gargoyle swung wide and crashed into Jake. His hand slipped out of Rachel's and he soared through the mist. Stone faces with hollow eyes passed by in a whirl. He hit the ground and all the air left his body.

'Jake!' Rachel screamed his name over and over.

'Don't stop!' he cried back. 'I'll meet you at the mouth of the cave!'

He got to his feet. Nothing appeared to be broken. Eyes narrowed, he peered into the dust clouds. It was difficult to tell from which direction he had been propelled. The green light shone weakly through the dust and gave him little sense of his whereabouts. The stalagmites had been the only signposts in the cave, and *they* were now on the move. All he could do was run and hope for the best.

Shadows lumbered through the haze. Sometimes they were close enough for Jake to make out their crude features. He saw a gigantic shape stalk past, its three heads turning this way and that. One colossal form pounded the earth with spade-like fists. Another jumped into the air and landed a few metres away from Jake. The ground trembled as each of the giants passed. They were like dinosaurs roaming through the mist of a primeval swamp.

Jake reached the cave wall. The best course of action was to grope his way around until he found the gap. It was a good plan. The only trouble was that the stone block against which he stood was *not* the wall of the cave.

Stunned, Jake could only watch as the 'wall' rose into the air. Easily the size of a double-decker bus, the largest of the stalactites towered above him, its great foot hovering over-head. Any minute now the foot would fall and crush Jake into a fine paste. It was stupid, but he didn't feel he could move. He held his breath and waited for death.

A second before the foot fell, he felt himself being swept into the air. A huge stone hand held him fast. His hair flew back as the creature raced across the cave, anxious to keep its prize for itself. A moment later, Jake was thrown to the ground, the giant's hand slapped across his body and he was trapped. He peered up at his captor.

The stalactite was not as large as some of its brothers, being roughly the height of Stonycroft Cottage. Bent almost double, its face sat in its chest. A pair of broad shoulders ended in somewhat stumpy arms, so that it had to lean to one side to hold Jake down. Its legs too were thick and short. It looked like exactly what it was: a boulder that had sprouted limbs. Hollow eyes and a crack for a mouth made up the face. The gargoyle raised its fist, ready to pound.

This time, Jake's brain did not seize up.

Deep in his mind, he flipped open the pages of his dark catalogue. He chose a particular area of horror fiction. *Think,*

think. Stone monsters . . . Beings created from the earth . . . The homunculus—a creature created by the ancient alchemists. Frankenstein's monster was a kind of homunculus. No, no, no. Medusa, the snake-headed gorgon? Her stare could turn people into stone. NO. Come on, come on. The Golem! Yes, the Jewish monster that was made from clay and animated by rabbis. But what good was that knowledge?

The creature drew back its hand. Its crack mouth widened into a smile. Fresh dust fell from between its massive fingers.

Emet. That was the word used by rabbis to animate the Golem. In the Hebrew language '*Emet*' meant 'Truth'. And to stop the monster all you had to do was lose the initial letter. '*Met*'—the new word—meant 'Dead'.

'*MET!*' Jake screamed. '*MET!*'

The hand swung down.

Of course! This creature hadn't been created by a rabbi. It was a being conjured by English witchcraft, perverting Hebrew mysticism. Could it be so simple?

'DEAD!'

The slab of the monster's fist stopped an inch from Jake's nose.

A final shower of dust rained across his face and made him sneeze. The monster had returned to its inanimate form. That relentless pressure on Jake's chest slackened and now he could wriggle free of the fist. Panting, he staggered to his feet.

Silence in the cavern. The magic word must have worked on all the creatures. Tiny white particles fell through the air.

The dust was settling. Jake strode out, making for the cave wall. He passed several golems, frozen into new positions. Each was too large to have passed beyond the entrance to the chamber, and so Jake guessed that this Omen must be limited to Crowden's Sorrow.

'Rachel!'

No answer. He prayed that these empty-headed monsters had not found her.

This time there was no mistaking the wall. The mist had dropped to a metre or so from the ground, and so Jake was able to see its full height. By a stroke of luck he also appeared to have arrived at the gap. With no sign of Rachel, he squeezed through the aperture.

'What the . . . ?'

This was *not* the entrance to Crowden's Sorrow. He had entered another chamber. Unlike the one at the top of the staircase, this had not been carved out of the rock but was a natural cell. It was larger too, about the size of two basketball courts laid end to end. In the centre stood a rock pool and, in the shadows next to it, a large block of solid ice. Jake's heart thundered. Although the green lichen grew inside the chamber, bathing it in that spooky glow, he took out his torch and shone the light against the block.

The hazy figure of a man loomed through the ice.

Emet—TRUTH—screamed at Jake. Keeping the figure of the man in view, he tried to listen to that truth. His senses flared, his thoughts burned. On unsteady legs, he moved across the chamber. With each step, it felt as if something was trying to leave him—as if his soul were splitting in two . . . No, that wasn't right. Not splitting, but trying to come together. To reform and make itself whole once more. His life up to now was the second half of a story—a tale that stretched back hundreds of years.

He laid his hand against the ice tomb.

'Who are you?'

The world-weary voice of the Witchfinder answered him.

I am my reflection. I am all that you are and more. I am all that you are and less. In despair, we shall find each other.

Jake ran his hand across the ice. It was not cold and yet the block was solid. He put his face right up to it and stared at the man beneath. He had never seen the Witchfinder's face in his dreams, and was frustrated to find that it was now obscured behind layers of thick ice. This was it—the answer his dad had promised—frozen in time. Jake's dreams must have been leading him to this place. Somehow the dead Witchfinder could stop the Demontide, without the need for sacrifices or weapons.

The secret remained out of reach.

Jake's finger slipped down the block and into a pencil-sized hole. The hole seemed to run deep into the ice, as if it had been drilled . . .

'Jake? Is—is that you?'

Jake nearly jumped out of his skin. The voice, weak and shivery, came out of nowhere. He recognized it immediately. The voice of a dead man.

Simon Lydgate emerged from the shadows of the chamber.

Fear, as deep as any ocean, stared out from Simon's face. The clothes that he had been wearing on the night of his 'death' hung from his body. Rings around his eyes made it look as if he hadn't slept for months. He shuffled forward, his gaze fixed upon the pool.

'I came from there,' he said. 'From the Nothingness. They kept me trapped: the librarian and the Mother and the Master. They will follow soon. All are coming to the Hollow, the Elders and the witches. The old enemies are gathering.'

Jake caught him as he fell.

'It's coming,' Simon whispered. 'The Demontide.'

'And he just appeared out of this pool?'

'That's what he said.'

'Jake, this is impossible. Simon Lydgate died on the night your mother was murdered. That's what you told the police.'

'They never found a body. Somehow he survived.'

Jake, Rachel, and Eddie were sitting in the Saxby's conservatory. The building was detached from the main house and hardly ever used. A perfect place in which to hide a boy who had returned from the dead. Simon lay sprawled on a battered old couch, unconscious, breathing steadily.

After leaving the cavern, Jake had found Rachel waiting outside with Eddie. Aside from the odd cut she had escaped unharmed. Eddie had helped carry Simon across the rocks and onto the beach. It had taken over an hour to get him up the hill to the Saxby residence. A few Hollow people had given them curious glances and whispered behind their hands. Word would spread like wildfire but there was nothing they could do about that. At least Dr Saxby was out of town for the afternoon.

Rachel laid a hand against Simon's forehead.

'His temperature's OK. I still think we ought to take him to hospital.'

'It'll lead to too many questions,' Jake said. 'The police will want to know where he's been these last six months.'

'And where has he been?'

Jake shrugged.

'Monsters,' Eddie said simply. 'They're real?'

'Afraid so, Ed.'

'I used to believe in monsters.' The kid twisted his hands in his lap. 'It was fun then, imagining that Dracula or the wolfman could break in through the window at any minute. I used to enjoy scaring myself like that. But in real life monsters aren't fun.'

Rachel wrapped an arm around her cousin.

'OK, Jake,' she said, 'I think it's time we heard your story.'

Chapter 17
Horror Stories

He didn't tell them the whole story. There were parts of it that he couldn't have explained to Rachel—things like her father insisting that a sacrifice was necessary in order to stop the Demontide. For similar reasons, he skimmed over his dad's abduction and imprisonment. He also left out his dreams of the Witchfinder and those peculiar experiences in which he had felt a connection with the long-dead man. What was the point of explaining such things when he still didn't know how the discovery of the Witchfinder's frozen body could help to stop the Demontide?

And so Jake told the story in its basic terms. Witches and demons were real. For centuries, the Elders of Hobarron had waged a war against the Crowden Coven. The aim of the Coven was to bring about the Demontide and the end of Man. Now it was looking as if they would succeed. Heralded by Omens—the toads, the mist, the stone monsters—the Demontide would soon break. In preparing for this day, the Elders had devised a weapon—a mysterious mechanical cube called, simply, the 'Incu'. The Coven feared this weapon and had killed Jake's mother in an attempt to discover its secrets. The irony was that the Elders believed the weapon to be useless.

'The Doorway,' Rachel said. 'That stone slab in the ceiling at the end of the staircase.'

'That's where the Demontide will start,' Jake nodded. 'It was mentioned in that old poem you told me: *Witchfinder, Witchfinder—Evil he saw—and used all his power—to seal up the Door.* I think that it was the Witchfinder who stopped the original Demontide . . . '

'Demons waiting behind the Door.' Rachel shivered and drew Eddie close.

'I think they gather there in force once in every generation,' Jake said. 'All of demonkind waiting for the Door to weaken. Waiting for their chance to break through and flood into our world.'

'And what will happen then?'

'Our time is over. Their time begins.'

'But why would this Coven want that to happen? These witches are human beings, too, aren't they?'

'I think so. But their magic comes from their familiars. Imagine what a witch could do with thousands of demons at his command.'

'And the Elders have stopped this happening,' Rachel said proudly. 'My father, your father, Dr Holmwood . . . '

The truth danced on Jake's tongue. No, he could not tell her.

'So why are they now afraid that they can't stop the Demontide?'

'Maybe it had something to do with Uncle Luke,' Eddie said. 'Maybe the witches killed him and . . . and . . . '

Jake cut in. 'Before my dad left on his business trip—'

'Strange, your dad heading off when the Demontide's just around the corner,' said Rachel.

'Before he left,' Jake persisted, 'he told me that, to understand the truth, I should find Sidney Tinsmouth.'

'That name sounds familiar.'

'He was the man who murdered Olivia Brown.'

'Of course! But why on earth would your dad want you to find *him*?'

'I don't know, but I think it's important that we do. The only clue my dad gave was that Tinsmouth lived in "the lion's head".'

'Wow. Cryptic,' Eddie said.

'Hold on.'

Rachel left the conservatory and crossed to the main house. She returned a few minutes later with her laptop. She tapped in 'Tinsmouth' and 'Lion's Head'.

'Good old Google . . . Ah. No direct matches. Did your dad say anything else?'

Jake thought back. It was difficult to remember that brief conversation with his drugged father. The threat of imminent discovery, nearly being eaten by a pair of ravenous hellhounds, almost drowning—all those things made his memories a bit jumbled. Finally, he admitted defeat.

Rachel tried the phrases in a few more search engines but with no clear result.

'The only "Tinsmouth" I can find is a cabinet maker in Stoke-on-Trent . . . '

Simon stirred. A shudder ran the length of his body.

'Cabinet,' he whispered. '*His cabinet . . .* '

Jake stood over his friend. He helped to lift Simon's head onto a cushion.

'Jake. Thank God. I thought that thing had killed you.'

'I've still got the scars,' Jake said. His eye was drawn to the puckered skin around Simon's throat. 'You've got them too. You saved my life, Simon.'

Simon managed a wry smile. 'There've been times during the last six months when I wished I hadn't. The things I've heard. The things I've seen. I thought I was going crazy. But it's all real—the darkness, the monsters . . . '

'Simon, I need to ask: *how* did you survive? I saw Mr Pinch tearing your throat out. I'm . . . I'm so sorry I ran.'

'If you hadn't, I'd have got up and kicked your arse myself.' The words came in Simon's trademark series of short, dry bursts. 'Truth is, I don't know what happened. One minute that thing was at my throat; the next? I must have passed out. I remember waking up in a car. Could've been minutes or hours later. It was still night, that's all I know— I could see the moon blinking through the trees. I was in the back of the car, curled up in the corner. There was a woman at the wheel, two men in the back with me. One had a short beard and was young-looking, the other was older with white hair. They were talking about Mother Inglethorpe and Tobias Quilp. About a plan that had gone wrong. Your mother had died and the weapon was still a secret. They were laughing about what their master would do to Esther Inglethorpe. "It'll be the box for her," the old man said. The young guy laughed, "That'll bring her down a peg or two." Then the driver spoke. She said their "amusement was misplaced". Mother Inglethorpe's plan was their best chance of finding out about the Elders' machine. "Don't worry," the old man said, "the Elders are powerless. Nothing can stop the Demontide now." Then the young guy noticed I'd woken. He held out his hand and spoke a few words. A yellow light flashed from his fingers and I lost consciousness again.

'The next time I woke up, the car had stopped. Hands bundled me out and into a deserted alleyway. There was something weird about the street . . . '

'Weird how?' Eddie asked, leaning forward.

Simon looked from Eddie to Rachel. 'Sorry, who are you people?'

Jake made the introductions.

'The sign said "Yaga Passage",' Simon continued. 'I could hear lots of cars, buses, people shouting in the streets nearby. We might have been in London, Manchester, somewhere big. Funny thing, though—this place didn't *seem* part of the city. It was dawn. I could see sunlight flooding into the street that joined up with the alley. But there was no sunlight here. I got the feeling Yaga Passage was always dark and cold.

Even the people who'd abducted me seemed afraid. They kept looking up and down the street, glancing at the windows. There were shadows on the blinds . . . '

Simon seemed to crumple in on himself. He shivered and ran a hand over his face. Rachel went to a bureau at the back of the conservatory. She returned with a glass and a half bottle of whisky.

'My dad's hidden stash. He thinks I don't know.'

She poured a glass and handed it to Simon. He drained it in a single gulp. When he returned the glass his gaze lingered on the girl.

'Then what happened?' Jake asked.

'I was taken into this shop. A bookshop. Hundreds and hundreds of old books. There was this little man behind the counter. The young witch called him "librarian", but his real name was Grype. He had this bird on his shoulder, like a vulture, only uglier.'

'His familiar.' Jake nodded.

'There were beetles dropping out of its feathers.' Simon shuddered. 'Grype helped them carry me to a cupboard at the back of the shop. That's where I stayed for the next six months.'

'Didn't you try to escape?' Eddie asked.

'I was kept drugged. Magically, I think.'

'Then how'd you get out?'

'One day the librarian came for me. Said that the Master had "requested my presence". There was something in his eyes that I had never seen before. He looked . . . frightened . . . Anyway, he hit me with another of those drugging spells.

Maybe I was becoming more tolerant to them because this time it didn't knock me out cold. I was groggy, but I could hear a lot of what was going on. Grype dragged me into the shop and through a curtained doorway. That's when we entered the Nothingness . . . Do you think I could have another drink?'

Simon's hand shook as he took the glass.

'Nothing living should ever enter that place,' he continued, wiping his lips. 'It was only fit for the dead. But it is *his* home.'

'Whose?'

'Crowden's, the Coven Master.'

'You saw him?'

'A glimpse. He was dressed in old-fashioned clothes: a dark cloak, a hat with a buckle, big leather boots. There was a cloth tied around his face. Behind him, in the shadows, there was this box. Like a magician's cabinet.'

Jake shot to his feet.

'The portrait.'

'Jake, are you OK?'

'The portrait from Holmwood Manor. Eddie, you remember I asked you about the second man in the picture with Tiberius Holmwood? That man had a buckle on his hat and there was a black box in the background. You see what this means?'

'Not exactly,' Rachel confessed.

'The leader of the Crowden Coven—the man now plotting the Demontide—is the *same* man as the one in the portrait. He was once friends with Tiberius Holmwood, the first of the Hobarron Elders, which makes him roughly four hundred years old!'

'Can't be,' Rachel protested. 'Maybe this guy's a descendant. Like Dr Holmwood is descended from Tiberius.'

'Then why the old-fashioned clothes?'

'And his speech,' Simon clicked his fingers, 'it was dated. From another time.'

'But how has he survived?'

'Because he lives in the Nothingness.' Simon's tones rang hollow. 'The empty, deathless place. His home.'

'Not his home,' Jake said. 'His prison. I think that was Crowden's punishment for trying to bring about the first Demontide in 1645.'

Eddie laughed. 'Some punishment, he got to live for ever!'

'No, it's a living death. An eternity of nothingness,' Jake said slowly. 'Personally, I can't think of anything worse . . . Go on with your story, Simon.'

'There isn't much more to tell. I overheard bits of what they were discussing. Nothing that made much sense. The next thing I know I'm crawling out of that pool.'

'I have a question,' Rachel said. 'Why did they release you?'

'Crowden, he said he wanted to "shake things up". I think he thought that my being here in the Hollow would achieve that.'

'It's a pretty crazy story,' Eddie said. 'There you are, going about your everyday life, and then—abracadabra—witches are holding you hostage in a broom cupboard.'

'That's it!' Jake shouted. 'Abraca-bloody-dabra!'

He snatched up Rachel's laptop and typed in the search phrases 'Tinsmouth', 'Lion's Head', and 'Abracadabra'.

'It was something my dad said. It struck me as weird at the time but it just got mixed in with all the other weird stuff. Result!'

He twisted the screen around so that the others could see:

ABRACADABRA!

The Magic Shop—jokes, novelties, card magic, coin magic, mental magic, tricks and illusions of all kinds. Step in and utter the magic word . . . Find us at Marmsbury Cove, just off the Lion's Head Parade. Proprietor, S. Tynsmawfe.

'We've found him.'

Fifteen minutes of explanations and arguments followed. Jake told Simon the story of Olivia Brown and Sidney Tinsmouth. He went on to explain how his father had told him that, in order to understand what was happening in the Hollow, he should speak to Tinsmouth. Rachel pitched in with her objections.

'I'm sure your dad didn't mean you should look up a convicted killer.'

'We're not even sure he *was* convicted,' Jake said. 'He's not in prison.'

'You saw him, Jake. You saw what he did to that little girl.'

'I know. I can't explain it, but there must be more to the story. We have to go to Marmsbury and find him.'

'I think Jake's right,' Simon said.

'Simon and I will go tomorrow.' Eddie started to object but Jake cut him short. 'I've got a job for you, Ed. I want you to go to the local library, research all you can about the town, the Witchfinder, Tiberius Holmwood, Crowden, anything you can think of.'

Night fell across Hobarron's Hollow. Inside the Saxbys' conservatory, the conversation had gone in circles with little more information or insights coming to light.

At last Jake got up to leave. Rachel stopped him at the door.

'This is crazy. The whole thing. It can't be real, can it?'

'Either it's real or we're all mad.' Jake smiled.

'I should speak to my dad.'

'You can't.'

'But why? Maybe if I told him the things we know, it could help.'

'Trust me, Rachel, telling your father will only make matters worse.'

'You almost sound like you're afraid of him. Is there something you're not telling me?'

'I don't want to hurt you. Just please trust me.'

'Only if you trust *me*.' She looked back at Simon and Eddie. They were sitting on the couch playing cards. 'Why didn't you tell them about what happened at the Door? Those symbols glowed when you touched them. And your voice, it changed. Jake, was that magic?'

'Honestly? I don't know what it was. Maybe Sidney Tinsmouth will be able to tell us something about it.' He glanced over Rachel's shoulder. 'Ed, are you ready?'

'He's ready,' Simon said, throwing in his hand. 'He's beaten me three times. The kid's a card-sharp.'

'My mum taught me how to play,' Eddie grinned. 'She's a demon at poker. Well, not literally.'

The unintended joke acted like a pin popping the tension. All the horror stories they had told each other fell away and the four of them shared their laughter.

'How old are you, Simon?'

'Seventeen.'

'You look older.'

'I feel older.'

After Jake and Eddie had left, Rachel went to the house and prepared a supper of cold chicken and salad. Returning to the conservatory, she pretended not to notice that Simon had drained the last of the whisky. The boy was sitting up on the couch, running fingers through his straggly locks of hair. Rachel handed him a plate of food.

'You're sure it's cool, me staying here?' he asked.

'My dad hardly ever comes down to the conservatory. As long as you don't snore too loudly, he'll never know.' She balanced a plate on her lap and picked at a stray lettuce leaf. 'So, how do you know Jake, exactly?'

'He used to drop by on his way home from school. We'd talk about old horror movies and stuff. He's a good friend.'

'I think you're birds of a feather,' Rachel said. 'You both seem lonely, lost, a little sad.'

'You certainly know how to cheer a guy up,' Simon smiled.

'It's weird, you have the same kind of relationship with

him that he has with Eddie. Older brother maybe. He looks up to you.'

'Trust me, he shouldn't.'

'Simon, just because you live rough doesn't mean . . . '

'It's not that.'

He got up and went to the conservatory door. Despite being starved for the last six months Simon had kept his brawny figure. His broad shoulders and thick arms strained at the shirt Rachel had borrowed from her father's wardrobe. His barrel chest rose and fell in quick bursts.

'I'm evil, Rachel.' Head turned away from her, he barked the words. 'Master Crowden knew it and my mother knew it. She said I was a curse.'

'I don't believe that.'

'You don't know me.'

'My dad has always told me that you can only judge a person by their actions. Talk is cheap, he always says, good intentions are worthless. It's what we *do* that matters. You saved Jake's life. Someone evil wouldn't have done that.'

Simon didn't appear to be listening. His eyes had glazed over and his breathing came ever faster.

'We lived by ourselves in the middle of nowhere,' he began. 'Mum said she couldn't risk me growing up near other children. My evil would infect them. For years it was just me and her. On Sundays, she'd go to church to pray for her soul. There was no point in praying for me, she said—I didn't have a soul to pray for. She'd dose me up with something or other and lock me in the cellar. That was what horrified me more than anything else during the last six months. Being locked up in that cupboard, it was like it was happening all over again. I thought I'd go mad.' Simon took a deep, shuddery breath. 'One day, my mother died . . . '

An unbearable pause followed.

'What happened to her?' Rachel murmured.

'I don't . . . ' Simon smashed his fist against the window. It was a miracle it didn't break. 'I can't remember. Everything after that day is a blur. It wasn't until I came to New Town that my mind settled. But I never got back the memory of that day, not until I was dragged into the Veil. I was slipping in and out of consciousness, but I overheard bits of what they said. Master Crowden, he . . . '

Rachel went to the boy. She took him by the arm and led him back to the couch.

'He said that I would betray you. All of you.'

'That's not true.'

' "He is evil," Crowden said, "evil incarnate." When he said those words, it was like I was being drawn back into the past. I saw flashes of what had happened. The darkness of the cellar. The whine of the front door opening. The sound of my mother's footsteps on the floorboards overhead. Pipes gurgling, water gushing, the click of the stove, a kettle on the boil. I would be let out soon. Fed. The door at the top of the cellar stairs opened and I saw her silhouette framed in the doorway. There was always the same expression of relief on her face when she saw me. "You've been good," she would say. "In that case, you can have some dinner." Only this time her face was different and she didn't speak. *She screamed.* The rest . . . ' He shook his head.

'Your mother was disturbed, Simon,' Rachel said gently. 'And after what's happened to you, it's no wonder your memories have become jumbled. But there's one thing I do know, you are *not* evil.'

'We'll see.' Simon ran fingers through his hair. 'We'll see.'

Jake saw Eddie safely home and then made his way back to Stonycroft Cottage.

He turned into the lane and stopped dead.

'Jacob Harker . . . '

The woman was dressed in a long robe with a hood pulled over her face. There was something familiar about her voice.

'What do you want?' Jake asked.

'I have news about your father.'

She stepped into the moonlight. The figure might have been made entirely of cloth. Even her hands were hidden beneath the robe.

'Adam is coming home,' she said. '*They* are bringing him back to the Hollow.'

'The Elders?'

The woman nodded. 'Tomorrow, at midnight, he will be brought by car through Wykely Woods. If you ever want to see him again be at the Steerpike Bridge. You may bring your friends but do not tell anyone else what you have heard.'

The stranger began to step back under the shadow of the birch tree.

'Wait!' Jake said. 'Who are you?'

'A friend.'

Jake started forward. In the same instant, the figure dissolved into the shadows. One moment she was there, the next she was gone, and Jake was alone in the lane.

His thoughts reeling, he entered the cottage and went straight to the kitchen. He poured himself a glass of water and drank it down. His father was returning to the Hollow. All the Elder families were gathering for the Demontide . . .

'There you are!' Aunt Joanna bustled into the kitchen. 'Where've you been all day?'

'With friends.'

'You look tired out. Do you want something to eat? I'm sorry I was away last night. Alice Splane is an old friend and . . . Well, I hope you managed all right by yourself.'

'Fine, thanks. Actually, I think I'm gonna head up to bed.'

'I'll bring you up a sandwich.'

Joanna went to the bread bin. Jake had reached the stairs when she called out.

'Oh, Jake, have you seen Lollygag?'

'Um. No, sorry.'

'Not to worry. He's probably sulking somewhere because of the diet I've put him on. It's cruel, I know, but that monster has to lose weight!'

He already has, Jake thought grimly—*he's half the cat he used to be . . .*

Chapter 18
Abracadabra

Jake hardly noticed the sights of Marmsbury Cove—
the long pier jutting out into the sea, the golden beach,
and the sunken flower gardens. Images of the day Olivia
Brown had died filled his head. Very soon now he would
be in the presence of the man who had ended her short
life . . .

'Are you sure you're all right?' Simon asked.

Jake took a deep breath of sea air and turned his thoughts
to other matters.

'I'm fine. Look, Simon, before we go any further, there are
some things I need to tell you . . . '

Jake filled in the parts of the story he had kept hidden
from Rachel. He told Simon how the Elders of Hobarron
had once murdered a young boy 'for the greater good'.
Somehow the sacrifice of Luke Seward had sealed the Door
and kept the world safe for a generation. Now, on the cusp of

another Demontide, the Elders were again tempted to sacrifice a child. Jake believed that *he* was that child.

'One man believes that this sacrifice is the *only* solution,' Jake said. 'Dr Saxby.'

'I see . . . Is Rachel close to her father?'

'Simon, she can *never* know.'

Simon looked out across the sun-sparkled sea. 'She's a special girl, Jake. Brave, clever, strong. Maybe you're underestimating her.'

The softness of these words, and the slight criticism behind them, made Jake bristle.

'Yeah, well you don't really know her.'

'No, I don't. I wouldn't underestimate her, though. She'll surprise you.'

It took a while before Jake could bring himself to speak. An irrational jealousy burned in his chest and he tried to put out the fire with a cold dose of reason. There was nothing in Simon's words to suggest he had any romantic feelings for Rachel. He was simply pointing out those strong aspects of her character that anyone might admire. Anyway, Jake had no right to be resentful towards Simon. He had risked his life on Jake's behalf, and now Jake needed his help again.

'There's something else I haven't told Rachel,' he said. 'I don't want her and Eddie putting themselves in danger on my behalf. As I was walking home last night, I was stopped by a woman in the lane . . . ' Jake told the story of his encounter with the cloaked stranger. 'I thought I recognized her voice from somewhere. I think it was the mutant-toad expert I told you about—Alice Splane.'

'But why would an Elder tell you this?' Simon asked. 'And what does she think you can do about it?'

'I don't know, but I need your help. Will come with me tonight to Steerpike Bridge?'

'Of course. Your dad's a great man, Jake. I'll do anything I can to help him.'

Jake's eyebrows drew together. 'You know my father?'

Simon turned back to the sea. 'I'd see him walking home along the canal some evenings. Sometimes he would give me a few quid, you know.'

A few quid? Jake thought that such generosity hardly made his dad 'a great man'. What wasn't Simon telling him . . . ? Another mystery to add to the collection. Figuring that, in the terrible scheme of things, this particular puzzle couldn't amount to much, Jake let it go.

'Come on,' he muttered. 'Sidney Tinsmouth's waiting . . .'

Mid-morning sunshine slanted through the windows of Hobarron's Hollow Library. There were no other visitors and so the command above the door—SILENCE AT ALL TIMES—was easily obeyed. Rachel closed another book of local history. Frustrated, she smacked her head against the reading table and glanced sideways at Eddie.

'Well, I've come up with nothing. What about you?'

'Pretty much the same,' Eddie said. He picked up one of the books he had been reading. 'A few bits and pieces on the Witchfinder, not much we didn't already know. It seems he died here in the Hollow not long after he arrived in 1645.

The following year, the locals built the mausoleum in his honour. There's no mention of the Elders or the Coven in any of this. The only scrap of information I didn't know was that, in those days, this place wasn't called Hobarron's Hollow.'

'Yeah, I'd heard something about that.'

Eddie nodded. 'It was known as St Meredith-by-the-Sea. Named after the church.'

'A holy name. It must have been a big deal to make a change like that in those days. I wonder . . . They honoured the Witchfinder with the mausoleum; maybe they also renamed the village in memory of him.' Rachel slapped her forehead. 'That's it! Eddie, it's so obvious! But I guess no one thinks too much about the meaning behind the names of villages . . . '

The sound of the library doors banging open cut Rachel short. Six shadows stretched across the floor. Dr Saxby entered at the front of the group while Miss Mimms brought up the rear. The old librarian shut the doors behind her and turned the key in the lock.

'Dad? What's going on?' Rachel asked, her gaze slipping between the adults.

Her father's voice came at her as hard as stone.

'Where is Jacob Harker?'

His companions flanked the doctor on both sides: Alice Splane, Eric Drake, Joanna Harker, Miss Mimms, and Mildred Rice. Eddie stared open-mouthed at his mother. The woman shivered but held her ground.

'I haven't seen Jake since yesterday,' Rachel said. 'Why do you want to know?'

'He *must* be found, Rachel. We know you were with him

this morning. Miss Daniels saw you talking in the lane leading up to the railway station. There was another boy with
him, a stranger. You will tell us what you know.'

'Why are you being like this, Dad? You're frightening me.'

'Good. You should be frightened. If we don't find Jacob
then there will be dire consequences . . . '

'You mean the Demontide.'

Now it was Dr Saxby's turn to be surprised.

'You're the Hobarron Elders,' Rachel persisted. 'Some of
them at least. It's your job to prevent the Demontide. We
want the same thing. Jake has been trying to find out how to
stop it. I don't know why he didn't want me to tell you, but
now we can put our heads together. We can . . . '

Saxby's face darkened. 'You will tell us where the Harker
boy has gone. Now.'

Terror caught at Rachel's heart. In her father's words she
caught a glimpse of the truth.

'You want to hurt him.'

The doctor turned to Alice Splane.

'Take her away,' he said. 'Do whatever you have to, but
find out where the boy has gone.'

Jake checked the map he had downloaded from the internet.
He had circled the magic shop in red. Without another
word, the boys set off.

Abracadabra stood in an alleyway just off Lion's Head
Parade. Unlike many of the drab shops, cafés, and amusement arcades that made up the seaside town, the magic shop

was bright and colourful. Several eye-catching displays had been designed to lure in passers-by. One window housed a beautiful miniature theatre. Giant playing cards, wizards' wands, polka dot handkerchiefs, and multi-coloured flags danced across the stage, all worked by invisible strings. In another window a small fountain had been set up. Despite the laws of gravity, the water started in the bowl of the fountain and tumbled upwards towards the spout.

The shop's central window had been reserved for the most baffling illusion. A mannequin dressed in magician's garb waved his wand over a top hat. Jake would have expected a jerky, robotic motion but the hand holding the wand moved smoothly. All at once, golden streamers exploded out of the hat. The magic man swirled his wand overhead and the streamers froze in midair. Like snakes obeying the command of a charmer, they whipped back into the box. For the life of him, Jake couldn't see how the trick was done.

A sign pointed towards the door—

> ## WELCOME TO...
> # ABRACADABRA!
> BEYOND THIS THRESHOLD YOU WILL ENCOUNTER
> ## MYSTERIES AND MARVELS,
> ## MIRACLES AND MAGICK,
> ## CONJURATIONS TO CONFUSE,
> ## ENCHANTMENTS TO ENTHRALL.
> CHILDREN OF ALL AGES, PLEASE STEP THIS WAY...

'Cute,' Simon said. 'Are you ready?'

The fear of his seven-year-old self rose up around Jake Harker. He was about to meet the creature that had haunted his dreams for the past eight years. Yet his fear was not limited to memories. He was also frightened of the things he might learn from the monster. Ever since his mother's death, he had yearned for the truth. Now he wondered if it might be better *not to know* . . .

Jake pushed open the door and entered the magic shop.

A bell jangled. From somewhere inside the shop came the mumble of voices. Jake stood on his tiptoes, trying to see over the confusion of shelves. The entire shop was a clutter of magical merchandise. If he hadn't known that the proprietor was one 'S. Tinsmawfe' he would have enjoyed browsing. There were top hats and wands, capes and crystal balls—even a magic carpet hanging from the ceiling. Moving between the shelves, he saw a hutch filled with rabbits and a cage of snow-white doves.

The voices became less muffled.

'I don't think I have enough pocket money, Mr Tyn. Will you save it for me?'

'Let's make a deal, Molly my dear. If you *promise* to learn the trick and show me next week, I'll let you have it free. How does that sound?'

Jake's heart jumped into his throat. That voice!

He raced towards the rear of the shop. In his haste he knocked against the shelves, sending toys and tricks flying across the floor.

He arrived just in time to see the murderer's long arm reach out for the child . . .

'GET AWAY FROM HER!'

A brown-haired, blue-eyed girl of about ten years old stared at Jake. Terrified of this furious stranger, she stepped back into the protective arms of Sidney Tinsmouth.

At the sight of Jake, the monster closed his eyes. His face crumpled. Tinsmouth quickly mastered himself and turned to the girl, a smile replacing the anguish.

'It's all right, Molly, don't be frightened. This is Jake. He's a friend of mine.'

Molly shook her head. 'He looks scary, Mr Tyn. He won't hurt you, will he?'

'Of course not.' Tinsmouth managed a dry chuckle. 'We just need to have a little chat, that's all. Now you take the cup trick and run along home. No charge.'

Tinsmouth dropped three tin cups and a small rubber ball into Molly's hand. Jake stepped back and allowed her to pass. She paused in front of him.

'You better not hurt Mr Tyn,' she said. 'He's nice and he's my friend.'

'I . . . I won't.'

The little girl looked at him, unconvinced.

'At first I thought you were angry,' she said, 'but you look more sad than angry. Mr Tyn's sad too. Even when he smiles.'

Simon opened the door for the child and, with a final frown, Molly left the shop.

The bell jangled.

'God save and protect her,' Tinsmouth said. His tear-blind eyes returned to Jake. 'I have dreaded this day. I have prayed and prayed that it would never come. But now that you are here, I must keep the promise I made to your father.'

The man nodded sadly.

'I will tell you the truth that has been kept hidden from you . . . '

Chapter 19
Oldcraft

They waited while Sidney Tinsmouth shut up shop. Locking the door and turning out the lights, he led the way into the back room that served as his living area. There was no window here and no electric light. Tinsmouth lit a candle and placed it on the surface of a rickety wooden table. The flame flickered, revealing a room as cramped as a prison cell. A camp bed with a mouldy old pillow and blanket had been set up in one corner. The framed picture hanging on the wall above the bed was the room's only decoration.

'Please sit down.' Tinsmouth indicated the chairs that stood around the table. 'I'm afraid there's very little I can offer you in the way of refreshment . . . '

'This is sick!' Jake exploded.

'What's the matter?' asked Simon.

Jake pointed at the picture. From behind the dusty glass, Olivia Brown smiled back at him.

'That's her. Olivia. The little girl *he* murdered.'

'I'm sorry,' Tinsmouth murmured, 'I didn't think. I should have taken it down.'

'Jake's right,' Simon growled. 'It's disgusting, you keeping her picture.'

'It's not what you think. I keep it as a reminder of the evil that I allowed into my heart. As a kind of punishment . . . '

'You deserve to burn in Hell for what you did.' Jake spat out the words.

'I agree,' Tinsmouth nodded. 'And, if I am right about the purpose of your visit, I will be burning there soon enough.'

'What do you mean?'

'The Demontide. Even if mankind can stand against it, a great many of us will wither in the darkness to come.'

Illuminated by the shifting candlelight, the man held his head in his hands. He couldn't have been much over thirty, but his shock of white hair and the lines around his eyes made him appear a lot older. The first pang of pity caught Jake by surprise. He spoke now in a softer tone.

'Tell us your story.'

'Before I begin, you must know that I don't expect your understanding or your forgiveness, Jake. The crime I committed that day claimed not only Olivia Brown—*you* were my victim too. Your father told me about your nightmares.'

'Tell your story,' Jake repeated.

Tinsmouth let out a long breath and began.

'Adam said that one day you might come looking for me. That if the weapon failed and the Elders decided upon a sacrifice, they might take him before he had time to tell you the truth. If that ever happened, then he would send you to me, and I would have to speak for him.'

'But why would my father send me to you?'

'Because he is my closest friend.'

Jake shot to his feet.

'That's not true! My dad wouldn't have anything to do with you. You're a filthy murderer!'

'Calm down,' Simon said. 'Let's hear what he has to say.'

Jake screwed up his anger and sank back into the chair.

'I understand your feelings,' Tinsmouth continued, 'but I'm telling you the truth. Your father saved me, Jake. He plucked me from the darkest, deepest pit of Hell and showed me the way into the light. He is the best man I have ever known . . .

'Let me start by telling you my history, what there is of it.'

The shopkeeper took the candle from the table and held it up to his neck. An ugly black mark, like a rope burn, scarred the skin all the way around.

'My fullest memories start on the day I was branded as a witch of the Crowden Coven. Everything before that day I remember in snatches. Sometimes I wake up in the dead of night, trying to cling to the ghost of a dream. Memories of my mother and father flash before my eyes. She was a small woman with blonde hair and crooked teeth; he smelt of old tobacco. I've seen an older boy in my dreams, a brother perhaps, I don't know. My past is a forgotten country, a landscape ripped away from me when I was ten years old. They came for me in the night—Mother Inglethorpe and Tobias Quilp.'

An image of Quilp—thin as a corpse, bloodthirsty, leering—flashed into Jake's mind. He saw the witch twirl his fingers and conduct his mother's death-dance.

'You see him, don't you?' Tinsmouth said. 'Him and his demon.'

Needle-sharp teeth. The pain as Mr Pinch bit down into his flesh. Jake grimaced. Tinsmouth reached out to him, a comforting hand. Jake slapped it away.

'Go on.'

'They took me. I must have done something to attract their attention. Some little feat of magic, I suppose. Spontaneous flight, speaking to the dead. Maybe I accidentally exploded the neighbour's budgie.' Tinsmouth smiled grimly. 'Whatever it was, it was enough to mark me out as potentially powerful. I remember . . . shadows at the window—a man and a woman hovering outside—the window opening by itself—hands reaching inside, reaching for me. Then . . . ' His long white fingers clutched at his neck. 'Nothing. A sleeping spell, I think. When I woke up I was in the presence of Marcus Crowden and his cabinet.'

'The nightmare box,' Simon whispered.

Tinsmouth's lips pressed into a hard line. 'You've seen it?'

Simon gave a brief outline of his story. When he had finished, Tinsmouth remained silent for a time.

'Hey, man, you're creeping me out. Why are you staring at me?' Simon asked.

'I'm sure it's nothing. Let us continue. The nightmare box: it is Crowden's demon—the so-called source of his black magic. It is a thing of pure evil and within it lies a dimension of torment and suffering. As I was dragged into the Master's presence, I could feel it whispering to me. It promised endless power, tempting me, drawing out the darkness within.' Tinsmouth's eyes glazed over with the horror of his memories. 'You see, boys, a dark witch is really made up of two parts: his magic and his evil. Witches like those in the Coven believe that all magic comes from demons, and that a young person who can work magic is actually drawing on the power of an invisible demon. To achieve full magical prowess that demon must be summoned and agree to work for the witch. A demon will only do so if the witch is devoted to evil. I loved my mother and my father. My young heart was theirs. I was *not* wicked.'

'What did Marcus Crowden do?' Jake asked.

'He made me evil.' There was no emotion in the man's voice, though tears ran down his face. 'By the time he had finished with me, I had forgotten my parents. Forgotten who I was. And what was left was a monster.'

'How?'

'He put me inside his cabinet.'

'While I was their prisoner, I heard . . . ' Simon trembled. 'One of the witches—Mother Inglethorpe—she had angered Crowden. He put her in the box for ten minutes. The little man who kept me captive laughed about it. Said that she looked barely alive when she came out. Ten minutes . . . '

'I was in the box for a month.'

Jake felt Simon's hand on his shoulder. He looked at the older boy and saw the grief and the tears. To his surprise,

Jake found tears streaking down his own face. Tinsmouth the murderer, white-haired, grey-skinned, looked like a little boy curled up on his stool.

'The things I saw,' he murmured. 'I'll never escape them. They twisted me into something new. When I stepped out of the cabinet, I embraced my place within the Coven. All that I had to do now was to summon my familiar, Mr Smythe, from the flames of the demon world . . . '

'There's something I don't get,' Simon interrupted. 'Why don't witches just keep on summoning demon after demon? Wouldn't that be easier than waiting around for the Demontide?'

Tinsmouth shook his head. 'It doesn't work that way. One demon per witch—that is the rule. It is the safeguard that was put in place aeons ago by . . . Well, that's a story for another day.

'I pledged my allegiance to Crowden and was given my brand. The Coven believe that it is a twisted tribute to all those dark witches that were hanged by the witchfinders. I know the truth: it is a leash by which our real masters bring us to heel . . . In any case, I had begun my magical career.'

A cold breeze whistled through the doorway. The candle fluttered. Tinsmouth jumped up, threw open the door and stared into the empty shop.

'What is it?' Jake asked.

'Ghosts maybe,' Tinsmouth said and returned to his seat. 'Where was I? Oh yes, my rebirth. For the next ten years I educated myself in the ways of dark magic. You see, according to the Coven, a witch's power comes from his demon, but it is just that: raw power. To work a spell you have to refine that power with mental application and ritual. In a simple transformation spell, for example, a demon can provide the energy, but you would need to find materials—fingernails, hair clippings, scraps of skin—from the person you wished to impersonate. Study is required for all magic. I was diligent, clever, naturally talented, and my soul was now as dark as any in the Coven. Dear God, the things I did with my hideous gift . . . But all of it was nothing compared to what was to come. The murder of an innocent child.'

Jake leaned forward. 'Why did you do it?'

'Because I could. Because I wanted to. Because it was fun.'

Silence, for a time.

'All I had heard for years was idle talk about the Hobarron Elders. How they had defeated our Coven for centuries, denying us the Demontide. They believed themselves superior in every way, and yet we knew that their power was fading. I wanted to make my master proud. I wanted to show the Elders that they were not invulnerable. I would strike at the very heart of them.' Tinsmouth took down the portrait of Olivia and held it to his chest. 'You know the result.'

'When you killed her, did you feel anything?'

'Nothing. Not a sliver of pity or remorse. I was glad. Yes, glad.'

'My dad told me you'd been arrested. That you were in an asylum.'

'What else could he tell you? I was taken to the cells underneath the Hobarron Tower, separated from my demon and tortured for information.'

'My dad wouldn't have tortured you.'

'He took no pleasure in it, Jake. Even then, before I knew him, I could see that. But this is a war, and good people do terrible things in wars.'

'Were you hurt?'

'Doesn't matter.'

'Show me.'

'I said it doesn't . . . '

'SHOW ME!'

Tinsmouth sighed. He lifted his shirt up to his chest. The skin was horribly scarred. Jake turned away in disgust.

'Adam Harker is a good man,' Tinsmouth insisted. 'He has helped many "dark creatures" . . . ' Tinsmouth's eyes flickered in Simon's direction. 'Not just misguided witches. The Hobarron Institute wants to lock them up, study them, dissect them, but your father has done what he could to keep the innocent safe.'

'If he didn't like their methods why didn't he just leave?'

'By staying he could use his influence to do some good. And then there was his work on the weapon.'

'The Incu box,' Jake said under his breath. His gaze switched back to Tinsmouth. 'What *is* the weapon?'

'All in good time . . . For you to understand why your father trusted me, we have to go back to my days in the Institute cells. My demon had been taken away for "study" and, without it, I started to dream for the first time in years. Pure dreams, without the ever-present taint of evil thoughts. I started to catch glimpses of the life Crowden had taken from me, bits and pieces of my mother and father. Your dad would watch me as I slept. For years, he had been working on a form of dream hypnosis . . .'

'Hypnosis.' Something stirred at the back of Jake's mind. It was no good, the memory was too hazy . . .

'The technique your father used on me was not wholly successful,' Tinsmouth continued. 'After my experience in the nightmare box, too much of my past self had been lost. Nevertheless, as I started to remember snatches of my child-hood, so your father began to see a change in me. In my sleeping face, he saw glimpses of the boy I had been. Through suggestion and hypnosis he stripped away the evil. After two years of Adam's help and training I had reclaimed my soul. That was when he broke me out of the Hobarron cells.'

The room seemed to be getting colder by the minute. Jake tried rubbing warmth into his arms.

'It was fairly straightforward,' Tinsmouth continued. 'As a senior Elder, Adam had the security codes to the entire building. He staged a power cut and, in the ensuing chaos and darkness, he smuggled me out. He had a car waiting nearby to whisk me to Marmsbury Cove, an out-of-the-way seaside town.'

Simon stood up and started pacing the room.

'Is there something the matter, Master Lydgate?'

Simon stopped abruptly. 'You murdered a little girl. Oh, I know you'd suffered at the hands of Crowden, that he'd twisted you. But it was still *you*. If I'm right, the nightmare box only drew out the evil already inside you. You murdered

Olivia Brown and you served a sentence of two measly years.'

Tinsmouth nodded. 'Jake's father thought the same. But you know, the darkest prison is one's own conscience. When I was brought to Marmsbury, Adam told me that I had not served my time for the murder. That perhaps my punishment would never end. You can see how I live, with the eyes of my victim staring down at me. I opened the shop to spread some happiness—it makes no profit and I give away my tricks. I never go out, never see anyone.' Tinsmouth tapped his forehead. 'In here is where I serve my time.'

'If you live like this I wonder why my dad set you free,' Jake said.

'Because of the Institute policy that, after a witch has been tortured for every scrap of information, he must be killed.' Tinsmouth shrugged. 'It makes sense. Most dark witches do not renounce evil. They have lived with it for so long that there is no way back. Remember, I had been a witch for only ten years.'

'But you've started practising magic again,' Simon said. 'Surely that's dangerous.'

'True magic is *not* evil,' Tinsmouth said. 'Adam Harker taught me that. More than any other Elder before him, Adam has studied the history of magic. He knows more about the subject than anyone, even Dr Holmwood—even Mother Inglethorpe and Tobias Quilp. Perhaps only Marcus Crowden himself could claim greater knowledge, but the Master's love of demons had blinded him to the truth.

Gentlemen, what I am about to tell you constitutes the greatest trick ever played on humankind.'

Tinsmouth leaned forward. The magician opened his palm. A golden flower of breathtaking beauty grew slowly out of his hand.

'*Magic does not come from demons.*'

The flower shivered, dropping its golden blossom across the floor. Then it withered back into Tinsmouth's palm.

'A simple spell but not a demon in sight.'

'Then how did you . . . ?'

'Oldcraft.'

'Oldcraft,' Jake echoed.

Some hidden chamber deep inside Jake's soul shuddered. The door to this forbidden place flashed in his mind's eye and then vanished again into a fathomless darkness.

'You recognize the word,' Tinsmouth said, his eyes alight. 'That's good. It means your father was right about everything! Oldcraft is the practice of pure magic. It is the magic of the world around us: of the earth, the wind, the sea. Centuries ago, before demonkind perverted our knowledge, we knew this truth. But, as we began to practise darker spells, born of greed and lust and violence, so mankind opened the door to demons. They are beings of pure evil, Jake. They made witches believe that magic could only be perfected with their aid. They destroyed much of the history of Oldcraft until only weak pockets of knowledge remained. Today, Wiccans and white witches work without demons, drawing on the magic of the earth, but their power is virtually non-existent. People with natural magical abilities like me can automatically tune into Oldcraft, but there are no good witches left to teach it, and we are soon picked up by dark covens and told the lie that our abilities come from invisible demonic forces.'

'But what do demons want with us?'

'We are their way into this world. Every time a witch summons a demon, the barrier between our world and theirs is weakened. They long to escape their fiery prison, even if it is only for brief periods of time. And they take delight in destroying us. We believe them to be our magical servants and yet *they* are the puppet masters. They whisper evil in our ears and we obey, murdering our souls in the process.'

'Why can't witches be told this?' Jake asked. 'If they knew . . . '

'The demons blind them to the truth. Oldcraft is laughed at as a crazy superstition. No dark witch would dare abandon his demon and risk his magic by believing such nonsense. Even a man as clever as Marcus Crowden cannot see the truth. And who is there now that could convince him otherwise? The last powerful practitioner of Oldcraft died over three hundred years ago. Crowden knew him, and to this day he believes that the Witchfinder unwittingly used invisible demons to power his magic.'

'Who was the Witchfinder?' Jake asked.

'His name was Hobarron.'

Chapter 20
Emet (Truth)

'After his sacrifice, the villagers honoured the Witchfinder by building him a grand mausoleum and naming their community after him,' Tinsmouth said. 'It really was the least he deserved.'

'You know his story?' Jake asked.

'Bits of it. No full record of the Witchfinder survives, just scraps of information. We know for a fact that he was the last true practitioner of Oldcraft. He had a natural instinct for magic, an understanding of its raw power. Some say he did not even need spells and incantations to work his will—conjurations came as easily to him as walking and breathing.'

'And he wasn't taken in by the demon lie?'

'Not him.' Tinsmouth smiled. 'He was blessed with two rare gifts. The first was his magical ability; the second was a sensitivity towards Evil. He could feel its power, see it plainly for what it was, and he was repulsed by it. This instinct was nurtured by his father, who was a preacher man and well-versed in the wiles of demonkind. His abilities led Hobarron into the life of a witchfinder.'

Jake remembered his dream in which he had walked inside the Witchfinder's skin. Tinsmouth was right—the man had had a *feel* for evil.

'But why be a witchfinder?' Simon asked. 'I've read about people like that. They were vicious men, accusing innocent people of witchcraft so that they could claim their reward.'

'On the whole, you're right,' Tinsmouth said. 'People like Matthew Hopkins, the Witchfinder General, were at best depraved lunatics, at worst money-grabbing murderers. Hobarron did not ask to be called "witchfinder", however, and his work brought him into direct conflict with Hopkins and his kind.

'When there was an accusation of witchcraft, Hobarron would go to the town and use his ability to sense demonic evil. He was a hard man and, if he found a witch truly *had* conspired with demons and had worked evil spells, he would gladly stand back and watch her hang. If, however, he believed the woman was innocent or, like him, a practitioner of Oldcraft, he would use all his powers to rescue her from the gallows. In this way, he probably saved hundreds of people. Each time he did so, he risked his own life, for it would have been very easy to accuse Hobarron himself of witchcraft. Despite the dangers posed to him by Hopkins and others, he found his work relatively easy. Stupid witches and their miserable demons were no match for *him*.

Emet (Truth)

'And then he was summoned to a little village on the coast. There he found the greatest evil he had ever known . . . '

'You know about the Demontide. You are aware of the danger facing not just this village but the entire world. It is your duty to tell us the whereabouts of Jacob Harker.'

'Why do you want to hurt him? What good will it do?'

'Those are questions, not answers.'

The cane lashed down and Rachel cried out. Another angry red welt blossomed from the flesh on her arm.

Alice Splane raised the stick again.

'If you talk, I will stop.'

'I won't tell you where he is.'

Thwack!

After being dragged from the library, Rachel and Eddie had been taken to Holmwood Manor. They were now seated in the great hall, their hands tied behind their backs. Those Elders that had abducted them stood on the staircase while Alice Splane did her best to get the truth out of Rachel. Their faces remained as hard as the stones from which the old building had been constructed. Only Mrs Rice and Dr Saxby flinched at the sound of the cane.

Now, as Alice turned to her son, Mildred Rice cried out. She bolted forward but the others managed to hold her back.

'Come now, Edward,' Alice said, 'you are a good boy, I know that. I'm sure you want to help us find Jake.'

'M-maybe,' Eddie stammered. 'But is Rachel right? Do you want to hurt him?'

'Just tell her, Eddie!' Mrs Rice shouted.

'You should do as your mother says, she only wants the best for you.'

'Don't listen, Ed,' Rachel murmured.

'But why do you want to hurt him?'

'You're just a child, Edward,' Alice Splane purred, 'you wouldn't understand.'

Eddie swallowed hard. 'You people are no better than the witches and the demons,' he said. 'You think you're good but you're bad.'

Rachel stared at her father. 'He's right, isn't he, Dad? I wondered why Jake wouldn't let me talk to you about all this. He was trying to protect me from the truth. That it's you, the Hobarron Elders, who are the *real* monsters.'

Alice looked at Malcolm Saxby. The doctor bowed his head in a silent assent. The cane whipped through the air.

'As I say, there is no full account of Hobarron's time as a witchfinder,' Tinsmouth said. 'A few old books hint that he kept a diary, but if so it has never been found. And so we can only be sure of a few details.'

Jake shivered again. The little room seemed colder than ever. And yet perhaps it was the sense of foreboding that made him tremble. Ever since the Witchfinder's name had been revealed, he had felt as if he knew the story that was to come. Knew it even better than the storyteller perhaps . . .

Emet (Truth)

'It was the summer of 1645 and the height of the English Civil War, the bloodiest and most brutal conflict in our history. Neighbour was fighting neighbour, brother killing brother. Hunger and fear stalked the land. When people are afraid they often cast around for someone to blame. Usually their victims are those that live on the outskirts of society: the hermit, the madwoman, and the witch. There is no record of what brought Hobarron to the village . . . '

'He'd heard there was a witch-hunt going on,' Jake said. 'He came to stop it.'

Tinsmouth gave Jake a curious look. 'How do you know that?'

'I dreamed it.'

'Fascinating . . . Well, whatever the reason, as soon as he stepped into the village he knew that something was wrong. The evil there was stronger than any he had felt before. By some means he traced it, not to the common people, who were so often targeted as witches, but to a group of wealthy landowners. There were thirteen of them in all. Their spiritual leader was a man called Marcus Crowden, the youngest son of a rich family. He had appeared in the village the previous winter, drawn there by dark forces. In social terms, the head of the coven was Lord Tiberius Holmwood.'

'We'd guessed that Crowden and Holmwood had been friends,' Jake said, 'but I didn't realize Tiberius was a coven member. I thought he had founded the Elders.'

'So he did. You see, the members of the original Crowden Coven were just a bunch of idle young lords and ladies dabbling with magic. They didn't know what they were getting themselves into. It was only when Hobarron came to the village and showed them Crowden's true purpose that they began to understand.'

'And what was his purpose?'

'Years before, Crowden had summoned a powerful demon to do his bidding. It took the form of his nightmare box. The demon whispered to him that, if he came to this village, he could use the combined magic of a coven to open a doorway into the demon world. When the Demontide broke across the earth, all of demonkind would serve him. And so he had recruited Tiberius Holmwood and his friends to help him. When Hobarron told the coven the truth, Tiberius cast Crowden out. He tried to help the Witchfinder, but there was nothing Tiberius could do. Hobarron had to face Crowden alone.

'The rest of the story we can only guess at. It is believed that Hobarron went down to the cavern and that a contest of some kind took place. Crowden lost and was imprisoned for ever in the Veil—that realm of nothingness that exists between the worlds of the living and the dead. Unfortunately, the Coven Master must have already summoned the Doorway into existence, and now the demons were ready to break through. Using all his magical ability, Hobarron managed to seal the Door, but at a cost. He had used a powerful freezing spell and the effects of it began to overwhelm him.'

'I saw him,' Jake said. 'A figure frozen in ice.'

Tinsmouth nodded. 'He had given his life to save the world, but he had not been wholly successful.'

Emet (Truth)

'Once in every generation the Demontide returns.'

'That's right. Because he had already used so much of his magic in the battle with Crowden, the Witchfinder had only been able to *seal* the Door, not destroy it. Every twenty-five years it had to be resealed using the blood of the Witchfinder.'

'But Hobarron was dead.'

'He had an heir. A little girl called Katherine Hobarron. She later married one of the original Crowden Coven, a man called Gerald Seward. And so the blood of Hobarron continued through the generations. According to a set of instructions handed down from Katherine's mother, each time the Demontide threatened, the youngest member of the family would be taken to the Door. Their blood would be spilled across it, sealing off demonkind for another twenty-five years. Due to the dark nature of the Door the blood had to come from an innocent—a child . . . '

'All those children were murdered?'

'Oh no. The bloodletting was a symbolic act, but powerful in magical terms. At first, only a little blood was needed. As the centuries passed, however, and the Sewards married into other families, so the true blood of Hobarron weakened. More and more of it was necessary in order to seal the Door. Then, one generation ago, the Elders found that they could no longer keep the Door closed. Not without a terrible sacrifice.'

'They needed *all* Luke Seward's blood,' Jake murmured. He remembered the brown smears he had seen on the stone door. 'But Luke had a sister. Why not use some of her blood and some of his?'

'The blood cannot be mixed. It must be pure. This sacrifice shook the Elders to their core. I don't think they ever really recovered,' Tinsmouth said. 'For some, like your father, the Elders of Hobarron had become the very thing they despised: destroyers of innocent life. Oh, they comforted themselves, saying that they had no choice, that it was either sacrifice the boy or face the end of mankind . . . Your father once told me that, if humankind is faced with a choice like that, and it chooses to murder a child, then it has given up its right to survive.'

'Wait a minute,' Simon said, 'surely if someone just went to Crowden and explained it to him. That if he opens the Door the demons won't serve him, that they're using him . . .'

Tinsmouth shook his head sadly. 'Don't you understand? Marcus Crowden would not listen. The man lost his mind many years ago. He has lived for centuries in the nothingness of the Veil—hundreds of years with only his demon to whisper to him. He has no idea about Oldcraft and the true nature of magic. No idea about the plans of his "servants" and of what waits behind the Door.'

'Surely he knows what waits. Demons . . .'

'More than mere demons,' Tinsmouth said. 'An evil so great even the Coven Master would shrink from it. There is a prophecy that, if the Door is opened, *He* will walk the earth once more. The oldest evil—the Demon Father himself.'

'Who is he?'

'Don't ask. I won't think of it,' Tinsmouth snapped. 'It won't happen. Your father has seen to that.'

'You mean his work on the weapon?'

'Adam and Claire Harker's miracle. It was an ingenious plan, to create a weapon of science and magic. The greatest defence against demonkind for over three hundred years.'

Jake's mouth ran dry. In his mind's eye, he focused on the image he had seen in the blueprint: the machine with dozens of wires running out from it. The box with a mysterious word stamped onto its side:

INCU

In a trembling voice, he asked:

'What is the Hobarron Weapon?'

Tinsmouth shook his head in disbelief.

'But, Jake, surely you have guessed?'

The magician stared at the boy.

'*You are the weapon.*'

Chapter 21
A Flight of Witches

The truth slammed into Jake with the force of a hurricane.

He was the Hobarron Weapon.

Every instinct screamed that this was so, and yet how could it be? The weapon was a machine. It had been constructed inside a laboratory by scientists overseen by his mother and father. It had been designed to stand against the Demontide, perhaps to end the threat of demonkind for ever. How could any of this apply to *him*?

'I don't underst—'

The door creaked open and an icy chill crept into the room. The same sensation that Jake had felt as he stood before the canal bridge on the night of his mother's death began to crackle inside him once more.

Tinsmouth shot to his feet.

'Stay here.'

Jake reached out and grabbed the man's arm.

'Don't go out there. She's waiting.'

'You sense her.' A sad smile spread across the magician's face. 'That's good.'

The bell jangled and the front door flew open. A bitter wind moaned through the shop. The magic carpet hanging from the ceiling fluttered, as if it was about to come to life and soar away.

'You can't face her alone,' Jake said.

'I must.' Tinsmouth stared into the darkness of the shop. 'It's time I made amends.'

Before Jake could protest any further, Tinsmouth waved a hand before his eyes. Lips mouthed a silent incantation and the muscles in Jake's arms and legs gave way. He was about to topple to the ground when Tinsmouth caught him. The man whispered in his ear.

'I'm sorry for the nightmares.'

Jake's eyes drooped and he felt himself drift into a troubled sleep . . .

Tinsmouth handed the boy to Simon.

'Hurry, there isn't much time.'

The shopkeeper pulled aside a curtain that covered part of the back wall, revealing a doorway.

'Whatever you hear, whatever you see, don't try to help. Go quickly.'

Simon bundled Jake through the door and into a back alley. The passage was narrow and strewn with cardboard boxes and bags of rubbish. Overhead, the sky had darkened and twilight shadows stole along the tiny backstreet. Surely it couldn't be night already! Simon looked up and saw that, to the west and the east, the sun continued to shine down. It was only here, in this little patch of Marmsbury Cove, that an unnatural darkness had descended. It was as if a storm had gathered over Lion's Head Parade, and yet there were no clouds in the sky. The shouts and cries from the crowds on the seafront had also vanished. Everything was silent, still, waiting . . .

Simon carried Jake to the end of the alley. He was about to move on into the street when he saw the witch. Outwardly there was nothing unusual about her—she was just a frumpy, grey-haired old lady leaning on a stick—but it was her voice that made Simon tremble. He had heard it before.

'Come out, come out, wherever you are.'

At first Simon thought she was calling to him. Then he saw the door of the magic shop open and Mr Tinsmouth step out.

The old lady's face darkened and she pointed a gnarled finger at the magician. Every shred of malice that she could muster went into the shriek—

'TRAITOR!'

Tinsmouth closed the door behind him. He stepped into the road and faced the demented old woman.

'You are right, Mother,' he said. 'I have been a traitor. I have betrayed my parents, my conscience, and my humanity. And now I am ready to answer for my treachery.'

'You speak very prettily for a dead man,' the witch sneered.

'How did you find me?'

'I followed Jacob Harker here. Imagine my surprise when

I saw the name over the shop door: S. Tynsmawfe. We were so proud of you, Sidney. The story of your victory against the Hobarron Elders has become legendary within the Coven and in the demon world beyond. You were the most promising dark witch I had ever known. Your ability was beyond Ambrose Montague's and Tobias Quilp's. One day you might even have surpassed my own talents . . . '

'Undoubtedly.'

There was no hint of arrogance in Tinsmouth's voice. He stated it as a simple fact.

'So, tell me,' Mother Inglethorpe said, 'what happened to you? Why did you become the Elders' pet?'

'A dear friend held up a mirror and showed me what I had become. What the Coven had made me. It was as simple as that.'

'Ungrateful child, we gave you your demon, your powers.'

'What power I had was not yours to give,' Tinsmouth countered. 'Demons do not hold the key to magic. We find that key inside ourselves.'

'Ah, I see it now,' Mother Inglethorpe smiled, 'the Elders tortured you for so long you lost your wits. Magic without demons! Impossible. Even those illusions we might conjure as children come to us through the invisible world of demonkind.'

Tinsmouth shook his head. 'They have deceived you, as they have deceived many who feel the trace of magic in their souls.'

'Enough. I will not bandy words with a halfwit. You will tell me now what you and the boy have discussed.'

Silent seconds slipped by. The witches faced one another like a pair of duellers, each holding their ground.

'Always a pity,' Esther snapped, 'to have to bring pain to an old friend.'

Her mouth moved but no words came out. Something throbbed beneath her clothes, flinched and moved up to her throat. Suddenly, the thing burst free, as if it had leapt clean out of her chest. It landed on the road, a creature about the size of a small dog, and fixed its eyes upon Sidney Tinsmouth.

'Say hello to Miss Creekley. You remember her, don't you, Sidney?'

'I do not converse with demons or listen to their lies.'

Simon gaped at the sight. During his captivity, he had caught glimpses of the bird-demon that accompanied the librarian wherever he went. That vulture had been hideous enough, but this creature struck true terror into his heart. He could feel the little hairs on his arms and neck shiver to attention.

The demon's body had taken the form of a large, powerful spider. Eight legs, barbed with vicious spikes, clicked across the road. Stripes of black and marmalade orange ran across the creature's body and down to its thorax. This egg-shaped segment pulsed, as if it housed a monstrous heart.

Simon's gaze crept along a spindly neck and up to the monster's head. His mouth fell open. The demon possessed the face of a beautiful young woman! She had a flawless, ivory complexion with just a hint of blood beneath the cheeks. Full lips, a cute little nose and a pair of bright green eyes completed the picture. Only when Miss Creekley began to speak was the illusion lost. Her lips drew back and revealed a set of hairy mandibles. Simon shuddered. He imagined kissing her, his lips brushing against those lethal spider-fangs.

'Ensnare him,' Mother Inglethorpe commanded.

Miss Creekley reared up onto her back legs. The pulsating thorax segment of her body jutted forward. She pressed her spinnerets against the ground and thick strands of webbing lashed out towards Sidney Tinsmouth. Within seconds, he had been spun into a sturdy cocoon with only his face still visible. Miss Creekley jerked the webbing and the magician toppled backwards. She dragged him across the ground and laid him at her mistress's feet.

'Now,' Mother Inglethorpe said, 'you will tell me all you know of the Elders' weapon. If you do, I will make your death an easy one.'

The demon stood over Tinsmouth, drool dripping from its fangs.

'Sssthh, let me taste him, miiissstress,' the thing purred.

'Do you remember how Miss Creekley's poison burns?' Mother Inglethorpe asked. 'How it will eat through your organs like acid? How it will fry your eyes out of your head? Speak, or you will know the agony of her bite.'

'Your threats are toothless,' Tinsmouth said, 'and so is your monster.'

His eyes blazed and Miss Creekley let loose a deafening scream. Those hideous fangs fell from her mouth, as if they had been wrenched out by an invisible dentist.

Dawn of the Demontide

'How is this possible?' Esther cried. 'Where is your demon? The Elders must have returned him to you. Where is Mr Smythe . . . ?'

Mother Inglethorpe stopped dead. She could do nothing but watch as the web cocoon started to wither and fall away. Tinsmouth rose and brushed the last of the decayed rope from his body.

'Smythe was returned to the hell fires years ago,' he said. 'My magic is untainted by demonkind. The power I now wield is the natural magic of the earth. It is Oldcraft.'

'Fairy stories! Lunacy!' Inglethorpe shrieked.

'Truth.' Tinsmouth reached out to his enemy. 'I can help you, Esther.'

The old woman looked from her familiar to her old pupil.

'Magic without demons? Is it possible?' She stifled a sob. 'I have committed so many foul acts, destroyed so many lives. Can there really be forgiveness for all my sins?'

Terror washed across Miss Creekley's pretty face.

'Miiissstress, what are you ssssaying? You know only I can grant your powersss.'

'Don't listen to her,' Tinsmouth said. 'Honestly, Esther, I don't know if our sins can be forgiven, but let us try and find out together. Let me help you, as I was helped.'

Mother Inglethorpe stepped towards Tinsmouth. She held out her hands to him.

'And my magic?'

'You will find it anew,' he said. 'A better, purer magic.'

'Miiissstresss!'

'You promise?'

Tinsmouth took her hand. 'I promise.'

'You're a fool!'

The witch wiped the phoney tears from her face. It seemed to Simon as he watched that Tinsmouth made no move to defend himself. He simply stood back and closed his eyes. Energy crackled between Mother Inglethorpe's fingers and she took her aim. The blast hit Tinsmouth and a large smoking hole appeared in his chest. He fell as if all the bones and muscles had been taken out of his body.

Simon laid Jake down on the cobbles. The witch had her back turned and did not see the boy emerge from the alley. Fists clenched, he pounded across the pavement. Something deep inside started to scream at him, howling and protesting against what he planned to do. It did not want him to help Tinsmouth. Instead, he felt that what it most desired was for him to join Mother Inglethorpe in her destruction of the man. Simon stopped. What was happening to him?

Tinsmouth caught sight of Simon. His fingers twitched and a small blue light danced into the air. It flew towards the boy and disappeared into his mouth. Like a string puppet, Simon was plucked a few centimetres from the ground. The toes of his trainers scraped the road and he was dragged back into the alley. He tried to call out but his voice had been hushed.

Misunderstanding the nature of the spell, Mother Inglethorpe laughed.

'Was *that* your great Oldcraft magic? Pathetic! Your spells are illusions and your hand-wringing grows tiresome. I do not believe that the Elders would ever have told an insect like you the secret of their weapon . . . Did you say something? Speak up!'

Tinsmouth struggled to breathe. His skin had turned a deathly white. It took all his energy to speak.

'I forgive you.'

A look of disgust bunched the old witch's features. She summoned Miss Creekley to her and hobbled out of the alley.

The moment she left, Jake woke from his slumbers and Simon found that he could move again. By the time they reached Sidney Tinsmouth the darkness had retreated and the summer sun was shining down once more.

Sidney looked up into the light, his expression calm, peaceful.

'Jake, get on your phone,' Simon instructed. 'Call an ambulance.'

Jake walked away in search of a signal. Simon squatted beside Tinsmouth. The wound at his chest was deep, ragged. The man shuddered and coughed up a mouthful of blood.

'Hold on. The ambulance will be here soon.'

'This is a magical wound,' Tinsmouth gasped, 'their medicine cannot help me.'

Simon took his hand. 'Why didn't you defend yourself?'

'No time. Not after I'd cast the spell on you.'

'There was no need for that. I can take care of myself.'

'It's true, you are very powerful.' A terrible shudder ran through Tinsmouth's body. 'Very powerful. But you must control your nature. It will be hard, I know that, but you must try. Don't—don't betray him . . . ' Tinsmouth turned and looked at Jake. 'Be true to the boy and to yourself. I'll be watching . . .'

His eyes fixed on an invisible figure standing in the doorway of the magic shop. Tears rolled down his face as he recognized the ghost. He held out his hands, as if waiting for someone to pick him up. To raise him to the light.

'She has come for me,' he said. 'Am I forgiven?'

Jake ran back, the mobile phone clenched in his fist.

'Ambulance is on its way.'

Simon closed the magician's eyes.

'He's gone.'

The train rattled through the night, its destination the tiny village of Hobarron's Hollow.

'You shouldn't go back,' Simon said.

Jake stared out of the window. Trying to ignore his pale reflection, he watched the black hedgerows flash by.

'I have to.'

'Why?'

'For the same reason you saved me from Tobias Quilp and Mr Pinch,' Jake said. 'Because it's the right thing to do.'

'Don't be so simplistic,' Simon argued, 'we're talking about life and death here.'

'Tomorrow we may all be dead.'

'We don't know that. All I've heard so far is vague prophecies and rumours. Maybe the Door will hold, maybe the demons won't get through. And even if they do, who's to say they'll be strong enough to take over the world? There's only one certainty I've heard—if you go back, the Elders *will* sacrifice you.'

'Sacrifices have already been made. My mum, my dad, Sidney Tinsmouth, you . . . '

'And they will all have been for nothing, if you go back.'

'Simon, I have to,' Jake repeated.

'Why? Because that poor man said you were the weapon? Jake, he was crazy with guilt and grief. He didn't know what he was saying. Anyway, that thing you described to me—that box of wires—"the Incu"—*that* is the weapon. Must be.'

'I can't explain it,' said Jake, 'but what he said *feels* right. I *am* the weapon. Maybe I'm descended in some way from the Witchfinder. Maybe that's why I've dreamed about him.'

'OK, let's say you are the weapon. From what you've told me, the Elders *and* your dad have said that "you" *don't work*. You're offline, buddy. Fritzed. Defunct. So what good are you anyway?'

The wheels clattered on the track. Dark shapes flew past the window.

'Maybe you're right,' Jake said at last. 'Maybe Tinsmouth was crazy; maybe *I'm* crazy, wanting to return to the Hollow. But the Demontide is going to happen and I have to try and stop it. If I don't, if I run away, I'll have betrayed my mother and father.'

'Your dad told you never to go to the Hollow.'

'I will have betrayed what was important to them. They stood against the darkness, Simon. I have to stand against it too.'

Simon crossed his arms and slumped back into his seat.

'No point arguing with an idiot,' he mumbled. Then a grin spread across his face. 'Oh well, as long as there's a chance of death by witchcraft, I guess you better count me in!'

'Thanks,' Jake said in a quiet voice. He reached over and gripped his friend's shoulder. 'It means a lot, having you with me.'

'Nowhere I'd rather be . . . '

A shape brushed past the window.

'What the hell?'

Thwish, thwish, thwish.

Human forms swept by, hurtling faster than the train, rocketing through the night. Their capes spread out behind them like dark wings. Jake snapped his fingers.

'Quickly, the map.'

Simon took the Ordnance Survey map they had brought with them out of his bag. He spread it across one of the empty seats. Jake leaned over and scanned the area. He jabbed his finger at a thin belt of green heading west from the coastal village of Hobarron's Hollow. It was marked 'Wykely Woods'.

'We were too busy gabbing to notice—we're here.'

Simon's hand shot up to the emergency stop cord. The brakes squealed, the wheels screeched, and the boys were jolted back into their seats. The lights flickered. In the snatches of darkness, they glimpsed another shadow shoot past the train. The ticket collector's angry tones echoed down the carriage.

'There's a fifty pound fine for misuse of the cord, you know? Who pulled it?'

His gallery of suspects was limited: Jake and Simon were the only passengers. Neither responded to his interrogation. Simon stuffed the map into his bag and opened the carriage door. The boys jumped down onto the track, vaulted a fence and started running across the open field beyond. The ticket collector stood in the doorway, his face an ugly shade of purple.

'Hooligans!' he shouted. 'I'll be contacting the police as soon as we get to Hobarron's . . . What the——?!'

All the anger and outrage drained from the man. The sight that greeted his eyes sent him reeling back into the carriage. He dropped into a seat and, like a wide-eyed schoolboy, pressed his face against the window. It was a hallucination. Had to be. That tuna sandwich he had bought from the canteen at teatime *had* tasted a bit iffy. He slapped his face, rubbed his eyes, but the illusion persisted.

Two boys running across a moon-drenched field, and above them . . .

Dark forms flying through the night sky. Like witches from a fairy story.

Chapter 22
Slaughter at Steerpike Bridge

Like a colony of bats, the witches passed across the face of the moon. They flew in tight formation, a dozen perhaps, all making for the bank of trees that marked the edge of Wykely Woods. With minds fixed upon their destination they did not notice the figures that tracked their flight.

Jake's eyes never left the Coven—it seemed that *these* witches did *not* ride broomsticks; their transports were far more grisly and unusual. Three metres or so in length, the thick-bodied snakes curled and twisted beneath their riders. One of the witches swooped down to the tree line, and Jake saw that the bit of a harness had been fitted into the snake's mouth. The sight of the creature stirred the pages of his dark catalogue. He had read somewhere that marshland witches used to shape snakes out of peat and ride them across the water. These monsters must be a variation on that old legend.

One by one, the snakes and their riders disappeared between the trees. Jake and Simon reached the forest minutes later. Simon took out the map.

'Steerpike Bridge is about a mile east of here.'

They set off again.

Tree boughs came together overhead and formed a green canopy that shut out the moon. The beam of the boys' torches provided the only light. Their feet thumped across the sun-hardened ground and Jake's mind raced ahead of him.

What would he do when he reached Steerpike Bridge? His rescue idea had been to stop the convoy by creating some kind of diversion. While Simon distracted the Elders, Jake would try to free his father. It had been a vague plan at best, and now there was the added complication of witches and flying snake monsters! What was the Coven doing here?

'There's the road!' Simon whispered. 'The bridge can't be far.'

The boys slowed to a trot. They kept to the shelter of the forest and followed the road for another five hundred metres. Gradually it began to widen and cut further into the forest. A watery chuckle told them that they were approaching the river that ran under Steerpike Bridge. Simon raised his arm and barred Jake's way.

'Kill the torches. There're people up ahead.'

He was right. Huddled together on the old bow-backed bridge, ten or more cloaked figures waited. Simon jerked his head sideways and they moved on, careful to avoid the telltale crunch of twigs underfoot. They stopped a good distance away from the group.

'Elders,' Jake whispered. 'But where's the Coven?'

'They won't be far.' Simon checked his watch. 'Ten to midnight. Are we sticking to that crazy-ass plan of yours?'

'Unless you can think of something better?'

The minutes passed with agonizing slowness. Every rustle from the forest, every call of a night bird tore at Jake's nerves. The Elders on the bridge, although more composed, often snapped their heads in the direction of the forest sounds. Bit by bit, Jake's eyes became accustomed to the darkness. He could make out the black and silver thread of the river running nearby—watched it slip into the stone mouth of the tunnel . . .

His mind shifted to the bridge at the Closedown Canal. The tunnel beneath which true evil had lurked. Jake's fingers tingled.

Simon grasped his shoulder. 'They're coming.'

The sound of the convoy rumbled towards them. The Elders stood up a little straighter and formed two lines on either side of the bridge. Headlights blinked between the trees.

Jake turned to Simon, his face horribly pale.

'It's a trap.'

'What? Jake, what're you doing . . . ?!'

Jake broke cover just as the first armour-plated Mercedes arrived on the scene. Not a hint of panic showed on the driver's face as he swung the car to the right, avoiding Jake by inches. A chorus of screeching brakes sang out from the other vehicles. The passenger door of the first car opened and the grim figure of Dr Holmwood emerged.

'Hello, my boy. I wondered if we'd see you tonight . . . '

'Get them off the bridge!' Jake shouted.

He spun round and waved at the Elders, still motionless on Steerpike Bridge.

'Get away from there!' He turned back to Holmwood. 'The Coven, I can sense them. They're under the brid—'

The explosion swallowed Jake's warning.

A pillar of blinding white light tore out from beneath the bridge. The blast knocked Jake to his knees and bent him backwards, like a stalk of corn flattened by the wind. His skin crackled under the liquid fire of the explosion. The white light fell back and a hellish scene of burning trees and broken bodies came into view. The driver of the car that had swerved to avoid Jake sat upon the ground and cradled the arm that had been blasted from his shoulder. A man ran into the forest, screaming, every inch of his body ablaze. Large red pools glinted in the firelight and gore and body parts littered the forest road. Without counting each limb it was difficult to tell how many of the Elders had died. Certainly everyone on the bridge must have perished.

Jake tried to get to his feet but the pain was too great. He looked down at his hands. No longer pale, his skin was now a molten mass of black and red. Fear and despair shivered inside him.

This was the end.

'Over here! I've found him!'

A man's voice, cool and cultured. Jake managed to look up

into a grandfatherly face, the cheeks cracked with burst blood vessels. The man wore a patch over one eye. In his right hand he held a length of hardened peat that had been sculpted into the shape of a serpent.

Mother Inglethorpe loomed into view.

'Do your best to heal him, Montague,' she instructed. 'There'll be little point in the Master torturing the child if he's already half-dead. I'll get someone to retrieve Adam Harker and follow you back to Yaga Passage.'

The man called Montague crouched beside Jake. He held his hand over the boy's scorched features and a faint red glow flowed from his palm. Deliciously cool, the magic spread like a mask across Jake's face and began to ease the pain and heal the burns. As his vision cleared, Jake could make out the figures on the ground all around him.

'M-my friend, Simon. Please, find him, Hel-help him. And the others?' he pleaded.

'Don't push your luck,' Montague said. 'Healing of any kind goes against my nature, but Esther's right—we must make you presentable for Master Crowden. Now, don't try to touch your face, the mask will fall away when the magic's done its work . . .'

'Please—they're hurt. They're dying.'

'Yes, rather wonderful, isn't it?'

His spell almost complete, Ambrose Montague grasped his patient by the scruff of the neck and lifted him from the ground. One long white finger pointed towards the sufferers.

'Do not pity them,' he said. 'They are the lucky ones.

When the dawn comes, when the Demontide breaks, many will wish for deaths as easy as these.'

Jake watched as the witches picked their way between the slow-dying Elders. Like a victorious army they mocked their vanquished foe and ignored the pleas for mercy. Pen and paper in hand, Mother Inglethorpe seemed to be taking an inventory of those present. She was clearly pleased with the magnitude of the slaughter, and yet a trace of anxiety remained on her face. There was no sign of Dr Holmwood or Simon Lydgate. Jake closed his eyes. Though he could do nothing to block out the screaming, he could at least shut out the sight of this one-sided battle.

Lost in the darkness, voices reached out to him. They sang an ancient song, their tones rustling, creaking, sighing. Sadness dripped from each note, melancholy from every strange syllable. The cries of fear and pain were silenced. The dying and the injured stared into the forest. Surely it was his imagination, and yet Jake felt convinced that the voices came from the trees . . .

'Nature's lament for the passing of Man.' Montague looked down at Jake. 'The last Omen. It is time to say goodbye to the world you knew, Master Harker.'

Montague tapped his peat cane against the ground. The snake came to life, hissing and snapping against the hand that held it. The old witch didn't flinch as he fitted the harness into the creature's mouth. Then, without the slightest effort, he lifted Jake onto his back. Jake struggled but the explosion had left him very weak.

'If you fight me, I will very likely drop you,' Montague

said, 'and I have used up all my healing magic for one night.
Now, hold tight.'

There was nothing Jake could do except obey.

Montague leaned forward, whispered a few words to the
snake, and a second later the thick body twisted beneath
them. As the tail lashed, the witch and the boy were lifted
into the air. They burst through the branches and out into
the starless night sky. Their work done, the other witches
joined the flight from Wykely Woods. Jake looked back and
saw the boughs of the forest moving in slow waves, as if ruffled by a breeze. The lament of Nature stayed with him long
into the night.

Dr Holmwood sat upon the stairs of his ancestral home, lost
in thought. He hardly heard Malcolm Saxby's dry little
cough.

'The numbers are in, sir. Seventeen dead, including
Cynthia Mimms and Eric Drake. No trace of Jacob or Adam
Harker . . . '

'I heard it, Saxby.'

'I'm sorry?'

'The lament of Nature for the world of Man. After the
explosion, I thought my eardrums had ruptured, but then I
heard the singing of the earth, of the trees . . . '

'Sir, we have to take stock. Prepare ourselves and—'

'What time is it?'

'Quarter to two.'

'Three hours until dawn,' Holmwood sighed. 'Even if we

followed the Coven to London, somehow managed to retrieve the boy, there would be no chance of getting him back here in time. The Demontide is now inevitable.'

Saxby slapped his palm against the banister.

'I don't understand it. How could the Coven have known we were bringing Adam to the Hollow?'

'Marcus Crowden knows our ways,' Holmwood said. 'He is well aware that *all* Hobarron Elders must be present at the Demontide.'

'Yes, but how did he know the route we would take, and at what time we would pass through the woods? How did he arrange for Jake to be there?'

'That's a point.'

'You telephoned me that morning with the plan for us to meet you at Steerpike Bridge. I passed on the message to the other Elders. There was no break in the chain. It had to be someone working within our own ranks that informed the Coven.'

'Or someone who was in the house when the phone call was received. Someone who overheard the plan. Someone who has already shown a marked reluctance to help our cause.'

Holmwood's head snapped in Rachel's direction.

'Your daughter, for example.'

Rachel and Eddie Rice were still tied to their chairs. Despite being beaten by Alice Splane, neither had betrayed the whereabouts of Jake Harker.

'Rachel?' Dr Saxby said in an anguished voice. 'She wouldn't. She's tried to protect Jake . . . '

'So she says,' Holmwood whispered. 'But her refusal to tell

us his whereabouts has resulted in our losing him to the Coven. Maybe her motives are not as pure as she pretends. Let us ask her.'

The two men descended the stairs and made their way over to the children. Exhausted and frightened by the day's events, Eddie had fallen into a kind of trance. He stared at the people around him, neither seeing nor hearing.

Dr Saxby knelt down in front of his daughter.

'Rachel, I need you to be honest with me, can you do that?'

An expression of disgust tightened the girl's features. She looked down at the bruises on her arms and turned her face away from her father.

'I won't tell you where Jake is,' she said. 'Now leave me alone.'

'You may think you're being very noble, Miss Saxby,' Dr Holmwood seethed, 'but your silence will be the death of every person in this room. Worse, by your obstinate refusal to talk you may already have condemned this world to oblivion. I pray that your treachery runs no deeper than mere foolishness.'

'What do you mean?'

'I will ask you plainly: are you a spy working on behalf of the Crowden Coven?'

'What?'

'Did you eavesdrop on a conversation between your father and me? Did you then pass on information to Marcus Crowden and his witches?'

'I don't know what you're talking about.'

'We shall see.'

Holmwood stalked out of the hall. He returned moments later with a small black box, secured with a chain and pad-lock, which he placed in front of Rachel Saxby.

'If she has performed magic in recent days, if she's opened a portal to the Veil, then we shall soon know. The traces of the spell will be all around her. *It* will sense them.'

'Dad? What's he doing?' The fear was evident in Rachel's voice.

As Dr Holmwood fitted the key into the padlock, Saxby laid a hand on his arm.

'Please, Gordon. It could have been any one of the Elders who betrayed us. This is just a hunch. There's nothing to suggest that my daughter . . . '

'If she's innocent, we will know soon enough,' Holmwood said. 'But if she's guilty . . . '

The doctor opened the box.

Mr Pinch squinted in the light. Kept away from his witch for over six months, Tobias Quilp's demon was a shadow of his old self. He pawed weakly inside his coffin and tried to raise himself up. What little strength he had left him in an instant and he collapsed back into the box. Like a maltreated dog, he mewled quietly to himself . . .

And then that old cruel light sparked once more in the creature's eyes. His nostrils quivered with excitement. Mr Pinch could smell magic. His tongue slurped across his lips and, with fresh energy, he grasped the sides of the box. A pair of yellow eyes stared in the direction of the children.

'Enough!' Saxby cried.

Dr Holmwood slammed the lid shut. The box rattled as the chain was looped around it and the padlock refitted. Holmwood called one of his assistants over and the box and its horrible cargo was taken away.

'It was her,' Holmwood said, leading Saxby into a corner. 'She's the Coven's spy, and indirectly responsible for the deaths of seventeen Elders.'

Saxby shook his head. 'She might've overheard the plans and informed Crowden, but she wouldn't have known about the ambush. My daughter isn't a killer.'

'The fact is, Rachel betrayed her own people,' Holmwood insisted. 'And now she must make amends.'

'How?'

'She is related to the Seward family, is she not? She is of Hobarron blood?'

Saxby staggered back against the wall. His face turned the colour of sour milk.

'No. She—she's my *daughter*!'

'You were ready enough to sacrifice Adam Harker's son for the greater good.'

'But he's different. My Rachel's blood will not be strong enough. She is another generation on from Luke Seward, and his blood barely held back the Demontide last time. It won't work.'

'Not with one sacrifice, I agree.' Holmwood's eyes fell upon the boy sitting in the chair next to Rachel. 'But if we drain *both* of them . . . '

'Impossible. The blood of two children can't be mixed; it must be pure. The Door will reject it.'

'The situation calls for desperate measures, Saxby. This is our only chance now.'

'Please, Gordon,' Saxby caught at Holmwood's sleeve. 'Remember how the murder of Luke Seward haunted you? That's why you set up the Institute—so that it would never have to happen again!'

'You sound like Adam Harker,' the doctor said. 'You are not my conscience, Malcolm, and we have no other option left. They *must* be sacrificed.'

Chapter 23
The Witchfinder Returns

They flew high over the city. A parade of London landmarks swept by—Covent Garden with its big old colonnades, Admiral Nelson atop his column, the great stretch of the Mall with the windows of Buckingham Palace shining just beyond.

Ambrose Montague tugged at the rein and the snake's head turned eastward. Jake glanced over his shoulder and saw the phalanx of witches fall into line. There were ten of them in all. One of the witches towards the back, a large man with a heavy black beard and broad shoulders, was carrying something on his back. No prizes for guessing that his burden was the unconscious Dr Adam Harker. Even in this desperate situation, the prospect of seeing his father after all these weeks lifted Jake's spirits.

Suddenly, a powerful shaft of light swept across the Coven, dazzling each of the witches so that they had to struggle to keep control of their snakes. It was with some surprise that Jake saw the source of the light. A guard or policeman stationed on the ramparts of the Houses of Parliament guided the spotlight up and down the line of fliers. His eyes as round as dinner plates, he held a walkie-talkie up to his chin. Before he could give his report, Ambrose Montague pointed his long forefinger at the man and muttered a few words.

Jake lunged forward and grabbed hold of the witch's wrist. A bolt of dark magic shot out from Montague's finger and missed the guard by inches. It hit the spotlight and shattered the glass. Montague threw his arm back and caught Jake a blow on the shoulder.

'Sentimental idiot,' he cried. 'You might have killed us both! If the Master hadn't insisted you be brought to him unharmed I would gladly throw you into the Thames!'

As he spoke, they flew over Westminster Bridge and Jake saw the great old river far below. A mass of dark, choppy water, it reflected the sky. The heavens rumbled and Jake looked up. Shoulder to shoulder, thunderclouds towered above the city like a scrum of grey giants. Bursts of lightning lit up their bellies while their thunder-voices rattled angrily between them.

Montague saw the danger and made a downward motion with his hand. A few of the younger witches took fright and zoomed past their leader, plummeting towards the arrow-shaped bulk of Waterloo Station. With a barked curse, Montague followed. He had descended several metres when one of the thunder giants roared and took a swipe with its lethal fist.

The bolt struck Montague square in the chest. Even as he let go of the old man and jumped back along the length of the snake, Jake felt the raw power of the lightning. It fizzed into his body and made his heart spasm. For a moment, his senses disappeared into a white glare, similar to that of the Steerpike Bridge explosion. The smell of burnt flesh brought him round.

Threads of smoke rose up from the body of Ambrose Montague. He dropped the reins and slumped forward. Then the old man tipped to the left and, with heavy grace, slipped off the back of the snake. Rolling and tumbling like a clumsy high diver, Montague plunged towards the Thames.

The moment the witch disappeared into the depths of the river, his magical force vanished from the world. Beneath Jake, the snake ceased its writhing flight and returned to the inanimate peat from which it had been conjured. Cold air roared around Jake, buffeted him to and fro and flipped him like a pancake. His eyes narrowed into slits and he saw the river below grow larger and larger. He had read somewhere that, if hit from a great height, water could be as hard as concrete. Maybe the impact would kill him instantly . . .

And then the memory of flying returned to him.

It hadn't been a dream. He *had* escaped from the river at Green Gables. He *had* flown! A flight of pure magic, powered by Oldcraft, and without the need for silly peat snakes. It had taken the fear of death to reawaken the memory, but now it flooded through him. And with it, the power returned.

The power that he had inherited from the Witchfinder?

He held out his hand . . .

Fingers locked around his wrist. Pain as bright as fire crackled across his shoulder as he was tugged upwards. His feet swished through the water and then the river was dropping away from him again. He looked up into the face of Mother Inglethorpe. The witch gave him a hard stare and kicked at her snake. Jake wondered how the old lady could possibly carry a nine stone teenager. Perhaps the prospect of standing before her master empty-handed had given her supernatural strength.

They passed over Waterloo station and dropped into a little gas-lit street. A sign identified this place as 'Yaga Passage'. It was dark and dismal, the walls mottled with moss and covered with tattered old theatre posters. Mother Inglethorpe did not wait to land before she released Jake. He hit the cobbles and rolled into the gutter. The fall and the pain of his rescue was enough to make him feel sick. He got to his feet without throwing up, but his reflection in the shop window opposite did not help to steady him.

His face was gone. In its place was a crusted yellow mask with two eye slits and a hole for his mouth. Filled with horror, Jake's hands went to the mask.

Mother Inglethorpe landed in front of him. She tapped her snake against the ground, turning the serpent back into its earthen form. Then she slapped Jake's hands away from his face.

'Don't touch it or the magic will fail.' She smiled a devilish smile. 'You've been horribly burned, my child. The spell is rebuilding your scorched skin; it is keeping the pain at bay.'

One of the witches who had overtaken Montague stepped forward. She was a pretty young woman with deep blue eyes and a strong chin. A green beetle with the head of a miniature dog sat in the folds of her hair.

'Dr Harker has been taken into the shop,' she reported. 'Mother, what has happened to Ambrose Montague?'

The clouds grumbled. A strip of troubled sky loomed between the houses of Yaga Passage.

'Montague is dead.' Esther looked west, towards the river. 'The lightning took his life and the river claimed his body. Like the trees in the forest, all of Nature cries out against the Demontide. Still, it is most encouraging. Our Coven has never before witnessed the fourth and final Omen. The end is so very close now.'

Mother Inglethorpe's strong fingers locked on Jake's shoulder.

'Come, our Master waits.'

'Ow! What do they feed you at that old folks' home?' Jake cried.

Esther ignored the insult and turned him towards the bookshop at the end of the passage.

'"Crowden's Emporium of Forgotten and Forbidden Books",' Jake read. 'Catchy name. Did your big, bad master think that up all by himself?'

'I do so hope Master Crowden will share out the task of torturing you and your father,' Inglethorpe snapped.

Jake shivered but managed to keep the fear out of his voice.

'Bring it on, Mother Ugly.'

The door of the bookshop opened and a small man waved them through. As he was bustled into the shop, Jake caught sight of movement in the window of the building across the street. A monstrous and yet strangely feminine figure stared back at him. Though her face remained hidden in the shadows, her eyes shone, the light within enticing. Eight arms writhed at her sides. Before Jake could see any more the door slammed behind him.

'You're late,' the little man spat. An ugly bird on his shoulder squawked at both Jake and Mother Inglethorpe. 'The Master has heard what happened with Sidney Tinsmouth. He is not pleased.'

'He'll be pleased enough when he hears of our achievement tonight. Seventeen Elders dead by our hand!'

A cry of triumph rose up from the witches now assembled in the bookshop. Chirrups and squawks, hisses and barks sounded out as their demons joined in the victory call.

'The followers of Hobarron are scattered. By our efforts the Demontide is now assured. Oh yes, *and* we have brought the Elders' second-in-command to pay tribute to our Master.' Esther fixed her enemy with a malicious grin. 'And you, miserable librarian, what have you done to merit a place at our side?'

'I have brought him news. I-I have served him faithfully!'

The Coven laughed as one.

'Crawl back into your hole, little bookworm!' Mother Inglethorpe bellowed. 'There are no rewards for cowardice in the Crowden Coven!'

A ball of red light crackled in her hand . . .

'ENOUGH!'

Strong as a gale-force wind, a blast of icy air accompanied the command. It tossed papers from the desk and threw books from their shelves. Many of the witches cringed. Other than the quiver of her bottom lip, Esther Inglethorpe displayed no fear.

'You dare to play games at a time like this?' There was no sign of the speaker. The arctic tones echoed out of a doorway towards the back of the shop. 'You will join me in the Veil, Mother Inglethorpe—my nightmare box is waiting.'

At the mention of Crowden's cabinet all Mother Inglethorpe's bravado abandoned her.

'Take the boy through to the office,' Grype instructed. 'The rest of you, stand guard.'

Inglethorpe dragged Jake behind her. Still weak from the explosion, he could not resist. They had reached Grype's office when one of the Coven whispered under his breath, 'Guard against what? The Elders are finished!'

Jake stepped into the back room and saw the truth of those words standing before him.

Dr Adam Harker was slumped against the wall. He was very pale and his hands trembled at his sides. A soft moan purred at the back of his throat while his head continued to rock back and forth.

'What have you done to him?' Jake shouted.

Mother Inglethorpe laughed. 'Nothing. This was how we found him.'

'The Institute did this?'

'A strange band of "good guys" are they not?' she said. 'No more talk now. The Master awaits.'

Inglethorpe shoved Jake and his father through a curtained doorway and into the emptiness of the Veil.

At first, Jake could see only the swirl of grey vapour and the door by which they had entered this dimension. The frame stood without walls while the mist tickled the scarlet curtain. The ground felt marshy beneath his feet, almost as if it was struggling to hold him up. He glanced at his father. Like the new world around them, Adam's face remained lifeless, empty . . .

'Welcome to my home, Dr Harker.'

The nightmare box glided with ghostly ease through the Veil. Walking before it was a man dressed in old-fashioned clothes. The cloth that covered his face did nothing to muffle the ringing tones of his voice. He came to within an arm's length of his guests and stopped. Two bright eyes played between Jake and his father. Then the Master's attention switched to Mother Inglethorpe.

'I hear that you have murdered Sidney Tinsmouth.'

'I could not help myself, Master. His existence made a mockery of our Coven. For these last eight years we have celebrated him as a fallen martyr and . . . '

Crowden held up a hand. 'Did I order his execution?'

'Please, if you had seen him, talked to him. He spoke of demonic deceptions, of power coming from the earth . . . '

'Did I order his execution?'

'He was a vile traitor! And the lies, Master! Magic without demons! Oldcraft!'

'DID I ORDER HIS EXECUTION?'

Crowden bellowed and the mouth of his nightmare cabinet swung open. Jake stared into the box. A deep, dark well of pain and suffering, it offered a glimpse of the demon dimension. A dimension that was about to smash its way into this world . . .

Sidney Tinsmouth was inside that thing for a whole month, Jake thought, *just a little boy, alone in that nightmare* . . . Now that he began to understand what Tinsmouth had suffered, Jake's anger raged against the cruelty and injustice of it. No longer fearful, he grabbed hold of the Coven Master and swung the monster around to face him. Caught off guard, neither Crowden nor Mother Inglethorpe reacted.

Jake spat in Crowden's face.

'Of course you ordered his execution! The day you took him from his parents and forced him into that living demon, you condemned him to death. You twisted his soul, made him evil . . . '

It did not take long for Crowden to recover himself. His cloth mask rustled as he intoned the spell and a stream of dark magic flashed from his palm. It struck Jake between the eyes and he flew through the air. The soft ground saved him from breaking his neck. The pain that roared inside his head was almost too much to bear and it was only the crisp, cold air of the Veil that kept him from passing out. He tried to move but his body had frozen. All he could do was stare across the ground, back in the direction of his father and the witches.

'Jacob Harker,' Crowden sneered. 'I am told that, beneath this mask, you now have a face to match your fiery spirit. Rest assured, young Harker, if your father does not answer my questions I will strip the healing spell away and burn the flesh from your bones.' He turned back to his second-in-command. 'There is no time to punish you just now, Mother, and if the Demontide goes as expected perhaps I will forget your little mistake. Now let us turn our attention to the good doctor.'

Adam Harker had remained insensible throughout the attack on his son. He did not seem to see Crowden, Inglethorpe, Jake, or the Veil.

'The Institute have used powerful drugs on our friend,' Crowden said. 'Bring him back to us, my dear.'

Relieved to have been forgiven, Esther now jumped at the chance to impress her master. She passed a hand across Adam's face and whispered gently in his ear. The man flinched, his hands twitched, his breathing came in gasps. It was as if he was waking from a deep sleep. His gaze fixed on Crowden.

'Dr Harker,' the Master bowed. 'You will tell me everything you know about the Hobarron Weapon.'

Crowden snapped his fingers and Jake rose into the air. Another gesture and the boy swept towards his father. Stopping a few metres in front of Adam, Jake's arms shot out from his sides. It felt as if invisible ropes had been lashed around his wrists and pulled taut. Pain throbbed in Jake's chest and shoulders.

'Speak,' Crowden commanded, 'or watch your child be torn apart.'

Adam stared into his son's eyes. His words came in calm waves.

'Listen to my voice, Jake. Only to my voice. You cannot hear Master Crowden. You do not feel any pain.'

'What's this?' Crowden laughed. 'Hypnotism? Whether or not he feels pain, he will still die unless you tell me what I want to know. What is the weapon, Dr Harker? How can it threaten the Demontide?'

The invisible ropes strained. Jake heard his joints crackle and a sickening jolt of agony ran through his arms.

'Dad, it hurts!'

'Listen. Look at me.' Adam managed a smile. 'It doesn't hurt. It isn't real.'

It felt real. The sweat pouring out of Jake began to dissolve the healing mask. It came away in yellow flakes.

'Tell me!' Crowden hissed. 'This is your last chance. At my next command his arms will be torn from their sockets. Save your son, Dr Harker. TELL ME!'

Adam's eyes bored into Jake.

'Remember, Jacob. Remember, Josiah. Comic books and horror stories. All those tales I told you, every one of them designed to reawaken the past. Devils and vampires, werewolves and witches, spells, incantations, potions, poltergeists and gremlins. Ghosts and demons and monsters. Remember your dark catalogue. Remember the days of your forgotten life, before you were Jacob and when you were Josiah . . . '

Cracks appeared in the magic mask.

Piece by piece, it fell away.

Master Crowden caught sight of what lay beneath and cried out.

'No! That—that cannot be!'

'Remember the Hollow, the cavern, the Door, and the Demontide. Remember when you were first there. Remember Tiberius Holmwood and Marcus Crowden and all those innocent people you saved. Remember that you have faced the darkest horrors of this world and triumphed against them. Remember that I love you and that I believe in you. You are my son . . . '

Memories raged around Jake. He felt as if he was drowning in a past both recent and centuries old. He gasped for breath. It glimmered before him . . .

Terrifying.

'You are Jacob Harker.'

Impossible.

'You are the Weapon.'

Beautiful.

'You are Josiah Hobarron.'

The truth.

'*You are the Witchfinder.*'

290

Chapter 24
A Desperate Experiment

The last crumb of Jake's mask fell away.

He turned a startled face towards Marcus Crowden.

The witch master recoiled.

'It *is* you . . . Josiah Hobarron!'

Jake shook his head. It was impossible. How could *he* be the long-dead Witchfinder?

'You have returned to face me once more,' Crowden said. He managed a bitter laugh, though fear quivered at its edges. 'The original Hobarron Weapon!'

The master and his favourite witch began to step back into the mists of the Veil. In retreat, his dark spell was broken. The invisible ropes around Jake's wrists melted away and he fell to the ground. Adam caught hold of his son and broke his fall. A look passed between the Harkers and, like a pair of hunters closing in upon a dangerous prey, they followed the witches.

'You appear a little younger than you were,' Crowden observed, 'but there is no mistaking your face. How have the Elders conjured you from the grave? Such strange and powerful magic . . . '

Crowden came to a stop. He held out his hand in warning and the Harkers paused.

'But you do not know what you are—*who* you are. If you did, you could have broken the binding spell I cast upon you just now.' The Master crooked his head to one side. 'Why have the Elders kept your identity a secret, old friend?' His gaze flickered to Adam. 'Perhaps it is because this new version does not possess the powers of the old Witchfinder. Let us see.'

A red flame sparked between the Master's fingers. His eyes darkened until they resembled two black suns.

'When last we met you fought me with the most ferocious, primal magic I have ever known. Now you return in the form of this child and hope to beat me again?'

The Master's gloved hand reached up to his cloth mask.

'You will fail, Witchfinder.'

He tore the mask away.

Jake had expected a horrific vision to be revealed. Instead, the face of Marcus Crowden was one of the most beautiful he had ever seen. A strong jaw, sharp cheekbones and a delicate nose: features that might have been carved by angels. The only imperfection was around the mouth, which was distorted by a permanent sneer. Deep in his memory, Jake found an echo of this face. He had seen it before, lit by candlelight in the dank depths of a cavern.

A Desperate Experiment

Mother Inglethorpe stared open-mouthed at her master.

'You wonder why I keep myself covered?' Crowden caressed his features. 'It is because this face is a pale reflection of who I am. My true self is a thing of darkness!'

Crowden thrust out his hand and a scarlet stream of light soared towards Jake. Automatically, Jake held out his own hand. Just before the pulse hit, Adam rushed forward and pushed his son out of its path. Landing on his side, Jake glanced back in time to see the hex strike his father in the shoulder and spin him round. A scent of burnt skin, similar to that which Jake had smelt when Ambrose Montague had been hit by the lightning, filled the air. Adam crumpled to the ground.

'No one to save you now, boy conjuror,' Crowden smiled. His fist crackled with fresh energy. 'Tell me, where is your fire? Where is the magic of old?'

At that moment, the sound of battle broke out from beyond the curtained doorway. Glass shattered, voices shrieked and cursed. In his surprise, the magical light disappeared from Crowden's hand. The curtain was ripped aside and Mr Grype hurried into his master's presence.

'Monsters,' he panted, 'they've broken into the shop. Dozens of them.'

'What?'

'They've come from Yaga Passage. *She* is their leader. They have already killed most of the Coven and are breaking their way into the back office. We must flee.'

'But these are dark creatures!' Crowden exclaimed. 'Why do they fight *us*?'

'They fight for him!'

Grype pointed at Adam, still unmoving on the ground.

'For once, the librarian is right,' Mother Inglethorpe said. 'We must make haste to the Hollow. There is less than an hour until dawn.'

'What about him?' Crowden stared at Jake with a mixture of hatred and wonder.

'If you are to survive in the living world, you must conserve your magic,' Inglethorpe said. 'If you weaken before the Door is opened then you will be dragged back to this prison. Grype and I will conjure the portal. Come!'

The three witches turned their backs on Jacob Harker. Grype's vulture-demon fluttered down to perch on his shoulder; Miss Creekley rustled free of her mistress's dress; Crowden's cabinet hovered behind its master. Joining hands, the witches pooled their magical forces. They whispered a few words and the mist before them formed into an oval gateway. At the edges, it took on the hue of rough, reddish stone. Grype entered first, followed by Inglethorpe. Before joining them, Crowden looked back at Jake.

'Do not attempt to follow.'

He stepped forward and the portal dissolved around him.

The strange woman that Jake had seen in the window when he arrived in Yaga Passage now helped to carry his father back through the curtained doorway and into Grype's office. Between them, they lifted the unconscious

Adam onto an old sofa. Then the woman disappeared for a few minutes before returning with a bowl of water and some bandages.

'It's real deep,' she said, cleaning the wound at Adam's shoulder. Her voice was low and sweet, and put Jake in mind of the great open prairies and misty bayous of the American South. 'The magic that did this is some of the darkest I have ever seen.'

The creature leaned over Adam. A concerned expression pinched her brow. Even when standing, she moved like a dancer, her hips swaying, her eight arms writhing, as if she was responding to some unheard music. Apart from those impossible arms, her appearance was that of a beautiful middle-aged woman with rich ebony skin.

'Why did you help us?' Jake asked.

'Because, long ago, your daddy helped *me*. He has aided many of my kind over the years.'

'What are you?'

Two hands were busy bandaging Adam's arm while another covered him with a blanket and a fourth smoothed his brow.

'We are the so-called "dark creatures". We live at the border between the world of Man and demonkind.'

'Are you demons?'

'No. Pure demons can only exist in your world as demonic familiars—servants to witches—a position they secretly loathe. Some of us dark creatures *are* related to demonkind. Vampires, for example, are demon cousins, and few of them can resist their evil heritage. For the most part we are just like human beings—some are bad, most are good. Your father knows this and he has helped to protect us.'

'From the Hobarron Institute?'

'Them, and others. We thank him by keeping an eye on the Crowden Coven. When I saw you arrive here tonight, I decided to call in a few friends and crash the party . . . '

'Thank God you did, Pandora.' Adam blinked up at them. His hand went to his shoulder and he grimaced. 'Could you leave us for a few minutes? I must speak to my son.'

'Certainly.'

'Oh, and Pandora? We will be needing a portal. Perhaps your friends can rustle something up? Quick as you can.'

Pandora nodded and went to the door. Before disappearing into the shop, her gaze fell upon Adam. The worried look in her eyes made Jake feel uneasy.

Adam propped himself up on his good arm and smiled sadly at his son.

'So, I guess you've got a lot of questions.'

Jake went and sat behind Grype's desk. He took a moment before he spoke.

'I am Josiah Hobarron, the Witchfinder?'

'Yes . . . And no.'

'Dad . . . '

'I'm not trying to be mysterious, but the fact remains: he *is* you, but you are more than him.' Adam sighed. 'Let's start at the beginning. If I know my son, you'll have tracked down Sidney Tinsmouth and worked out a lot of the story for yourself.'

Jake nodded. He would tell Adam about what had happened to Tinsmouth later. Now was not the time.

'Good.' Adam took a deep breath. 'Luke Seward was the best friend I ever had. When I became an Elder, and was told why he had been sacrificed, I decided I had to find another way to stop the Demontide. The problem was this: in the beginning, just a smear of blood from a child descended from Josiah Hobarron was enough to seal the Door. But, as the blood weakened with every new generation, the Elders found it took more and more to keep the Door closed. Not only that, but the Door itself was a living thing and, over the centuries, it had grown hungry for the blood of children. It was difficult to see how we could ever seal the Door again *without* a sacrifice.

'And then a thought struck me: one person *had* managed to lock the Door without a drop of blood being spilled. The Witchfinder had sealed it with magic. The solution was obvious—we had to bring Josiah Hobarron back to life. But how?'

The sound of voices casting a spell came from outside the office door. Jake barely heard the chant.

'By this time, I had taken my degree in psychology and I was working at the Institute. In my first few days there I met a young scientist called Claire Peterson. We clicked immediately. She was funny, clever, beautiful . . . ' Adam's voice tightened. 'As we became closer, Claire started telling me more and more about her work. She was a genetic biologist and—'

'Genetic? I knew Mum studied biology before switching to engineering, but—'

'We'll come to that. Through Claire's knowledge of genetic science, I began to see a way in which we might bring the Witchfinder back. If it could be done, then it would be the miracle the Elders had been searching for. With Dr Holmwood's approval, I told Claire about the Institute's secret mission. She needed a lot of convincing!' Adam laughed. 'But finally she came on board and we started work.

'When the Witchfinder originally sealed the Door, he had used some kind of freezing spell. It seemed that the spell had got out of control, backfiring on Hobarron and freezing him in a block of ice. Unlucky for him, but fortunate for our plan. We took a team of scientists to the cavern and started drilling.'

Jake nodded, remembering the hole he had felt in the ice block.

'We reached the body and managed to scrape away a number of skin samples. Now our experiment could begin.'

Dimly, Jake started to see the truth. He felt the first stirrings of dread and disgust.

'We had to be careful,' Adam continued. 'What we were planning was against international law, and yet I thought it was worth the risk. I won't bore you with all the complexities of the science. To put it simply, we took an egg from your mother and removed the nucleus—that's the genetic material that comes from the mother. Then we implanted cells taken from Josiah Hobarron's skin into the egg. The egg was then transferred to a machine that fused and activated it. Finally, we implanted the egg back into your mother where it developed into a healthy baby boy. The experiment was very complicated. We had to use magic to stabilize the process and—'

'Stop it,' Jake said quietly. 'Just tell me what I am. I want you to say it out loud.'

'Jake, listen to me . . . '

'Say it!' He shot out of the chair. 'SAY IT!'

Adam could not look at his son.

'You're a clone. An exact copy of Josiah Hobarron.'

A heavy silence followed. Jake's world reeled around him.

'I don't understand. I'm a clone of the Witchfinder. I'm the weapon . . . Then what was the "Incu" box?'

'I'm sorry?'

Jake explained about the blueprint he had found on the night of Adam's abduction. The diagram of the machine labelled 'Hobarron Weapon: Incu'.

'You've linked that blueprint to your mother's work in engineering and come to the wrong conclusion,' Adam said. 'The Hobarron Weapon was *never* a machine.'

'But Mum—she told Quilp the weapon was an engine. A machine of ferocious power.'

'She said that to protect you. To throw Quilp off the scent. And, like you, the Coven assumed that, because Claire was involved, the weapon *had* to be a machine.' Adam sighed. 'The doctors working on the weapon project expected you to be very weak when you were born. A special piece of equipment had to be built to keep you alive. The full title of the machine was the "Hobarron Weapon: *Incu*bator". It's where we placed you after you were born.'

'Born?' Jake echoed. 'I was *never* born. Not really. Mrs Rice, she said I was "no child of God". I was made. I'm an experiment!'

'No. You're my son. Your mother . . . '

'I don't think she ever loved me,' Jake said. 'Not really. She was always so cold. So distant. Did she just think of me as a science project?'

'The experiment changed her,' Adam admitted. 'Despite the miracle of your life, she felt that what we had done was wrong. That was why she turned her back on genetic science and became a mechanical engineer. It's true that your mother sometimes found it hard to separate *you* from *how* you had come into the world, but she *did* love you. In the end, she gave her life to save you.'

'But why, Dad? Why did you do it?'

'I did it to create a weapon that we could use to end the Demontide once and for all. Only the magic of the Witchfinder could bind the Door without bloodshed. We knew from the stories that Hobarron's magic was a natural part of who he was. All I had to do was reawaken that ability in you.'

'The comic books,' Jake said.

Adam nodded. 'The years were passing and there was no sign of you possessing any magical ability. I decided to try two approaches. I would fill your world with stories of monsters and witches, hoping that the magic part of you would respond. The second approach was even more desperate. There is a theory that memories can be encoded in a person's DNA and, just like a father or mother passing on their hair or eye colour, they may pass on these memories too. I tried hypnotism, probing deep into your unconscious mind while you slept, trying to seek out any trace of the Witchfinder's past . . . '

'It worked,' Jake said. 'I've heard his voice. I've dreamed about him.'

Adam's eyes widened. 'Then you can really feel the magic? You can seal the Door?'

'I've felt his power,' Jake said. 'But to stand against Crowden?'

Adam rose and walked towards his son. He took the boy's face in his hands.

'You must try or this world will fall into darkness.'

The office door opened and Pandora stepped inside.

'If you're ready, we've summoned the portal.'

Chapter 25
The Final Sacrifice

Step by stumbled step, the man dragged the children across the bay. A rope in each hand, Dr Holmwood squinted through the rain. It was as if the years had rolled back and he was cast in the role of murderer once more. Everything was the same—the fury of the storm, the tug of a straining leash, the pleas of a child-voice in his ear. He had made a promise that this would never happen again . . .

Alice Splane, Joanna Harker, and Walter Drake—the dead postmaster's brother—helped to hurry the children across the bay. Eddie Rice's mother had descended into hysterics when told of the Elders' plan. The poor woman had always been haunted by the horror of what had happened to her brother all those years ago, and now some of her closest friends were preparing to do the same thing to her son. Joanna had tried to calm her but the woman had ranted and raved. Eventually Dr Saxby had sedated her.

The Final Sacrifice

Holmwood stole a glance at the man walking beside him. The rain made it difficult to tell if Malcolm Saxby was crying or not. Was it wise, allowing him to join them? Wouldn't any father try to save his daughter when the time came? Perhaps, but what if the father knew that, in so doing, he would risk the destruction of the world? No, Saxby could be trusted to see it through.

Fifteen minutes of climbing across the rocks brought the party to Crowden's Sorrow. They stood for a moment in the shadow of the cavern, catching their breath. Dr Holmwood felt the tug of the rope in his hand. Like Eddie Rice, Rachel had been drugged before they left Holmwood Manor. The mild sedative was no match for this child's fierce energy and her will to live.

'Don't do this,' she said. 'I haven't spied for the Coven, I swear.'

Holmwood tried to look at the girl and found he could not.

'I'm sorry, there is no other way.' He shouted so that his voice could be heard above the storm—'Come on! Time is against us.'

The mouth of the cavern waited, ready to swallow them. No moonlight penetrated and so the Elders switched on their torches. Yellow beams swept across the dripping rock and made a hazy path for the party to follow. The voice of the storm echoed into the cave, its fury rumbling ever deeper as they stepped further into the darkness.

Reaching the false wall, Holmwood moved to his right and shepherded Rachel into the vast space beyond. Here the green moss that covered every surface gave off its phosphorous light, making the torches unnecessary. Holmwood towed Rachel the last few metres to the foot of the giant staircase.

'The stone men,' Dr Saxby murmured. He looked around at the dozens of stalagmites and stalactites, positioned across the floor like giant chess pieces. 'The third Omen . . . '

'They're golems. My friend Jake stopped them with a single word. *Met. Dead.* Jake was brave. Rachel was brave.'

It was the first time Eddie had spoken. Now he looked around him, as if coming out of a dream. His gaze turned towards Rachel and he started to tremble.

'Why have they brought us here?'

'Are you going to tell him, Dr Holmwood?' She switched to her father. 'Or you?'

Grief washed over Dr Saxby's face. 'There's nothing I can do. If we don't try to stop the Demontide then we will *all* die. If only you hadn't betrayed the Elders . . . '

'That's enough,' Holmwood said. 'Let's finish this while there's still time.'

Alice, Joanna, Walter Drake, and Dr Holmwood formed a circle around the children. Unable to watch, Dr Saxby retreated to the cavern's hidden entrance and buried his face in his hands.

'The knife,' Holmwood said.

Alice Splane took the long, curved dagger from the folds of her cloak. The letters 'JH' glimmered at the hilt. The Elders held Rachel still while Alice pressed the blade against her throat. Four voices rose up in a sing-song chant—

'Hobarron—Elder of Elders—showed us the light, and so we fight against the darkness. Let us spill the Finder's Blood. Finder's Blood to seal the Door. Finder's Blood to vanquish Evil. Finder's Blood to hold back the Demontide.'

The blade nicked Rachel's skin.

A trickle of warm blood rolled down her neck . . .

'STOP!'

All eyes turned to Eddie Rice.

'Please, don't hurt her. It was me. *I'm the one that betrayed you . . .*'

The hand wavered and the knife slipped from Rachel's throat. Eddie took a long, shivery breath.

'I'm the Coven spy.'

If Dr Holmwood was surprised he didn't show it. His question came in a calm voice.

'Why?'

'Because my mother told me the truth about what happened to Uncle Luke.'

Holmwood shook his head. 'Impossible. She was an Elder, sworn to secrecy . . . '

'She told me in her dreams. Every night she spoke in her sleep, reliving the memory over and over. You thought that she was tucked up in bed when you came to take Luke, but his cries woke her up. She watched you drag him from the house and, when his body was found, she knew that *you* had murdered him. Uncle Gordon and his friends. She grew up and became an Elder herself, but the memories of that night haunted her. She spoke of the sacrifice in her sleep: the Finder's blood—a child's blood—being used to seal the

Door. I knew that, when the Demontide came round again, it might be *my* blood that was taken. And so I contacted the Coven. I offered to spy for Marcus Crowden if he could save me.'

'When Dr Saxby called your mother, when he told her about the plan to bring Adam Harker to the Hollow, you were listening in.'

Eddie nodded. 'I contacted Crowden and passed it on. But I fooled him into thinking I was Rachel, just in case he ever decided to come after me.' The boy gave Rachel a grief-stricken look. 'I'm sorry, I was just so frightened.'

'How did you do it?' Holmwood asked.

'The Manor is full of old magic books left by Tiberius Holmwood. In one of them I found a spell that could transform my appearance. All I needed was a few fingernails or strands of hair from the person I wanted to impersonate. I've used the spell on Jake, too, making him think that the woman who told him to be at Steerpike Bridge was Miss Splane.' Eddie reached out to Dr Holmwood. 'So, you see, it's all my fault. I'm the one who betrayed the Elders. Please, let Rachel go.'

An ominous rumble echoed from above. The eyes of the children and the Elders swept up to the top of the great stone staircase. The sound of cracking, splitting rock reminded Rachel of the noise of the stalactites as they shrugged themselves free of the cavern roof. Holmwood made a gesture with his hand and the sacrificial knife returned to Rachel's throat.

'I'm sorry, Eddie,' he said, 'but in the end it doesn't

matter who betrayed our cause. This is not a punishment, and we take no joy in what we do.'

He nodded at Alice Splane and, with the help of Joanna and Walter Drake, she managed to turn Rachel round. With an arm clamped across the girl's chest, Alice pressed the knife against the left side of her windpipe, ready to sweep it across her throat. Through a mist of tears, Rachel stared at her father. Dr Saxby peeked at his daughter from between his fingers, shook his head and moaned. The wind whistled into the chamber, swept around the circle of figures, whipped their clothes and stung their eyes. The glow of the luminous moss seemed to fade a little and the shadows lengthened across the ground. Rachel could hear the little boy sobbing quietly behind her.

'Don't be frightened, Eddie. It'll be over soon.'

She swallowed.

The voices rose up again, completing the ritual chant.

'Now let us spill the Finder's Blood. Finder's Blood to seal the Door.'

The frantic beat of her heart slowed and a strange kind of calm settled over Rachel. The only emotion that still niggled at her was sorrow. Sorrow that she would never see *him* again. She conjured a picture of the boy to keep her company in the darkness that was to come.

'Finder's Blood to vanquish Evil. Finder's Blood to hold back the Demontide.'

The hot words of her murderer sighed in Rachel's ear.

'I'm sorry.'

And then . . .

The knife fell from Alice Splane's hand and clattered to the ground.

Stunned, Rachel turned and watched Alice totter backwards in the direction of the stairs. Finally, the dead woman crumpled into a heap.

Joanna Harker was the first to break out of the trance. She ran across the chamber, dropped to her knees and scooped her friend into her lap. The bullet hole in Alice Splane's head stared back at her like a third eye.

A hard voice rang through the cavern.

'A gun is such an undignified weapon, but I cannot waste my magic.'

As one, the group turned towards the speaker.

Three witches emerged into the green light of the chamber: a little man, an elderly woman, and their leader, a figure of angelic beauty. Only his smile, cold and crooked, marred his perfect face. A black box, the size and shape of a magician's cabinet, swirled behind him. With lightning movements, he handed the pistol to the toad-like man on his left, removed his glove and thrust his hand out towards the Elders and the children. A stream of red light shot out from his palm, split into five branches and wrapped itself around Rachel, Eddie, and the Elders. Meanwhile, the old woman had conjured her own light stream, lashing it around Dr Saxby. With a gesture from the witches, the Elders and the children were dragged across the ground and pinned to the cavern wall. The handsome man smiled and went to inspect his prisoners.

Reaching Rachel, he held out his hand and stroked her face.

'My spy,' he purred. 'See, I have kept my promise. Your pretty neck is unscathed.'

Eddie opened his mouth to speak. A glance from Rachel stopped him.

'I know this one,' the old woman said, stopping in front of Joanna. 'It's Adam Harker's drunkard of a sister.'

'You killed my Alice!' Joanna cried.

She strained, trying to break free and attack the Coven leader. The ring of light kept her locked to the wall as securely as any manacle.

'And here is Dr Holmwood,' the leader said. His gaze passed over the old man's features. 'So like my old friend Tiberius. You are the descendant of a traitor, doctor. A traitor and a coward.'

'Josiah Hobarron showed him the light,' Holmwood said. 'Showed him the insanity and the evil of your plan, Master Crowden.'

Crowden clenched his fist and the loop of magical energy around Holmwood's neck tightened.

'And you thought that bringing the Witchfinder back would save you?' Crowden sneered. 'He's just a boy. A miserable child.' He relaxed his palm and the pressure around Holmwood's throat eased. The old doctor spluttered and choked. 'Don't worry, I'm not going to kill you. Not yet. You must be here to witness the end.'

Crowden walked to the foot of the giant staircase. His lips quivered with excitement. He held out his hand, index finger upraised, and made a beckoning gesture. The sound of splitting rock thundered through the cavern. From the top of the stairs a cloud of dust belched into the air. Great cracks splintered along the walls, tearing the primeval stone apart.

'Nothing can stop it now!' the Coven Master shrieked. 'No sacrificial blood. No Witchfinder returned from the grave. The Door is coming!'

He turned to the helpless Elders.

'The Demontide has dawned!'

Pandora had cleared the shop of her fellow dark creatures and now took her leave of the Harkers. There were no tears and yet the emotion in her voice could not be mistaken. Careful not to brush against his injured shoulder, she wrapped eight arms around Adam.

'Thank you for helping me all those years ago. For showing me the kind of person I should be. I'm going to miss you, Adam Harker.'

Again that mournful look entered her eyes and Jake glanced at his father. He was grey, stooped like an old man, his breathing ragged. The bandage wrapped around his shoulder was already stained with fresh blood.

The writhing, almost hypnotic movement of her limbs began once more as Pandora turned and walked out of the shop. She was so graceful that it was difficult to believe that she had taken part in the carnage of the last hour, but the evidence was all around. The bodies of nine witches littered the floor.

'It sounded like she was saying goodbye for good,' Jake said. 'Like she didn't think she'd see you again. Dad, are you . . . ?'

'Don't ask.'

Jake thought he was going to be sick. A great weight seemed to press down on his chest.

'I need to know.'

'No, you don't,' Adam insisted. 'You have to be focused. Crowden is stretched very thin now. He is using every last scrap of his magic to live outside the Veil. That's your chance.'

'I don't think I can do this,' Jake murmured.

Adam drew his son close. 'I believe in you.'

'You don't. You tried to get me away from the Elders, remember? You said the weapon wouldn't work.'

'But you've found yourself, Jake. The journey you've taken has brought you to the truth. You've heard Hobarron's voice in your dreams, you've felt the magic of the Witchfinder. Whatever power was his now rests in you . . . '

Jake held up his hand and stopped his father mid-sentence. 'I am him. The same DNA, the same blood.'

'Yes.'

'You said that the Door couldn't be sealed because the blood of Hobarron had weakened. That the DNA had been diluted. But *my* blood is *his* blood. Surely just a little of it could lock the Door . . . '

'Don't you think we thought of that?' Adam said. 'I told you, the Door is a demon itself, and it has grown hungry over the years. No, Jake, you must use your magic to destroy it once and for all.'

'But even Josiah couldn't do that.'

'The Witchfinder had to use his magic to send Crowden to the Veil. This time Crowden is weakened—all your power can be used on the Door.'

Jake shook his head, disbelieving.

'You don't have to do this, of course,' Adam said. 'We could walk away.'

The portal pulsed before them, an oval doorway of brilliant blue light. Surely only death waited beyond . . .

Jake's eyes narrowed.

'I am the Hobarron Weapon. This was what I was made for.'

He stepped into the light.

Chapter 26
Dawn

Standing in the old graveyard at the top of the hill, Simon Lydgate looked down on Hobarron's Hollow. He saw roofs with missing tiles, streets clogged with rainwater, the stark branches of trees stripped naked by the gale. Power lines had fallen and the streetlights flickered on and off, as if reflecting the lightning that flashed overhead.

Simon turned his back on the Hollow and walked towards the Witchfinder's tomb. He stared at the frescoes that covered the walls, his eyes skipping between paintings of angels and demons. A bright stab of pain seared through his body. It had nothing to do with the injuries he had sustained after the Steerpike Bridge explosion. Thrown back into the forest, he had been knocked unconscious by the blast, but had suffered only minor cuts and bruises. No, this pain was deeper than anything physical. It went straight down into his soul. It had drawn him to the tomb, and now it spoke to him—

Hear me . . .

In an untouched corner of Simon's mind, a shape moved.

Soon I shall burst into this world and bring with me all the dark majesty of our kind. You *must be there to greet me . . .*

A great shudder racked Simon's body.

Simon . . .

The shape reached out—

My son.

Without knowing it, Simon had moved to the door of the mausoleum. He grasped the handle and pulled. His touch was light and yet the old door, sturdy, solid, its lock rusted over, was torn from its hinges. A cold power surged out from Simon's heart. He tossed the door aside and stepped into the tomb.

He had expected to find a stately coffin carved out of finest marble. Instead, the interior was just a dusty, cobwebbed shell. A large rectangle of granite, about the size of the mausoleum door, occupied the middle of the room. Simon knelt beside it and ran his fingers over the smooth surface.

At his touch, a long crack appeared in the stone. Wherever his fingers moved, splinters followed, until a dozen had etched their way across the slab. A great rumble echoed inside the mausoleum and the ground quaked underfoot. Simon jumped up and pressed his back against the wall. Dust puffed out from the cracks and, in one smooth motion, the entire slab disappeared into the earth.

The voice spoke again.

Dawn

Follow the Door, my child. I await you, in the darkness.

As the words faded, a blade of brilliant sunshine cut through the mausoleum door.

Dawn.

Jake and Adam dragged themselves out of the pool. They rolled onto the bank, panting hard and soaked to the skin. Jake stared up at the rocky ceiling. It took a moment for him to realize that he was now in one of the cavern's little side chambers—the one in which he had found Simon Lydgate. It made sense. Simon must have been plunged through a portal on the Yaga Passage side and come out at this same gateway. Simon. In all the terror and excitement he had hardly thought of his friend. Had he survived the explosion? Again, there was no time to give it much thought. Adam was already on his feet. His back to Jake, he peered out into the main chamber.

Jake was about to join his father at the chamber entrance when he stopped dead. His eye had fallen on the block of ice and the figure sealed within. He walked slowly across the chamber and placed his hand on the frozen surface. Wiping an oval in the condensation he stared at the hazy outline of the man. The Witchfinder's face remained obscured by glinting, crystalline layers.

Jake's hand moved across the ice and found the hole from which the Witchfinder's DNA had been taken—scraps of skin that had been used to create a new life. Palm down, his hand retraced the path back to the level of the man's face. A sudden fiery sensation coursed down his arm and into his fingers. At the tips, a blue flame flickered. Stronger than any torch, its light pierced the dimness of the ice.

It was like looking into a mirror. The face of the Witchfinder may have appeared a little older, but the features were identical to Jake's. The blue light sparked in the dead man's eyes.

Their gaze met . . .

'We *are* the Witchfinder . . .'

Slowly, Jake turned, and left his other self.

He had reached the chamber entrance when an invisible force lashed out and struck him like a hammer blow. He slumped back against the wall.

Evil.

'The strongest I have ever known. Yes, I have felt this malice once before.'

His voice sounded deeper than before, the patterns of speech those of a distant time. Adam looked from his son to the frozen man and back again.

Jake smiled.

'I am him. He is me. Is that not what you wanted?'

Stunned, Adam could not bring himself to answer.

'No time for a regretful heart, Dr Harker. The Door has come. Now we shall see what magic I have left in me.'

He stepped into the large chamber.

Transfixed by the rumble from above, Crowden, Mother Inglethorpe, and Mr Grype all had their backs turned to the Witchfinder. Most of the prisoners were looking in the same direction, their eyes focused on the shower of dust that rained down from the hole in the roof. Only one among them turned and looked at Jake, as if *she* felt his presence.

Jake whispered a few words. Both familiar and strange, they were accompanied by the swish of his hand through the air. Rachel's mouth dropped open in surprise as she saw the pale blue light streak out from Jake's fingers. It whipped around the group, touched each of them in turn, and then returned to the hand of the conjuror.

'Sleep,' Jake instructed.

The prisoners obeyed. Crowden's ring of light which had bound them to the wall fizzled twice and vanished. Jake held out his hand, cushioning their fall. With the thunder of cracking rock coming from above, the Master and his under-lings had noticed nothing.

'What are you going to do?' Adam whispered.

'Be ready,' came the answer.

Adam Harker stepped away. This fifteen-year-old boy, pale, lanky, brown hair falling over his eyes, certainly looked like his son. And yet a change had come over him. It was exactly the transformation that Adam had worked for all these years. Through hypnosis he had tried to get at those hidden memories and talents buried in the child's DNA. In cold, scientific terms, the Hobarron Weapon was fully func-tional at last. And now that Adam beheld what he had achieved, his soul shivered at the sight of it. He had moved beyond all natural laws and brought a dead man back to life. For the greater good, his mind insisted, and yet, deep down, he knew that what he had done was wrong.

Too late for second thoughts.

The Door was coming.

A final crack, like the splitting of a mountain, boomed through the chamber. Adam covered his ears and made a dash for the unconscious form of Dr Malcolm Saxby. With an eye on the witches, he searched through the doctor's pockets. He found what he was looking for in the holster strapped across Saxby's chest. As he reached for the gun, the air seemed to freeze around him. A large shadow swept across the chamber. Adam looked up and fear clutched at his heart.

The Door.

The slab of ancient granite fell to earth with an ear-splitting thud. Fine cracks splintered the rocky ground and aftershocks rumbled through the cavern. Embedded in the earth, the Door now faced the Master of the Crowden Coven. The stars and moons, the figures and faces that had been carved thousands of years ago by an unknown hand glowed with fiery light. This light also burned between the fresh cracks that ran all across the Door. A whiff of sulphur stung the air and lava began to sizzle between the fissures and splash across the cavern floor. Despite the volcanic flow the temperature in the chamber grew colder by the second.

Adam shivered, and not just because of the cold.

Slight, boyish, vulnerable, the figure of Jake stood in the presence of the demon Door, his hand outstretched . . .

'Four hundred years I have waited,' Master Crowden roared. 'Sixteen generations and more, locked inside a realm of nothingness.' Crowden's cabinet whirled behind him, mirroring its master's excitement. 'Centuries have passed, and I have felt each year, each day, each hour creep by. But now my patience will be rewarded.'

Mother Inglethorpe and Grype watched their master, the old woman jubilant, the librarian's face fixed into a wary smile.

'With a thousand demons at my command, I shall rule this world . . . '

'You are deceived.'

At Jake's words the witches spun round. Crowden pointed a shaking finger at the boy.

'Your voice, it has changed . . . ' He squared his shoulders and shrieked. 'You cannot deny me now! The Door *will* be opened!'

'I believe you're right,' Jake said.

His gaze flickered between the witches and the great granite slab. The Door shuddered. A spill of lava frothed between the cracks. Any minute now the flood of demonkind would break through and a new age of darkness would dawn across the world.

And HE would be at the forefront of the swarm . . .

The Demon Father.

The trident symbol in the centre of the Door glowed a deep, boiling red.

'The demons have played you false, Crowden,' Jake shouted. 'All these years, you have believed that they served you, gave you your magic. Lies. All magic comes from the ancient spirit of this world. From Oldcraft. How we wield it? That is our choice.'

'It is you who are deceived, *little man*,' Crowden laughed. 'Soon enough I shall teach you the depths of your folly. I shall pay you back tenfold for every year of my imprisonment. See now, the hour has come!'

The trident symbol cracked into tiny pieces and exploded out from the Door. An infernal wind rushed through the hole and threw the witches and Adam Harker onto their backs. Only Jake stood against it. Legs braced, eyes screwed shut, hands thrust out before him, he leaned into the blast. Above the wind a deep, throaty chuckle rang through the chamber.

'*Hear my proclamation: the Father of Demons shall lead his children through the Door.*'

Images rose up in Jake's mind: Eddie Rice, his father, his mother, Simon Lydgate . . .

'*We shall lay waste to the world of Man.*'

Rachel . . .

'*All shall perish at our hand.*'

A deeper memory stirred. The picture of a beautiful woman with cornflower blue eyes and golden hair swam before him. The love of his life. His soulmate from long ago. His Eleanor . . .

'*Kneel before me, Witchfinder!*'

'NO!'

Anger sparked in Jake's heart. It caught like a flame in the barrel of his chest and raged through his body. He released it in a river of molten magic, more powerful than he had ever known. At his fingertips, the pulse crackled into life.

Mother Inglethorpe saw it first. She staggered to her feet, pointed at Jake and began her spell. She never finished it. Adam aimed the weapon he had taken from Dr Saxby and squeezed the trigger. Fire whipped out of the barrel. Esther Inglethorpe jolted backwards, teetered, and collapsed to the ground. Wreathed in flame, the demonic Miss Creekley burst out of her mistress's dress. Her life force had been bound to the witch and now she was returning to the fire from which she had been conjured. Her spider legs ticked across the frozen ground as she careered about, her beautiful face screwed up with pain. Then, with a final crackle, the demon was gone.

The death of witch and demon had gone unnoticed by Jake.

He directed his magic at the Door.

The stream of light hit the granite slab and immediately started knitting the cracks back together. The stink of sulphur vanished from the air and, within a few seconds, every crack had been closed. The Door was almost sealed. All that remained was the hole where the trident symbol had been. Jake concentrated his gaze . . .

Again, Adam saw the movement of a hand, the mutter of a spell, but this time the gun jammed. He could not save Jake from Crowden's hex. The bolt paralysed the fingers that Jake had been using to work the binding magic. The light stream died.

'You will not rob me of my victory, Witchfinder!' Crowden shouted. 'I will rule this world!'

That deep voice rumbled through the hole again.

'*Pathetic creature.*'

Wide-eyed, Crowden turned back to the Door.

Following his master's gaze, Mr Grype shrieked. The librarian ran towards the chamber entrance, abandoning his master without a second thought.

'W-what . . . ' the Master faltered. 'What are you?'

A huge, blood-soaked eye with a dark slit for its pupil stared through the hole.

'*I am the Demon Father. I am YOU.*'

Crowden screamed as the great eye dissolved into a thick, black smoke and poured out of the Door. Jake shifted his body, channelling the magic into his good hand, but it was too late.

Like a giant snake's head, the smoke reared up in front of Crowden. In one jack-knife motion, it lashed out and struck its helpless victim. For a moment, the Coven Master's head became encased in the oily vapour. Then the smoke began to clear, and Jake could see that it was flooding into Crowden's eyes. The shape of the man's pupils sharpened into slits, the hue changed from black to blood-red.

The man who had once been Marcus Crowden touched his handsome face. He smiled, and the nightmare box swirled around its true master.

'My new life begins.' A warm voice, like Crowden's, but now with that deep, demonic edge. He gestured to the hole in the Door. 'Join me, my children.'

Thousands of demons answered his call. They teemed at the cavity, laughing, ready to break through.

Jake focused every scrap of energy into his good hand. The name of the unknown woman left his lips . . .

'Eleanor.'

. . . and he released the full force of his magic.

The Door was no match for such primal Oldcraft. The magic hit the ancient slab with the force of a five tonne wrecking ball. The portal to the demon world shattered on impact, leaving nothing behind—not a splinter nor a crumb of stone—just a cloud of grey dust that spiralled to the earth in a lazy cyclone.

The Demon Father cried out and fell to his knees. His mouth gaping, he seemed to be frozen by the enormity of what had just happened. Before the echo of the cry had faded away, Adam reloaded the gun and was at his son's side.

'The demon will soon tune into the magical abilities of his new body,' Adam whispered. 'But for the moment, he is weak, helpless.'

'Won't he have to return to the Veil?' Jake asked.

Adam glanced at his son. 'Don't you know the answer to that?'

Jake shook his head. 'I feel *him* fading. The power, the magic, the memories . . . '

There was no time to discuss the overlapping souls of Josiah Jacob Hobarron and Jacob Josiah Harker. The danger that now faced them came from another kind of possession.

'Marcus Crowden is gone,' Adam said. 'A new soul has taken his body. As such, the spell binding him to the Veil is broken. You have stopped the Demontide and shut off the portal to the demon dimension, but this creature will not rest until he has condemned all to darkness.' Adam aimed the gun at the back of the Demon Father's head. 'Now, bind him.'

Without thinking, Jake obeyed. A rope of blue light lashed itself around the Demon Father. Adam stepped forward and pressed the muzzle of the gun against the creature's head.

Jake shuddered. 'Dad. You're sure about this?'

A bead of sweat trickled down Adam's temple. He tightened his grip on the gun.

'What else can we do?' he asked. 'This is the Father of Demons, Jake. Can't you feel his evil?'

Though the instinct was fading, Jake reached out with his mind and sensed the malevolence of the creature. He tasted it like a bitter poison at the back of his throat, felt it burn his eyes and freeze his flesh. Evil, a thousand times stronger than the kind he had experienced on the night of his mother's death. Evil beyond that of Tobias Quilp and Mother Inglethorpe and Marcus Crowden. A primal force, cold and calculating, bent on the destruction of mankind. His dad was right. This was the only way. He took the gun from Adam's hand.

'What are you doing?'

'This is my duty and mine alone,' Jake said, a trace of Hobarron still in his voice.

Adam looked for a moment as if he was about to argue. Finally, he nodded and turned away.

'This isn't over, boy,' the Demon Father murmured. 'You may have stopped the Demontide but I shall not rest until this world is overrun by my children. Darkness and death will follow in my wake. We will meet again, Witchfinder. That I promise.'

Jake tried not to listen. His finger slipped on the trigger.

A roar as loud as the thunder that had raged across Hobarron's Hollow throughout the night now rang from wall to wall. Jake looked up in time to see a form bounding down the stone staircase. It ran at such a speed that it was impossible to make out exactly what it was. An animal perhaps, the size of a wolf but moving like an ape. What happened next passed in a blur. The creature took the last dozen steps in a single leap and landed in front of Jake and the Demon Father. The first blow knocked the gun out of Jake's hand. The second sent him sprawling across the ground. A third swept Adam Harker off his feet.

'The first of my children.'

The Demon Father's laughter sounded very distant in Jake's ears. He had hit his head as he fell and now he watched helplessly as the scene unfolded around him. The dark stranger swept the Demon Father up in his arms, as if he weighed no more than a newborn. A pair of catlike eyes, just like the demon's, blazed at Jake. Then the roar boomed through the cavern again—a cry that was somewhere between animalistic rage and the sound of a human being in utter despair. The creature turned and bounded back up the stone staircase, Crowden's nightmare box swirling behind it.

The roar faded as both figures disappeared into the light of an unsuspecting world.

Chapter 27
End of the Road

Jake woke to the sound of seagulls squalling overhead, to the hush of the sea and the chirrup of insects in the long grass. He could smell the dusty scent of warm stone, the freshness of rain-pummelled earth. Each sensation seemed like a celebration of the new day.

At the murmur of voices he opened his eyes and sat up. He saw a doorway full of light, shadows moving beyond it. He held out his hand to ward them off. Had the Door returned? Were those demons in his view? Or were they angels? That part of him that had died long ago now strained in his chest, as if wanting to break free. To join the angels and to find peace . . .

A hand closed on his shoulder.

'Easy, son.'

Adam pushed him gently back onto the ground. Jake looked up into the ceiling, then shifted his view back to the door. A line of crumbling gravestones rolled down to the cemetery gate. Of course, this was the Witchfinder's tomb. He must have passed out some time after the mysterious creature had rescued the Demon Father. Then Adam had carried him up the stone staircase and out of the cavern. He glanced to his right and saw the rectangular hole in the floor. It hadn't occurred to him until now that the Door had led into the tomb. It made sense, he guessed: the Elders must have built the mausoleum over the Door in order to hide it from curious eyes.

The Hobarron Elders. The last of them were now clustered around one of the larger gravestones. Dr Holmwood, Joanna Harker, Dr Saxby, Mildred Rice, and Walter Drake, speechless as they stood over the body of Alice Splane. Like Jake, the dead woman had been carried out of the cavern and laid upon the cold earth.

Standing a good distance away from the group, Rachel Saxby and Eddie Rice huddled together.

As Jake's senses reasserted themselves so the pain made itself felt. His back ached and the hand that had held the gun was so badly bruised he could barely move it.

'That thing—that creature—it came out of nowhere,' Jake murmured. 'What was it?'

Adam let out a long sigh. 'That was Simon Lydgate.'

'What?'

'I've known about him for a while now. I helped to keep him hidden from the Elders.'

'He's like Pandora,' Jake said slowly. 'One of the dark creatures.'

End of the Road

'Yes, and no. As Pandora told you, the dark creatures are kin to demons but they are *not* demonic. Simon is . . . different.'

'Different how?'

'I believe that he is half-demon.'

Jake gaped at his father.

'Even before he came to New Town to live rough, I'd heard stories about the boy. Stories that made me take an interest in him. All the talk was that Simon had been born of a human mother and a demon father. Such beings are very rare and their nature is unpredictable.'

'He'd changed. His body, his face . . . '

'His demon heritage showing through.' Adam nodded. 'I should never have allowed him to roam free.'

'But he rescued me from Quilp and Mr Pinch,' Jake said hollowly. 'That must stand for something.'

'I'm sorry, Jake, but his demon side has won out. Last night Simon saved the Demon Father.'

Jake focused on Adam. 'He saved *his* father, just as I would have saved you. That doesn't prove he's evil, in fact I think it shows that there *is* good in him. I'm going to find him, help him.'

Adam smiled. He leaned forward and ruffled Jake's hair, just as he had when Jake was a little boy.

'Dad . . . ' Jake took a shuddering breath. 'What am I?'

Adam Harker held his gaze.

'You are my son.'

'I'm not anyone's son.'

Jake got to his feet. He walked to the mausoleum door and stared out across the village.

'You're not my father, Claire wasn't my mother. I was grown in a laboratory from a dead man's skin. He is me and I am no one. Josiah Hobarron had a father and a mother; he was born like any other child. When I was facing the Door, when I was fighting the Demon Father, I had his memories. I felt what it was like to be whole. To be real.'

'You *are* real, Jake.'

'But now those memories are fading,' Jake continued. 'Josiah's experiences, his abilities, they're leaving me and I'm hollow again. What am *I*? Do I have my own soul? Am I just an experiment? An empty clone?'

Jake felt his father's arms around him.

'Your body is an exact replica of Josiah Hobarron's, but that does *not* make you *him*.' Adam took his son's face in his hands. 'You are my son, Claire's son. You were shaped by us and by all those who love you. Your spirit is your own.'

The Harkers held each other for a long time.

'So what now?' Adam asked.

'You're asking me?' Jake stood back, smiling through the tears.

'Seems you're the boss.'

Jake let out a long sigh. 'In the past twenty-four hours, I've been set on fire, had my arm almost ripped out by a witch, struck by dark magic and knocked unconscious by a half-demon creature. I'm tired, hungry, and every muscle in my body aches. I could eat a horse and sleep for a week. But the first thing I'd like to do? See my friends.'

Like a pair of wounded soldiers emerging from the smoke of battle, father and son stepped into the sunlight.

Down at the gate, Jake saw Rachel Saxby smile up at him. She looked tired, careworn, but that smile helped to lift his spirits. The sun was shining, his father was beside him, Rachel and Eddie were safe, and the world had not fallen into darkness. Life was good.

Only one thing could spoil this day, and it was standing right in front of him.

Lined up behind their leader, the Hobarron Elders waited for Jake like a reception party. Dr Holmwood stepped forward, his hand outstretched to Adam. Several minutes passed and finally the doctor lowered his hand.

'I—I owe you an apology, Adam,' Holmwood faltered. Standing directly behind the Institute head, Dr Saxby stared at the ground. 'You were right about everything. Your work, the merits of the experiment, the effectiveness of the Weapon.' His gaze flickered to Jake. 'We should never have doubted you.'

Adam spoke through gritted teeth. 'You imprisoned me. Endangered my son.' He turned to Saxby. '*You* would have sacrificed your own child. What kind of people are you?'

'We were wrong,' Holmwood said. 'But now we must forget our differences and work together again. I understand that, although Jake destroyed the Door, a powerful demon *has* escaped. From what we know of this creature he will not sit idle for long. We will need your help, Jake, if we are to find the Demon Father. To that end, I want you to join the Institute. You will be third in command under your father. A senior Hobarron Elder . . . '

'You take my name in vain, sir?'

Adam's eyes snapped towards his son. Jake's voice had changed again. It rang in the deep tones of the Witchfinder. Dr Holmwood covered his mouth with his hand.

'I will not have it, doctor,' Jake continued. He snapped his fingers and a small blue flame danced between the tips. 'No doubt you meant it well—this Institute of yours—but I have heard it said that the road to Hell is paved with good intentions. Hear me now, Elders of Hobarron: *this is the end of the road*.' He swept his hand through the air, scoring his message with a line of blue fire. 'You have become so fearful of evil that you have allowed it to take root in your hearts. Now I look at you and barely know the difference between your Institute and the Crowden Coven. Each so desperate to achieve its goal that human life mattered little. Oh, I do not doubt you wrestled with your conscience but the result was always the same. The innocent suffer by your hand. And so I say again, this is the end. No more Institute, no more Elders. It is finished.'

'But—but the Demon Father,' Holmwood flustered.

'He is *my* responsibility, and mine alone. I will find him and I will send him back to his infernal kingdom. Rest assured, he shall not escape me.'

The fire in Jake's eyes died and he walked away from the Elders. Adam caught hold of his son and turned the boy to face him.

'It's me, Dad . . . I guess he's still with me after all.' His voice was normal again. Jake gave a grim smile and continued on towards the gate.

Rachel rushed to meet him. She threw her arms around

his neck and held him close. Then she stood back and looked into his eyes.

'There's something different about you,' she said. 'You've changed.'

'I think we all have.'

'For better or worse?'

'Time will tell, I suppose.'

'Still mysterious.' Rachel grinned and her beauty shone through the grief and pain. It didn't take long for the happiness to fade. 'Do you know what happened to Simon?'

Jake hesitated.

'That's a long story, Rachel,' Adam said. 'Better told some other day.'

'He survived and we'll find him,' Jake added. He felt a gentle tug at his sleeve and looked down at the boy beside him. 'Hello, Ed.'

Eddie Rice's face crumpled. 'I betrayed you, Jake.'

In a few stuttering sentences he told of how he had made the pact with the Crowden Coven. How he had traded information in order to keep himself safe and how he had endangered the lives of those he loved. By the end of it, the boy's head was bowed and he could no longer speak. Jake squatted down to Eddie's level.

'Fear makes us do terrible things.' Jake wiped the tears from the kid's face. 'I forgive you, Eddie.'

'Still friends?' Eddie sniffed.

'Course.' Jake jabbed him playfully in the shoulder. 'Now, I think you should go and talk to your mum. She's waiting for you.'

Eddie looked back up the hill to where his mother stood a little apart from the rest of the Elders. Her face was pale in the sunshine, her hands pressed together as if in prayer. She took a step forward and held out her arms.

'She needs you,' Jake said.

Eddie gave a solemn nod. He ran to his mother and fell into her embrace.

'And what about me?' Rachel asked. 'Any advice as to where I should go?'

'Your father . . . '

Dr Saxby turned and looked down the hill, as if he knew that he had been mentioned. Tears filled Rachel's eyes and she shook her head. At this distance, the doctor presented a small, sad figure. Again, he lowered his gaze.

Saxby joined the Elders as they lifted the lifeless body of Alice Splane from the ground. Together, they carried the woman down the hill to the cemetery gate. Adam, Jake, and Rachel moved aside to let them pass.

'I'm sorry for what happened to Alice,' Adam said.

Without looking up, Joanna murmured, 'Thank you, brother.'

Neither Dr Holmwood nor Dr Saxby said a word. With stately pace, the group moved on to Alice's cottage.

Adam Harker winced. His hand went to his wounded shoulder.

'You all right, Dad?' Jake asked. He did not like the grey-ness of his father's skin and the pain in the man's eyes.

'I'm fine.' Dr Harker put his arms around Rachel and his son, drawing them close. 'Let's go home.'

NOW
Strangers at the Grange

No one had lived in the house for over a hundred years. Located at the outskirts of Little Muchly, the Grange was a large, rambling pile, built in the sixteen hundreds by a family whose reputation continued to haunt the village. 'Them up at the Grange' were still spoken of in whispered tones by the old timers hereabouts, and even the young people, who claimed not to believe in such nonsense, would shudder at the name of the long-dead family.

Crowden.

Old Mrs Ogleby, who ran the tearoom at the Little Muchly Museum on Wednesday and Thursday afternoons, spun the same tales to any visiting tourist.

'Right enough, we've a pretty village here, but don't you be deceived. Why, there's stories about this place that would have you shakin' clean out'f yer boots!

'It was *them* as brought the evil here,' she would continue, her single tooth clacking in her head. 'The Crowden family. Worst among them was the youngest son, known as Marcus. Powerful bad, he were, hungry for knowledge that no man ought to have rattlin' around in his head. Even the other Crowdens were afraid of that one. Witch, you say? To be sure, that's what they called him—master of witches. Though I did hear that to look at him you'd have thought he was an angel sent from heaven.

''istory has it that he left home one night and made his way upcountry. My old grandmother, who heard it from her mother who heard it from hers, told me that young Marcus had learned of a place where a whole army of devils were waitin' to be released. Thought that, if he could summon some kinda door and set them free, they'd serve him. Make him their king. No one knows how it turned out. Still, there is a legend that one day, yup, one day . . . '

Here Mrs Ogleby would pause and pour the visitors their tea—nice and strong, just the way tea ought to be. She'd wait until her audience could stand the suspense no longer . . .

'One day Master Crowden will return to Havlock Grange.' The old lady would give a smile and a wicked wink of the eye. 'Strangest part of the legend is that they say he will return a changed man. A man with the eyes of a demon . . . '

Now, with the strangers up at the Grange, Mrs Ogleby shuddered at her own story. If the gossip was right, there were three of them: a little toad-faced man who went by the name of Grype; an invalid boy who appeared to be in some kind of coma (he had been pushed into the house in a wheelchair on the day the strangers arrived—since then no one had laid eyes on him). All this was strange enough, but it was talk of the third man that made Mrs Ogleby's blood run cold.

No one knew his name. He was often seen standing in the windows of the old house, looking out across the grounds as if he was master of all he surveyed. He had a face that could shame the angels, so they said. At the bus stop, in the park, chattering away in the tavern, the local girls would talk of the handsome stranger, while that harmless old gossip Mrs Ogleby listened in.

'Isn't he *gorgeous*?' they would swoon. 'I'd love to see his eyes. I bet you could just drown in them. But he's always wearing those dark glasses, even at night. I wonder why . . .'

Sitting all alone in her cottage at night, Mrs Ogleby wondered if anyone had ever *really* listened to her stories.

A man with the face of an angel and the eyes of a demon . . .

My heartfelt thanks go to Deborah Chaffey, who placed me firmly on the Witchfinder's path. Thanks also to Jacob Chaffey for his encouraging early review and for lending my hero his name. I'd also like to acknowledge the aid of friendly alchemists Johnny Draper, Claire Wilson, Bryony Bowers, and Graeme Hills who listened patiently to early incantations and helped me conjure a few golden nuggets from a lot of base metal.

Witchfinder found its home through a series of magical links, beginning with the spookily talented Sarah Silverwood. Sarah introduced me to my brilliant agent Veronique Baxter, whose boundless enthusiasm brought *Witchfinder* to OUP. Stewed in the editorial cauldron of the wonderful Jasmine Richards, the book became infinitely more magical. To all these people, and to countless others who have nurtured my writing, I say—THANK YOU!

About the author

William Hussey has a Masters Degree in Writing from Sheffield Hallam University. His novels are inspired by long walks in the lonely Fenlands of Lincolnshire and by a lifetime devoted to horror stories, folklore, and legends. William lives in Skegness and writes stories about things that go bump in the night . . .

The trilogy continues . . .

WITCHFINDER
Gallows at Twilight

January 2011

www.witchfinderbooks.co.uk

The House of Bones

Lizzie Redfern grasped the lion's head knocker. She tried to lift the heavy brass ring clasped between the lion's teeth, but the effort sapped the last of her strength. Her legs gave way, her face smacking against the cold stone step. She felt no pain. She was beyond any sense or feeling now. The hunger that had gnawed at her for the better part of a week seemed to vanish.

Dimly, she heard the rasp of a bolt and the weary grumble of the old door. Candlelight dazzled. A figure stooped down, its ivory face pinched with concern. Arms encircled Lizzie and picked her up from the ground. A rush of words wafted into her ear.

'Here you are, my dear, just as my clever sister foretold. But you are such a little thing! Like a broken sparrow in my arms. Come now, into the warmth and the light.'

The sound of the unknown lady's dress was like the

rustle of a half-remembered lullaby. Twice Lizzie mustered
the energy to open her eyes. She saw glimpses of a gloomy
hall, and a staircase festooned with spider webs. At last, they
came to one of the upper rooms.

'Drude, my dear, I have brought our guest.'

The creak of another door. Lizzie managed to lift her
head. A face swam into view.

'Oh, but she is so thin, Lethe,' the woman called Drude
clucked. 'Bring her straight to the table, the broth is ready.'

Lizzie was placed onto a cushioned chair and felt the tap of
a spoon against her teeth. Rich, meaty stew salted her lips.

'Oh, how charming,' Lethe purred. 'See, Drude, how she
blinks in the firelight like a newborn pup.'

Lizzie felt a second spoonful of stew wash into her mouth.
Heat spread out from her stomach and spilled into her arms
and legs. By the time the spoon had scraped the last of the
stew from the bowl, Lizzie was sitting up straight and looking at her hosts.

They had called each other 'sister' but Miss Drude and
Miss Lethe were not at all alike. Miss Drude was dressed in
a threadbare nightgown stained with splashes from the
broth. Straggles of white hair poked out from beneath her
nightcap and brushed against a hawkish, warty nose.

Miss Lethe had the face of a playful imp. She wore a
gown of finest satin, and a cascade of golden hair rolled
down her back.

'There now.' Miss Drude dabbed Lizzie's lips with a hand-
kerchief. 'You must be feeling better.'

'I am, thank you, ma'am.'

'No need for thanks, my pet. But tell us, what has brought you here on so bleak a night?'

'I have been trying to find what work I can,' Lizzie explained. 'I came this night to the village not far from here—Little Muchly. A lady, she called herself "Old Sowerberry", told me to go to the Crowden sisters at the big house.'

'Dear Old Sowerberry.' Miss Drude showed a set of worn teeth. 'Yes, we have an . . . arrangement with that lady. She sends all needy children to our door.'

'Tell me,' Miss Lethe said, 'are you quite alone in the world?'

'Yes, ma'am. My mother died giving me life. My father—' Lizzie's voice cracked. 'He was killed in battle the month before last.'

Her gaze wandered around the room. A large curtain had been used to screen off the far end of the chamber. Within a few paces of Lizzie stood a grand stone fireplace with gargoyle faces carved into its columns. Flames crackled in the grate and cast restless shadows across the floor.

'Come,' Miss Drude muttered. 'Our sister calls.'

Hands locked onto Lizzie's shoulders. The sisters barged her through the room. They reached the curtain and Drude, no longer smiling, grasped the edge and tore it back.

'This is our youngest sister. Say hello, Frija.'

The woman sitting at a spinning wheel lifted her head. She was small and dressed in black. Although a thick veil covered her face, Lizzie felt sure that Frija was looking directly at her. Frija's fingers played through the spokes of the spinning wheel, turning it slowly, surely.

'I saw your coming, Lizzie Redfern,' Frija said.

'Who are you?' Lizzie whispered.

'I am the cloud spinner. My eye sees far and my hand speaks truth.'

Frija's fingers teased a strand from her spinning wheel and cast it loose. The fibre soared across the room and into a dark corner. Like a bright finger, it descended, touching on a large wooden chest. The lid was thrown back and, as the light strengthened, Lizzie caught sight of the trunk's contents.

A scream caught in her throat.

'Old Sowerberry sends any passing child to us,' Frija murmured. 'They come to beg a penny, to plead for the scraps from our table. They are never seen again.'

The finger-cloud brightened.

Arm and leg bones poked out of the trunk like the stalks of strange, headless flowers. Little skulls, some with clumps of hair still attached, grinned in the ghostly light. A leathery strip of flesh lolled from the mouth of one of the skulls, as if the dead child was poking its tongue out at Lizzie. The sight of these remains was frightening enough, but what chilled Lizzie most were the chips and notches scored into the bones. Teeth marks. She looked back at Lethe and Drude, and imagined the hungry women sitting at the table, chomping and gulping, sucking and slurping, wiping the juice from their chins. When the bones had been picked clean, they would be thrown into the chest. Such a small grave for so many children.

Lizzie thought about the delicious stew she had just enjoyed and her gaze switched back to the table. Fear sharpened her senses, and she noticed things that in the haze of hunger she had missed.

She saw the slick, red gruel dripping down the cauldron's belly. Smelt the faint stench of rotting flesh. Saw the chopping board at the end of the table, its blood-smattered surface littered with chunks of meat and scraps of gore. Six eel-black tongues had been heaped together, ready for dicing. A single, jellied eye, shucked from a child's head, sat upon the table and stared up at the ceiling. At one end of the chopping board, fingers and toes had been laid out like a row of little sausages.

Lizzie covered her eyes. She could no longer look at the cannibals' kitchen.

'Such a shame,' Lethe sighed. 'We had intended to keep you alive for a few weeks. Fatten you up; get some flesh on those bones. But I'm afraid Frija has forced our hand. Drude, my love, will you be a dear and fetch the axe?'